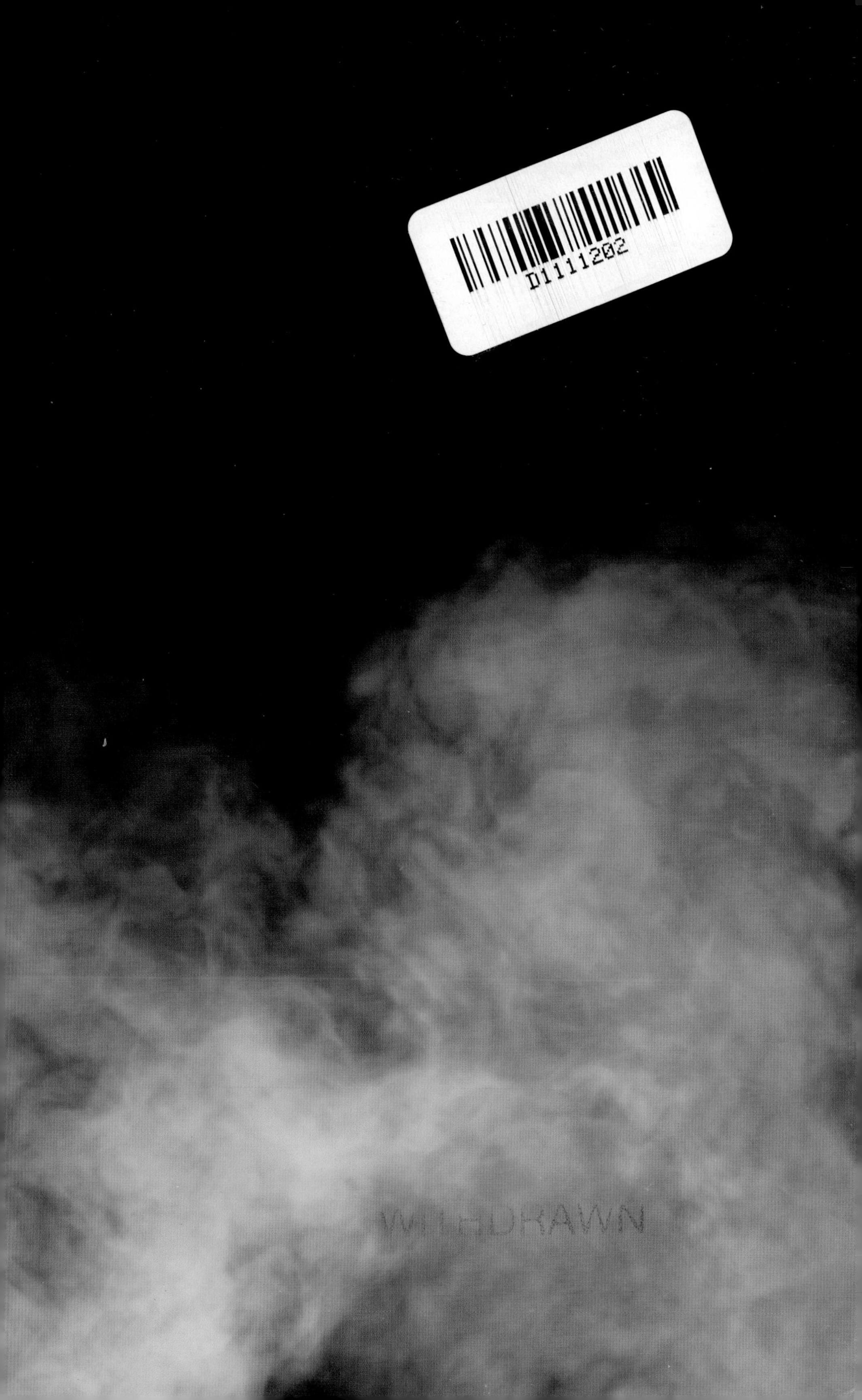

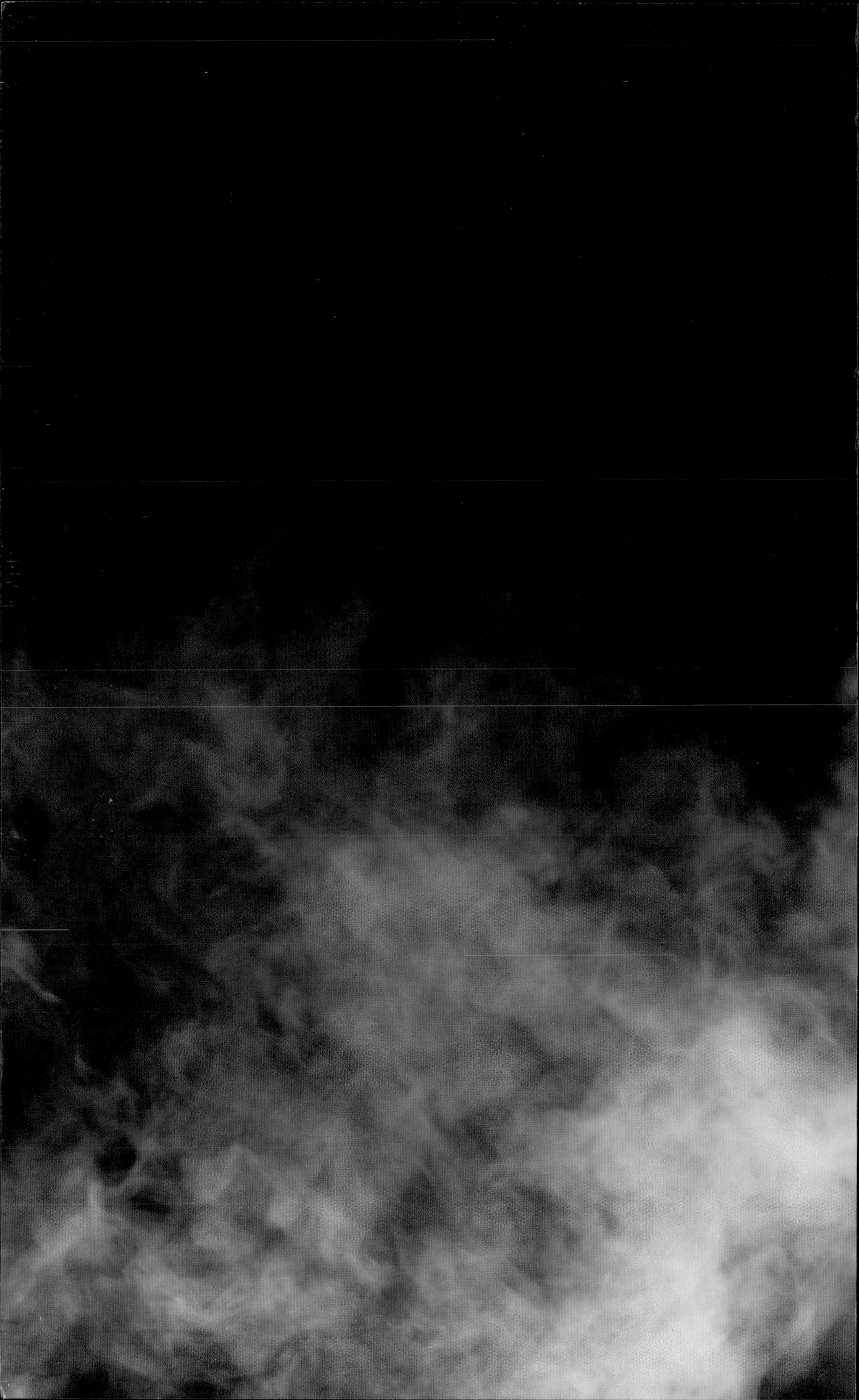

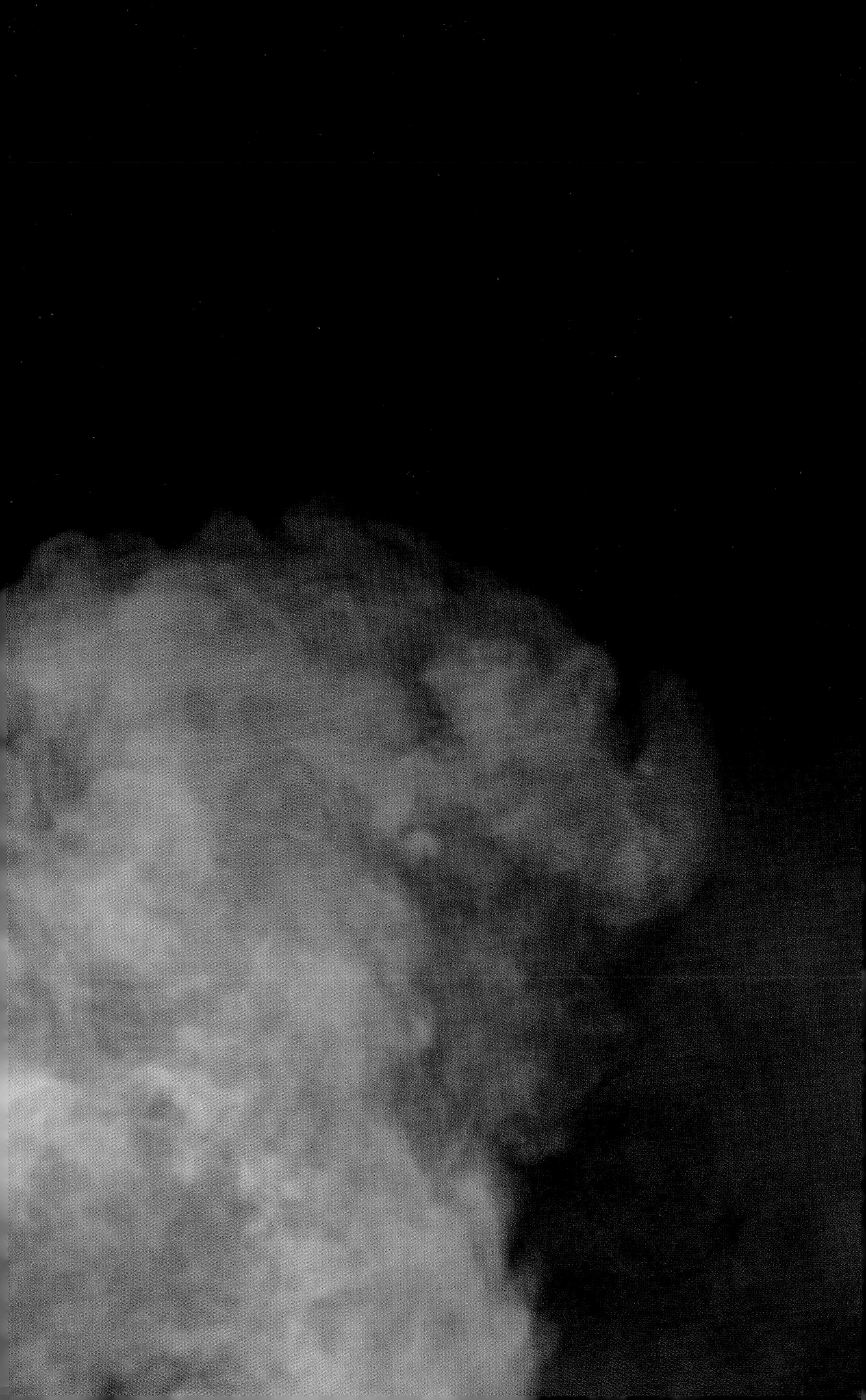

SIMON SPOTLIGHT
An imprint of Simon & Schuster Children's Publishing Division
1230 Avenue of the Americas, New York, New York 10020
This Simon Spotlight edition December 2022
Copyright © 2022 by Simon & Schuster, Inc. All rights reserved, including the right of reproduction in whole or in part in any form. SIMON SPOTLIGHT and colophon are registered trademarks of Simon & Schuster, Inc. YOU'RE INVITED TO A CREEPOVER is a registered trademark of Simon & Schuster, Inc. For information about special discounts for bulk purchases, please contact Simon & Schuster Special Sales at 1-866-506-1949 or business@simonandschuster.com. Designed by Nicholas Sciacca. Text by Matthew J. Gilbert. Based on the text by Heather Alexander. Art Services by Glass House Graphics. Art by Giusi Lo Piccolo & Onofrio Orlando. Lettering by Giuseppe Naselli/Grafimated Cartoon. Supervision by Salvatore Di Marco/Grafimated Cartoon. The illustrations for this book were rendered digitally. Manufactured in China 0922 SCP
10 9 8 7 6 5 4 3 2 1
This book has been cataloged by the Library of Congress.
ISBN 978-1-6659-1570-0 (hc)
ISBN 978-1-6659-1569-4 (pbk)
ISBN 978-1-6659-1571-7 (ebook)

YOU'RE INVITED TO A

CREEPOVER

THE GRAPHIC NOVEL

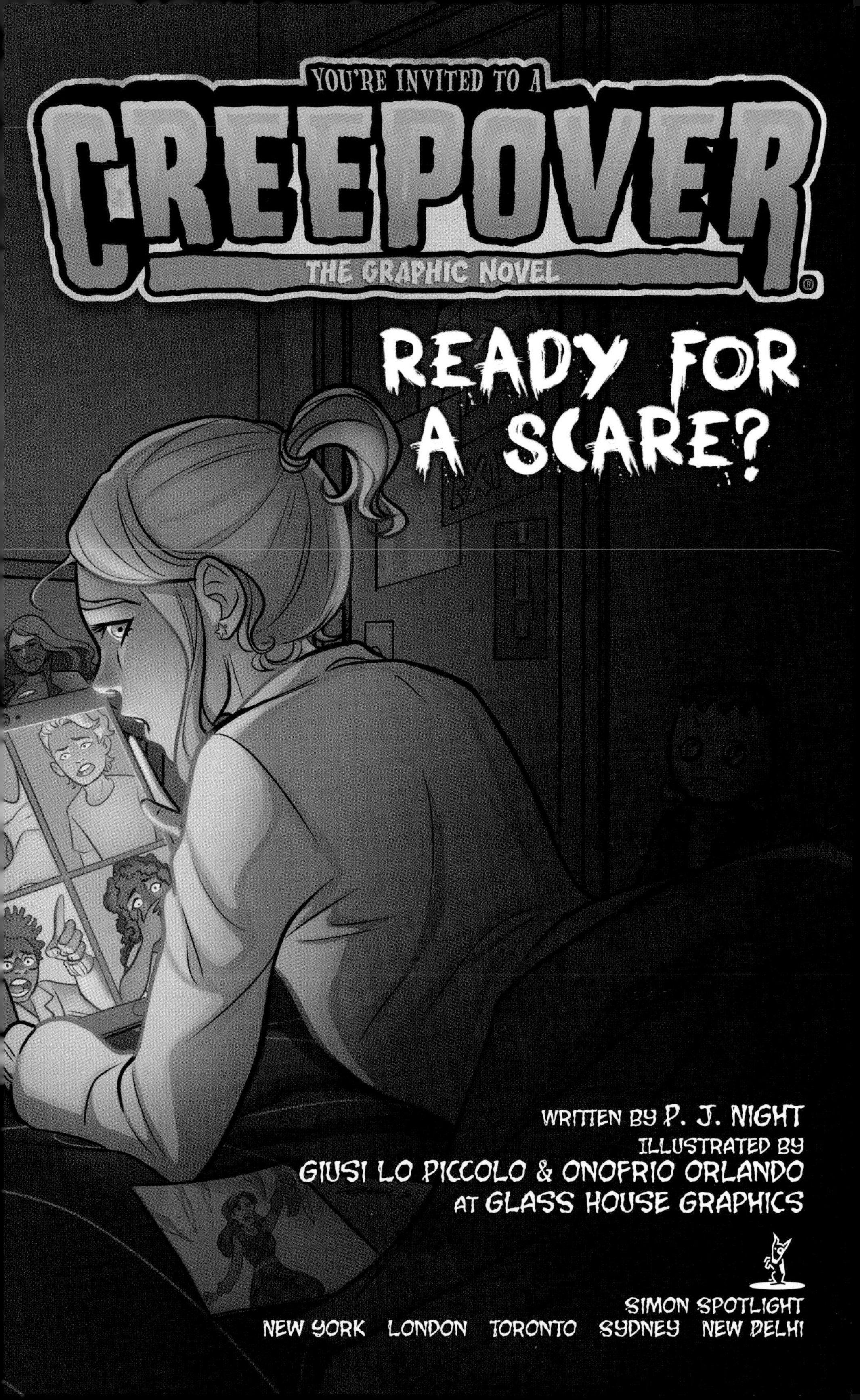

READY FOR A SCARE?

WRITTEN BY P. J. NIGHT
ILLUSTRATED BY
GIUSI LO PICCOLO & ONOFRIO ORLANDO
AT GLASS HOUSE GRAPHICS

SIMON SPOTLIGHT
NEW YORK LONDON TORONTO SYDNEY NEW DELHI

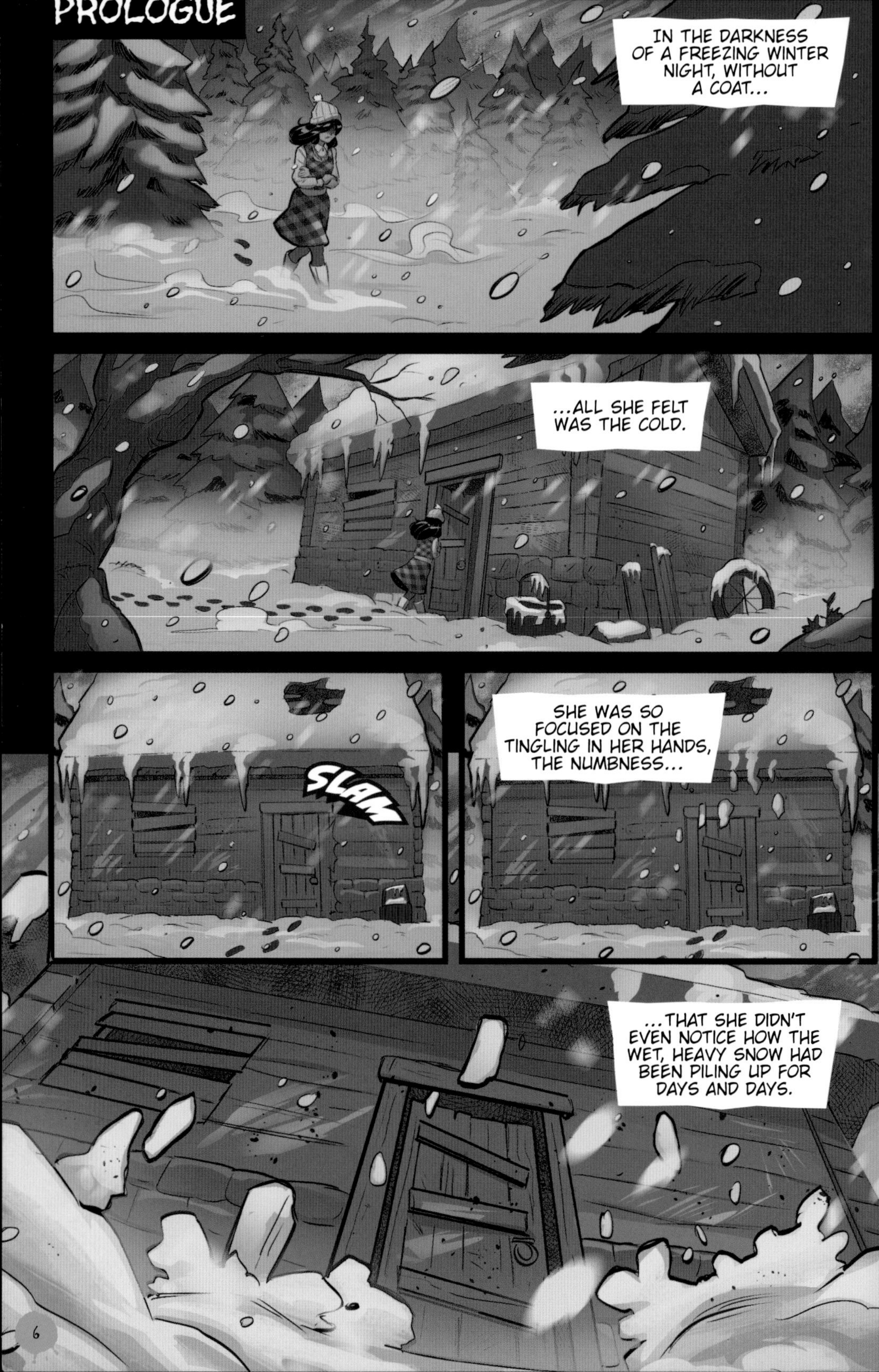
PROLOGUE
IN THE DARKNESS OF A FREEZING WINTER NIGHT, WITHOUT A COAT...
...ALL SHE FELT WAS THE COLD.
SLAM
SHE WAS SO FOCUSED ON THE TINGLING IN HER HANDS, THE NUMBNESS...
...THAT SHE DIDN'T EVEN NOTICE HOW THE WET, HEAVY SNOW HAD BEEN PILING UP FOR DAYS AND DAYS.

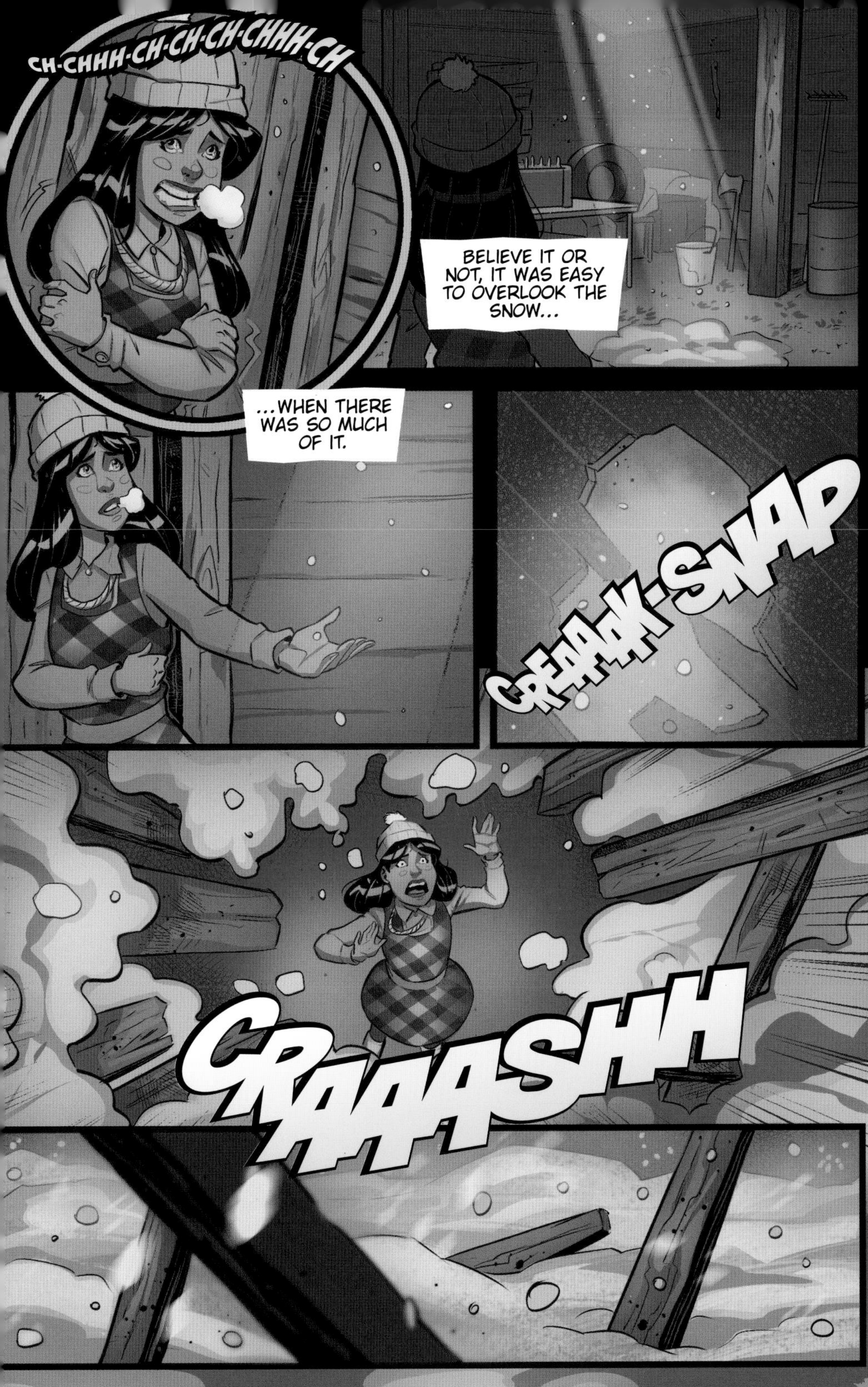
CH-CHHH-CH-CH-CH-CHHH-CH
BELIEVE IT OR NOT, IT WAS EASY TO OVERLOOK THE SNOW...
...WHEN THERE WAS SO MUCH OF IT.
CREAAK-SNAP
CRAAASHH

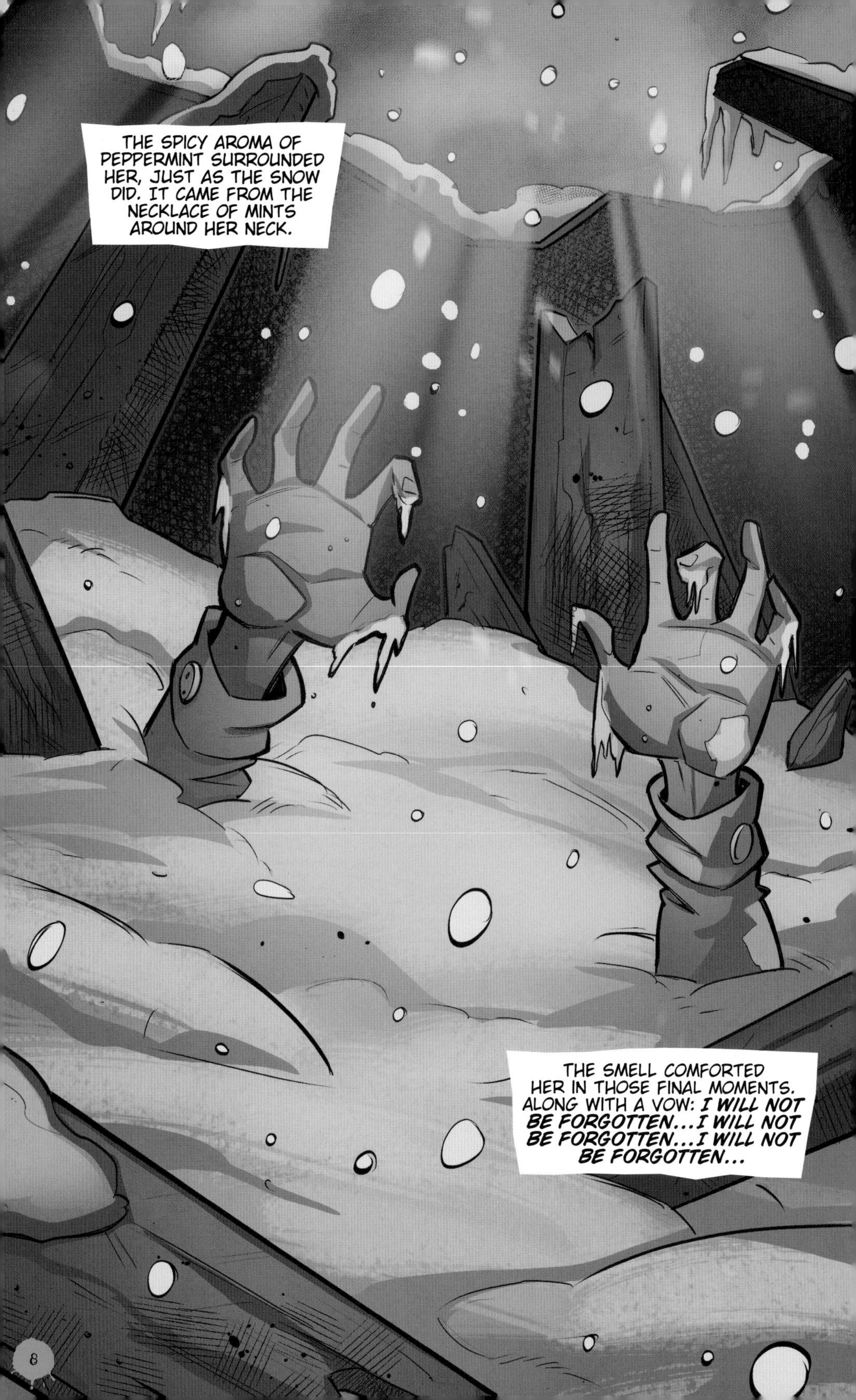
THE SPICY AROMA OF PEPPERMINT SURROUNDED HER, JUST AS THE SNOW DID. IT CAME FROM THE NECKLACE OF MINTS AROUND HER NECK.
THE SMELL COMFORTED HER IN THOSE FINAL MOMENTS. ALONG WITH A VOW: *I WILL NOT BE FORGOTTEN...I WILL NOT BE FORGOTTEN...I WILL NOT BE FORGOTTEN...*

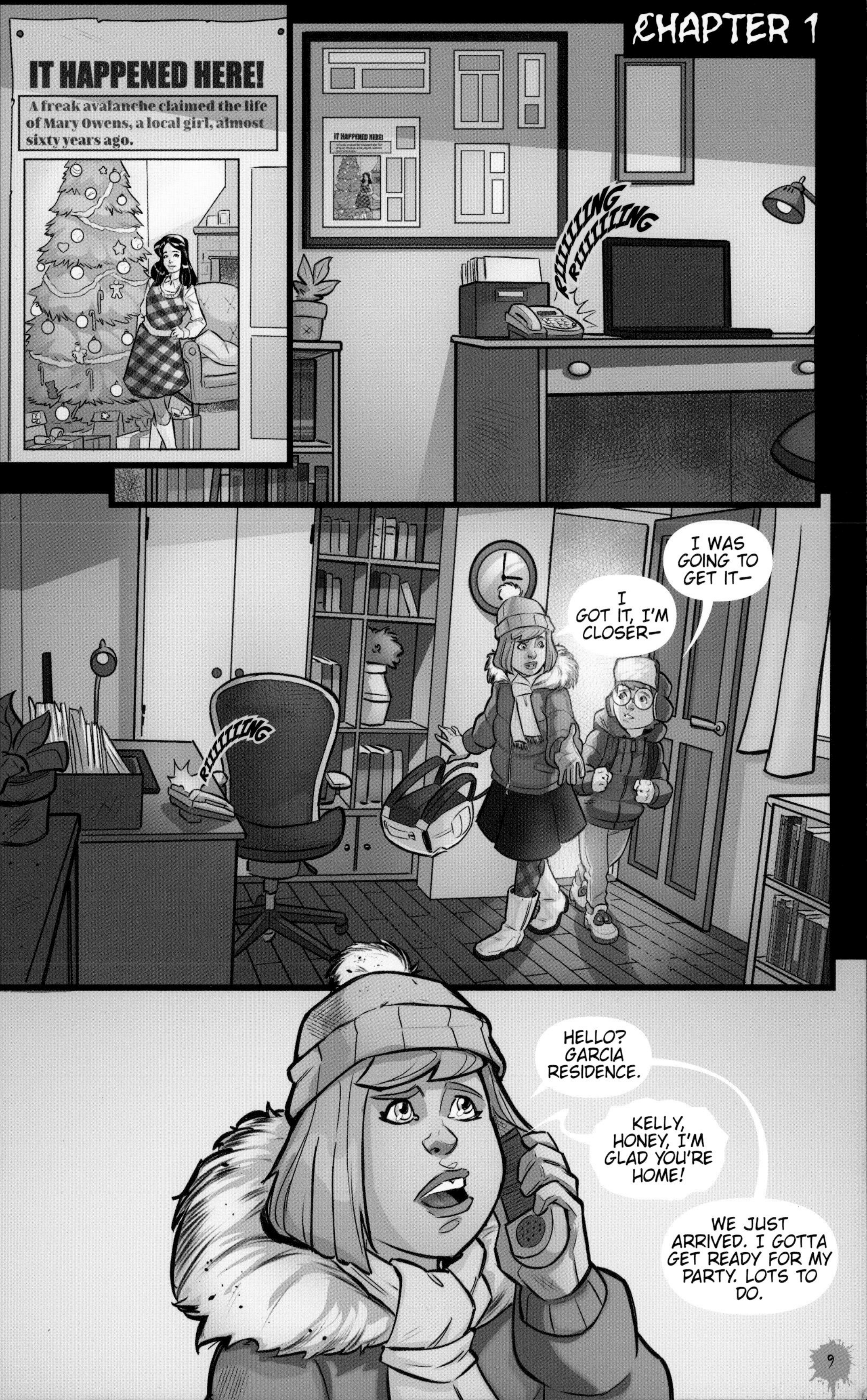

CHAPTER 1
IT HAPPENED HERE!
A freak avalanche claimed the life of Mary Owens, a local girl, almost sixty years ago.
RIIIIIIING RIIIIIIING
RIIIIIIING
I GOT IT, I'M CLOSER—
I WAS GOING TO GET IT—
HELLO? GARCIA RESIDENCE.
KELLY, HONEY, I'M GLAD YOU'RE HOME!
WE JUST ARRIVED. I GOTTA GET READY FOR MY PARTY. LOTS TO DO.

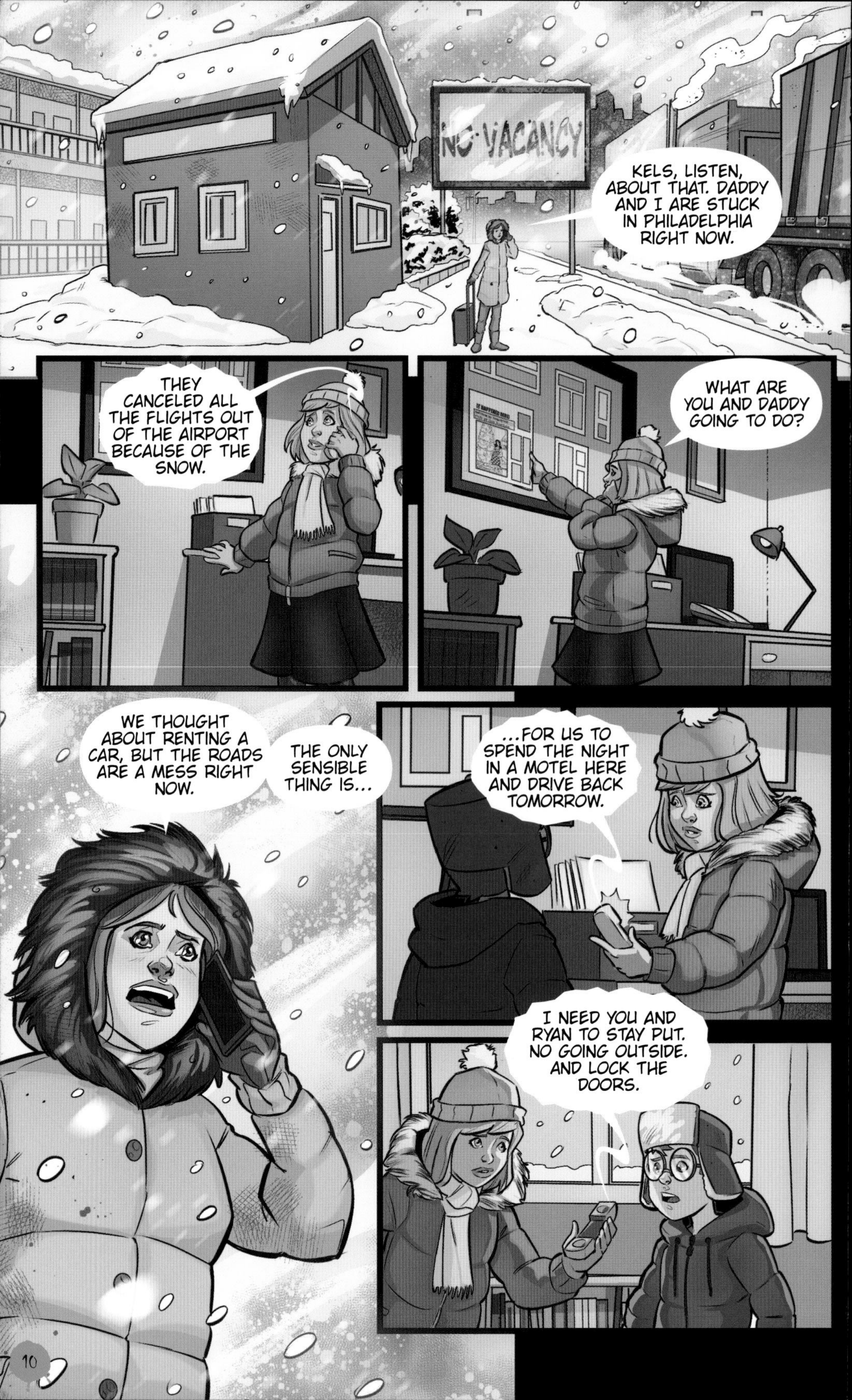
NO VACANCY
KELS, LISTEN, ABOUT THAT. DADDY AND I ARE STUCK IN PHILADELPHIA RIGHT NOW.
THEY CANCELED ALL THE FLIGHTS OUT OF THE AIRPORT BECAUSE OF THE SNOW.
WHAT ARE YOU AND DADDY GOING TO DO?
WE THOUGHT ABOUT RENTING A CAR, BUT THE ROADS ARE A MESS RIGHT NOW.
THE ONLY SENSIBLE THING IS…
…FOR US TO SPEND THE NIGHT IN A MOTEL HERE AND DRIVE BACK TOMORROW.
I NEED YOU AND RYAN TO STAY PUT. NO GOING OUTSIDE. AND LOCK THE DOORS.

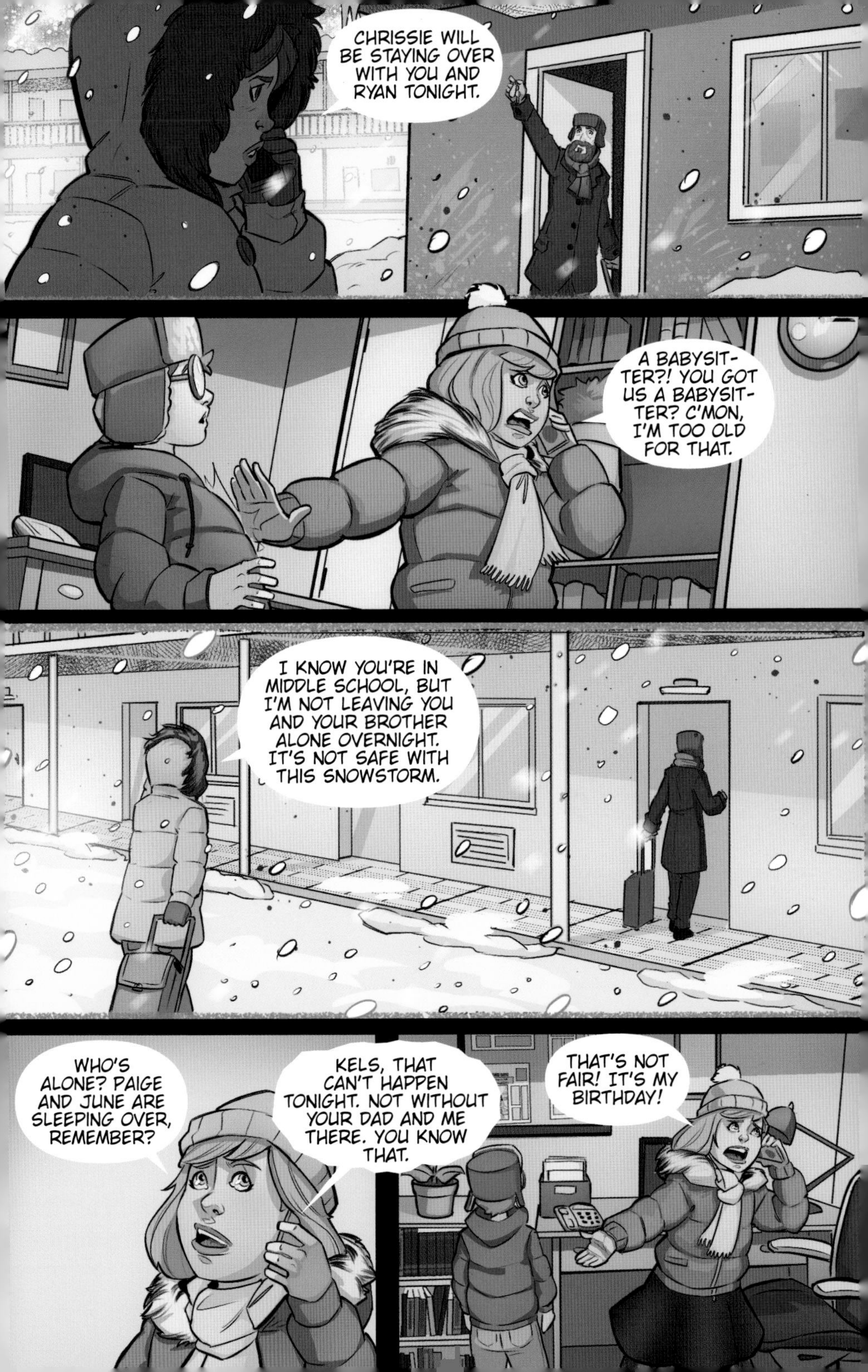
CHRISSIE WILL BE STAYING OVER WITH YOU AND RYAN TONIGHT.
A BABYSIT-TER?! YOU GOT US A BABYSIT-TER? C'MON, I'M TOO OLD FOR THAT.
I KNOW YOU'RE IN MIDDLE SCHOOL, BUT I'M NOT LEAVING YOU AND YOUR BROTHER ALONE OVERNIGHT. IT'S NOT SAFE WITH THIS SNOWSTORM.
WHO'S ALONE? PAIGE AND JUNE ARE SLEEPING OVER, REMEMBER?
KELS, THAT CAN'T HAPPEN TONIGHT. NOT WITHOUT YOUR DAD AND ME THERE. YOU KNOW THAT.
THAT'S NOT FAIR! IT'S MY BIRTHDAY!

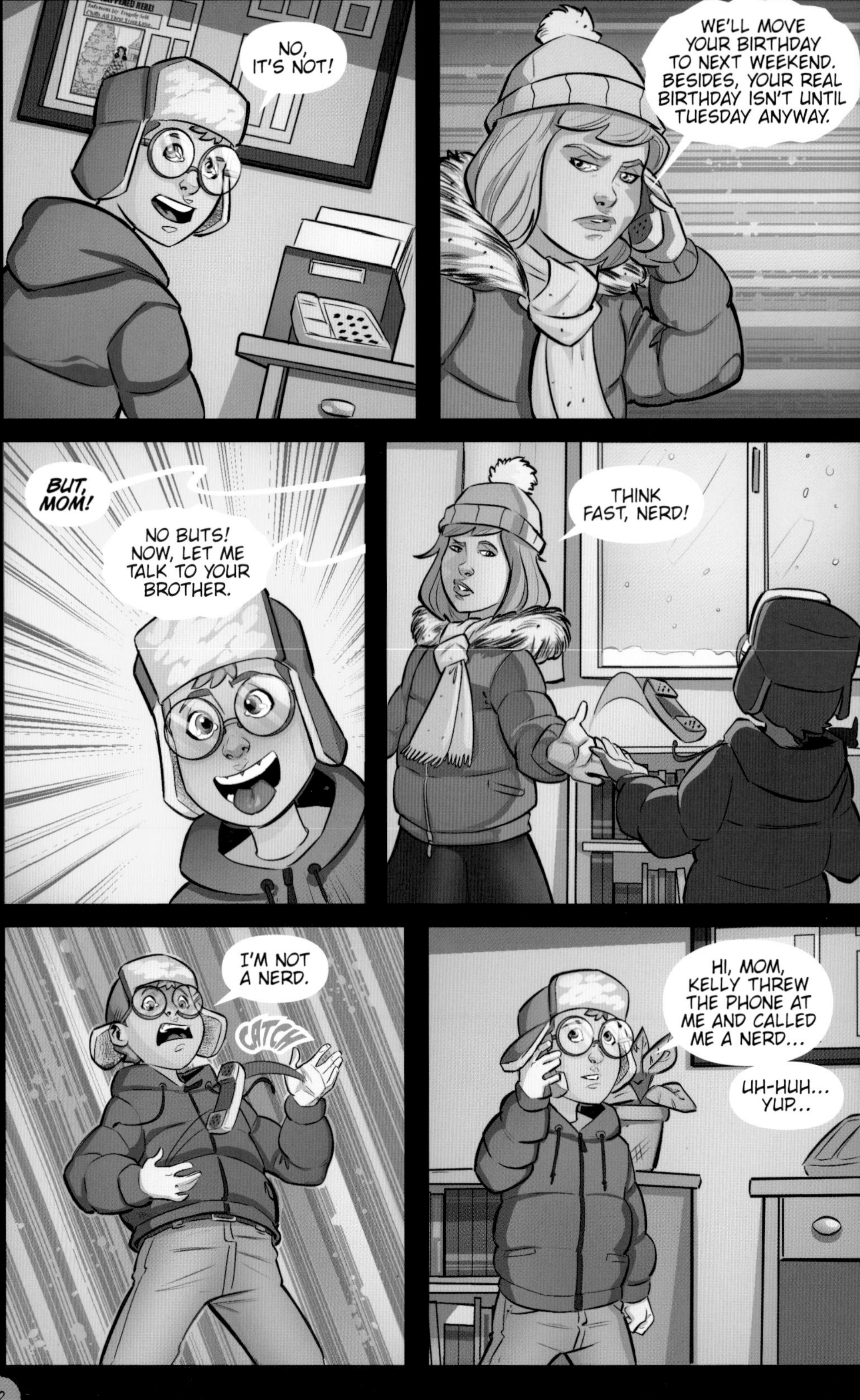
NO, IT'S NOT!
WE'LL MOVE YOUR BIRTHDAY TO NEXT WEEKEND. BESIDES, YOUR REAL BIRTHDAY ISN'T UNTIL TUESDAY ANYWAY.
BUT, MOM!
NO BUTS! NOW, LET ME TALK TO YOUR BROTHER.
THINK FAST, NERD!
I'M NOT A NERD.
CATCH
HI, MOM, KELLY THREW THE PHONE AT ME AND CALLED ME A NERD...
UH-HUH... YUP...

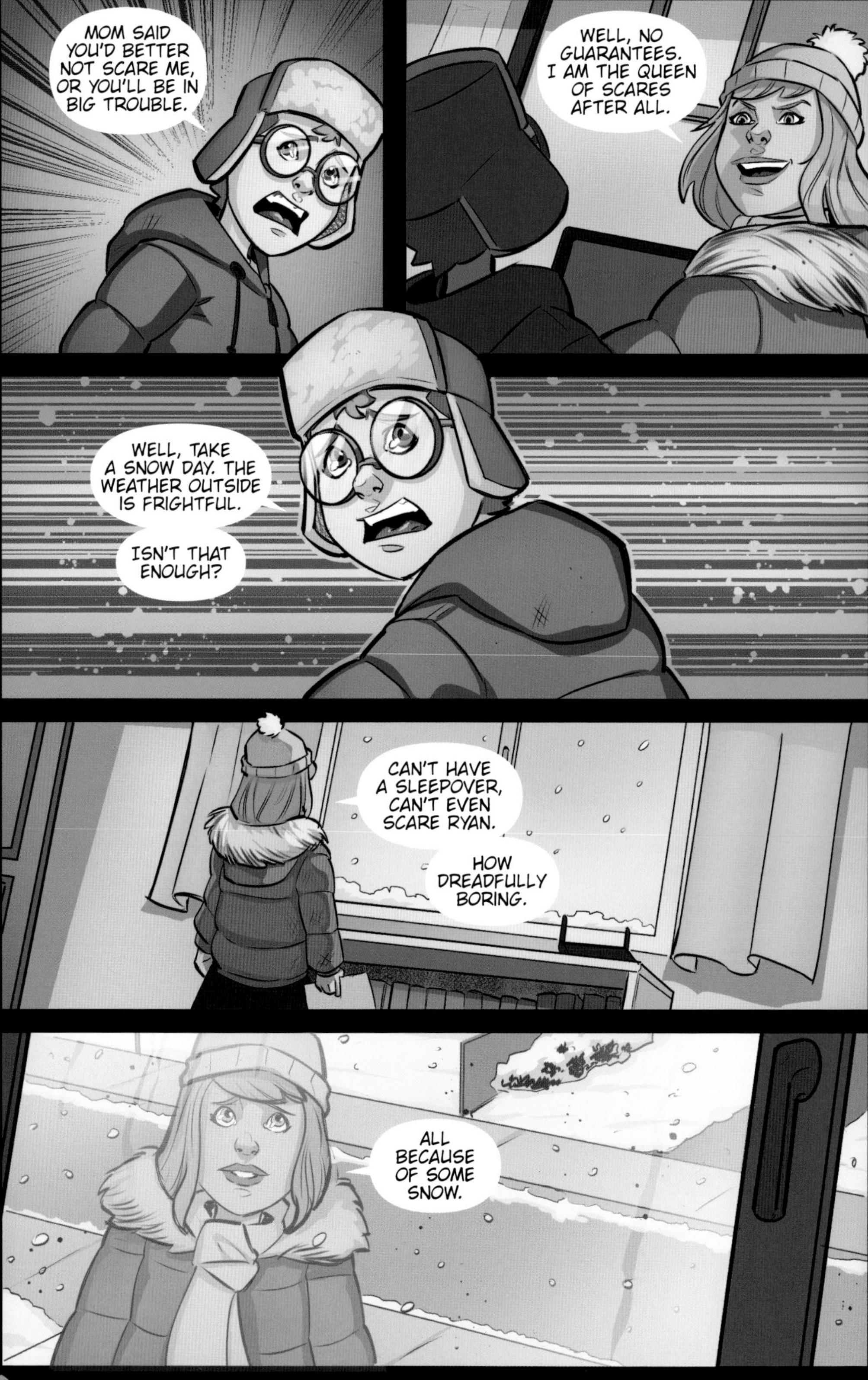
MOM SAID YOU'D BETTER NOT SCARE ME, OR YOU'LL BE IN BIG TROUBLE.
WELL, NO GUARANTEES. I AM THE QUEEN OF SCARES AFTER ALL.
WELL, TAKE A SNOW DAY. THE WEATHER OUTSIDE IS FRIGHTFUL.
ISN'T THAT ENOUGH?
CAN'T HAVE A SLEEPOVER, CAN'T EVEN SCARE RYAN.
HOW DREADFULLY BORING.
ALL BECAUSE OF SOME SNOW.

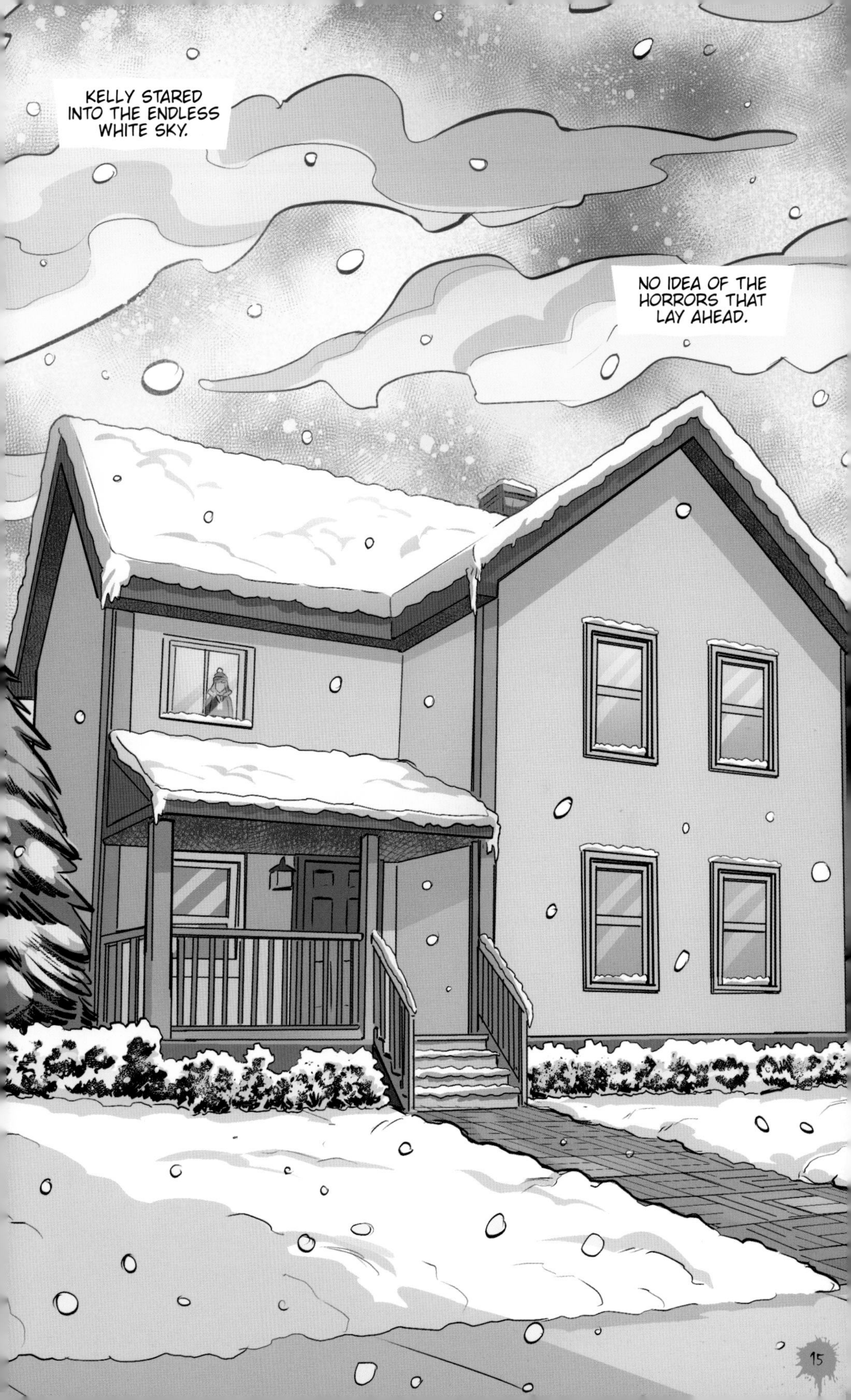
KELLY STARED INTO THE ENDLESS WHITE SKY.
NO IDEA OF THE HORRORS THAT LAY AHEAD.

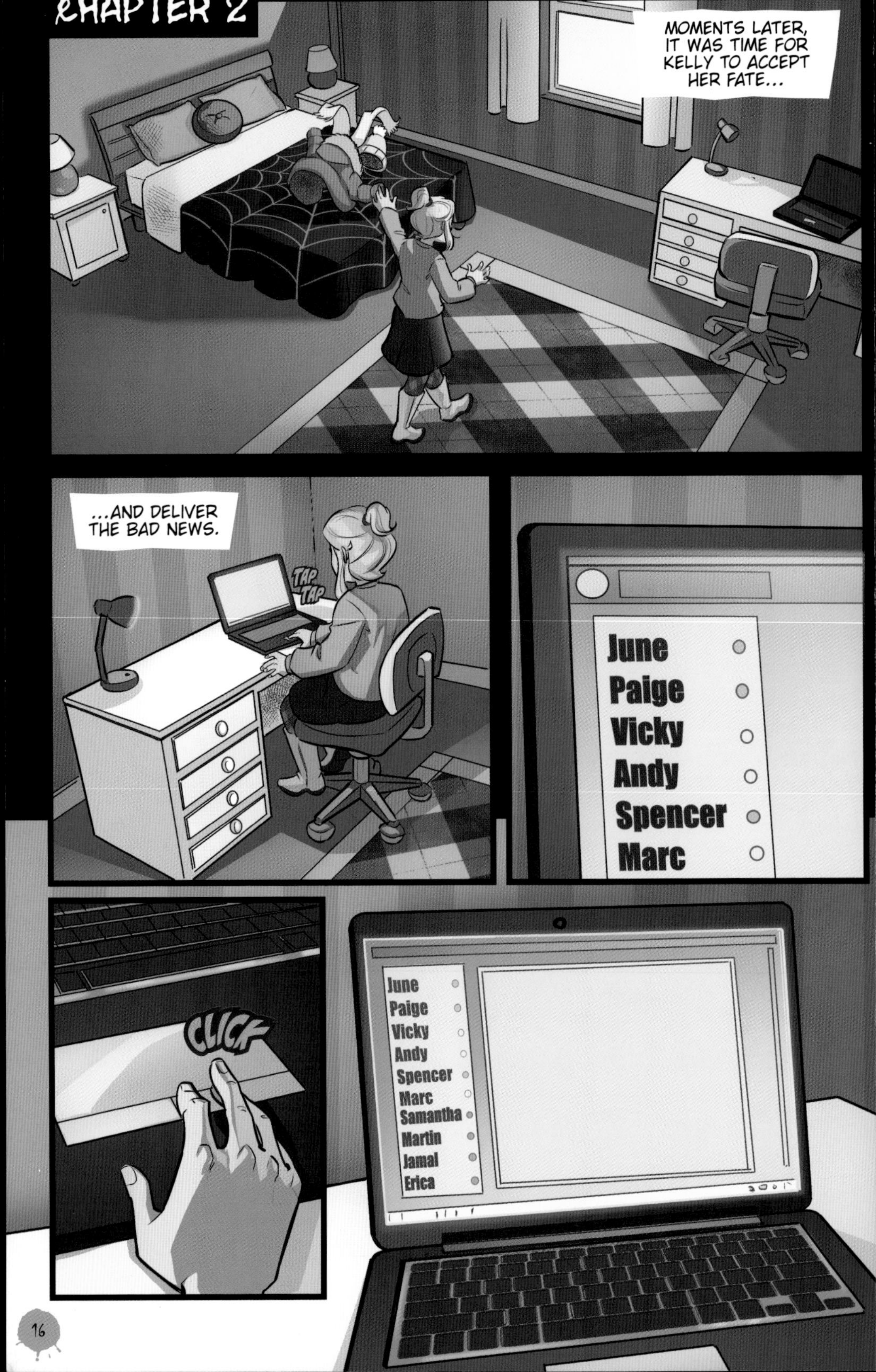
CHAPTER 2
MOMENTS LATER, IT WAS TIME FOR KELLY TO ACCEPT HER FATE...
...AND DELIVER THE BAD NEWS.
TAP TAP
June
Paige
Vicky
Andy
Spencer
Marc
CLICK
June
Paige
Vicky
Andy
Spencer
Marc
Samantha
Martin
Jamal
Erica

CHAT WITH JUNE AND PAIGE

KELLY

BAD NEWS.

JUNE

?

KELLY

No sleepover tonight. Parents trapped in Philly 😰

PAIGE

I heard. Can't believe your mom thinks Chrissie is gonna keep u safe! LOL

KELLY

I KNOW.
So not my idea!

JUNE

Hold up. Chrissie is babysitting???!!!!????

KELLY

NOT 👏
MY 👏
IDEA 👏

PAIGE

I mean, it is kinda scary at night alone 😨

JUNE

Better watch out, Kels!

KELLY

Whatevs.
So NOT scared!

JUNE

Sad about your sleepover. I have a present 4 u.

PAIGE

Yeah me 2.

KELLY

Thx! You guys r the best.
I have to move it to next weekend.
STINKS. Had so many great scares planned for u tonight.

PAIGE

Maybe I'm safer at home, haha.

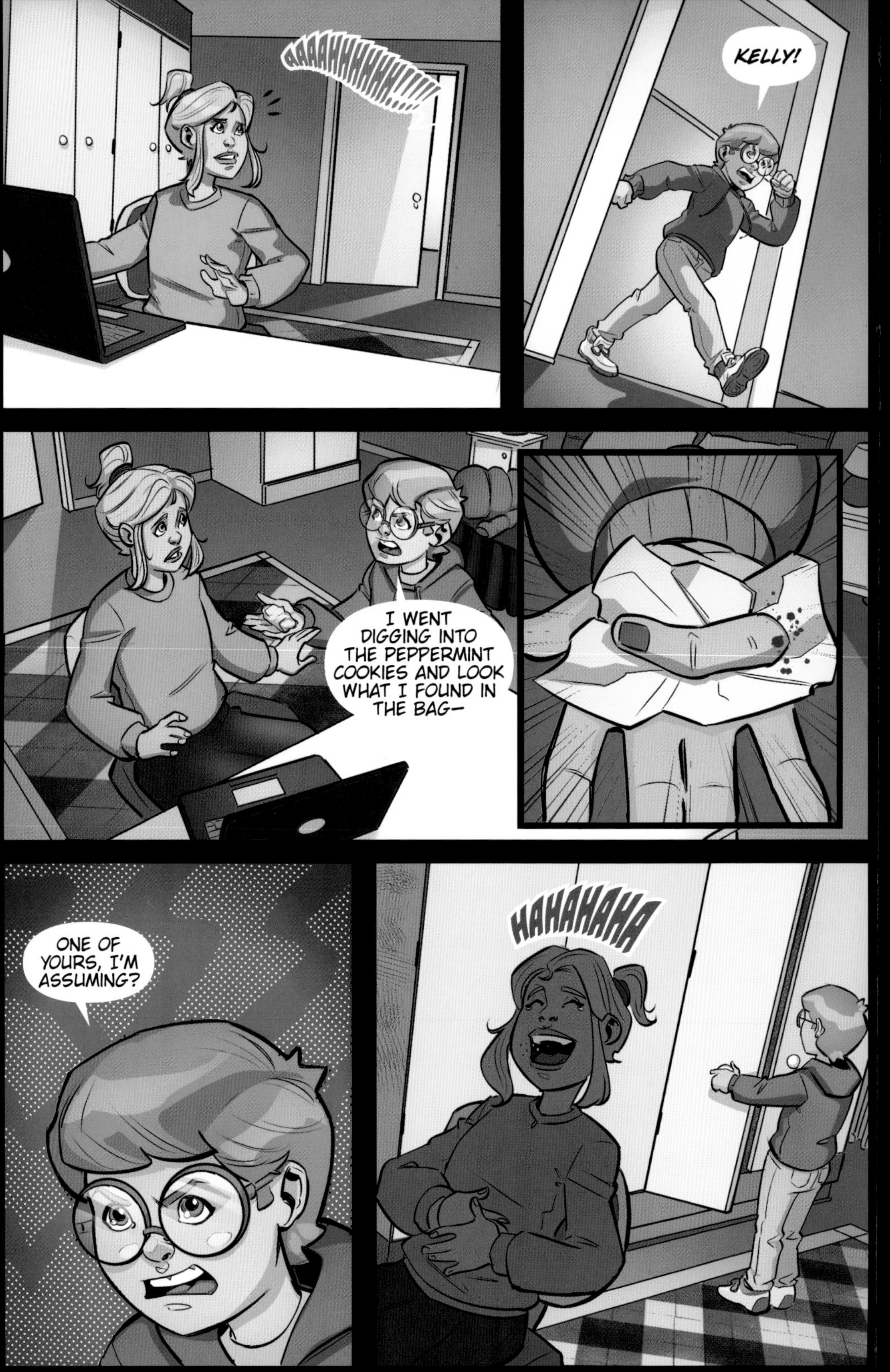
AAAAHHHHHH!!!!!!
KELLY!
I WENT DIGGING INTO THE PEPPERMINT COOKIES AND LOOK WHAT I FOUND IN THE BAG—
ONE OF YOURS, I'M ASSUMING?
HAHAHAHA

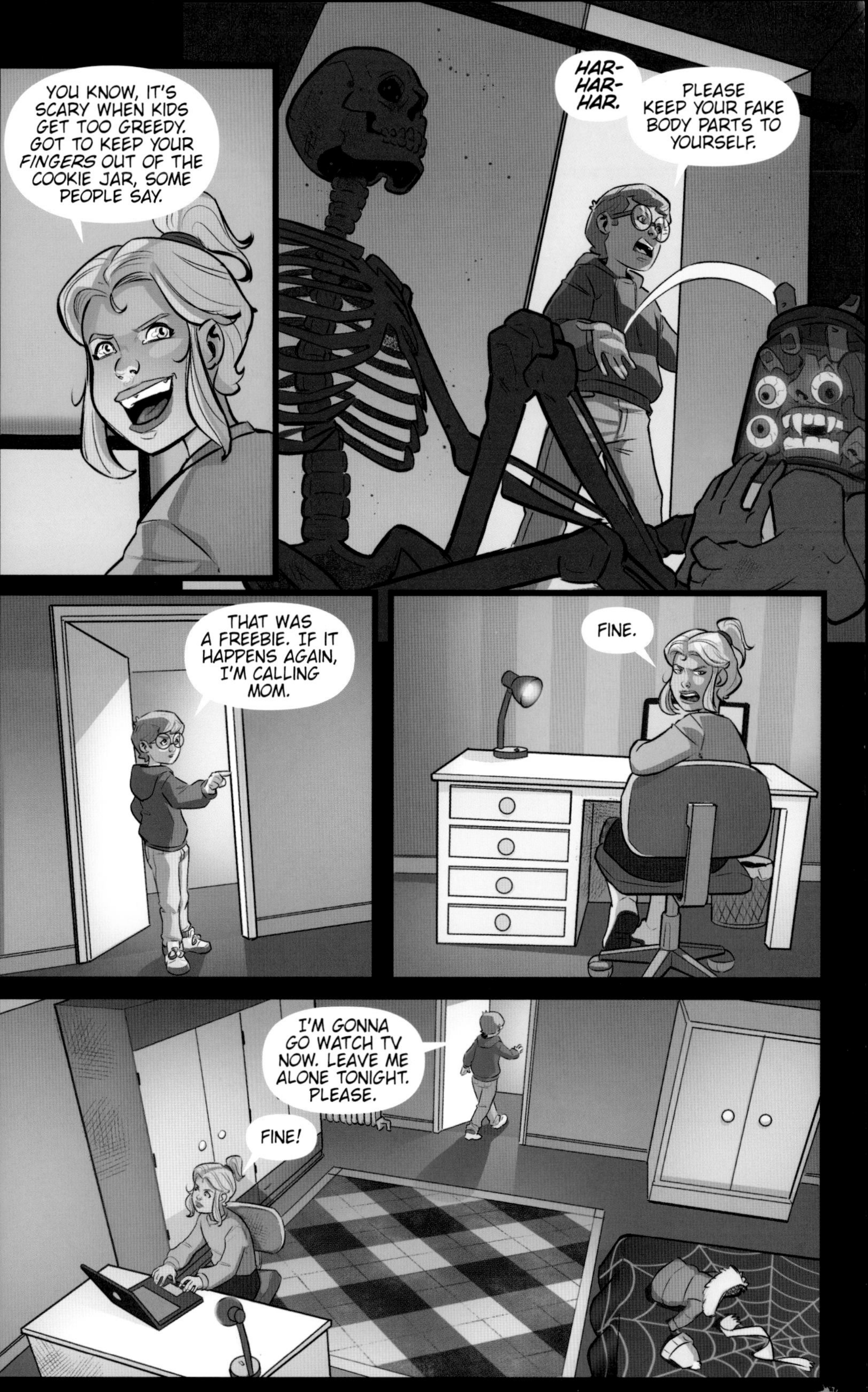
YOU KNOW, IT'S SCARY WHEN KIDS GET TOO GREEDY. GOT TO KEEP YOUR *FINGERS* OUT OF THE COOKIE JAR, SOME PEOPLE SAY.
HAR-HAR-HAR.
PLEASE KEEP YOUR FAKE BODY PARTS TO YOURSELF.
THAT WAS A FREEBIE. IF IT HAPPENS AGAIN, I'M CALLING MOM.
FINE.
I'M GONNA GO WATCH TV NOW. LEAVE ME ALONE TONIGHT. PLEASE.
FINE!

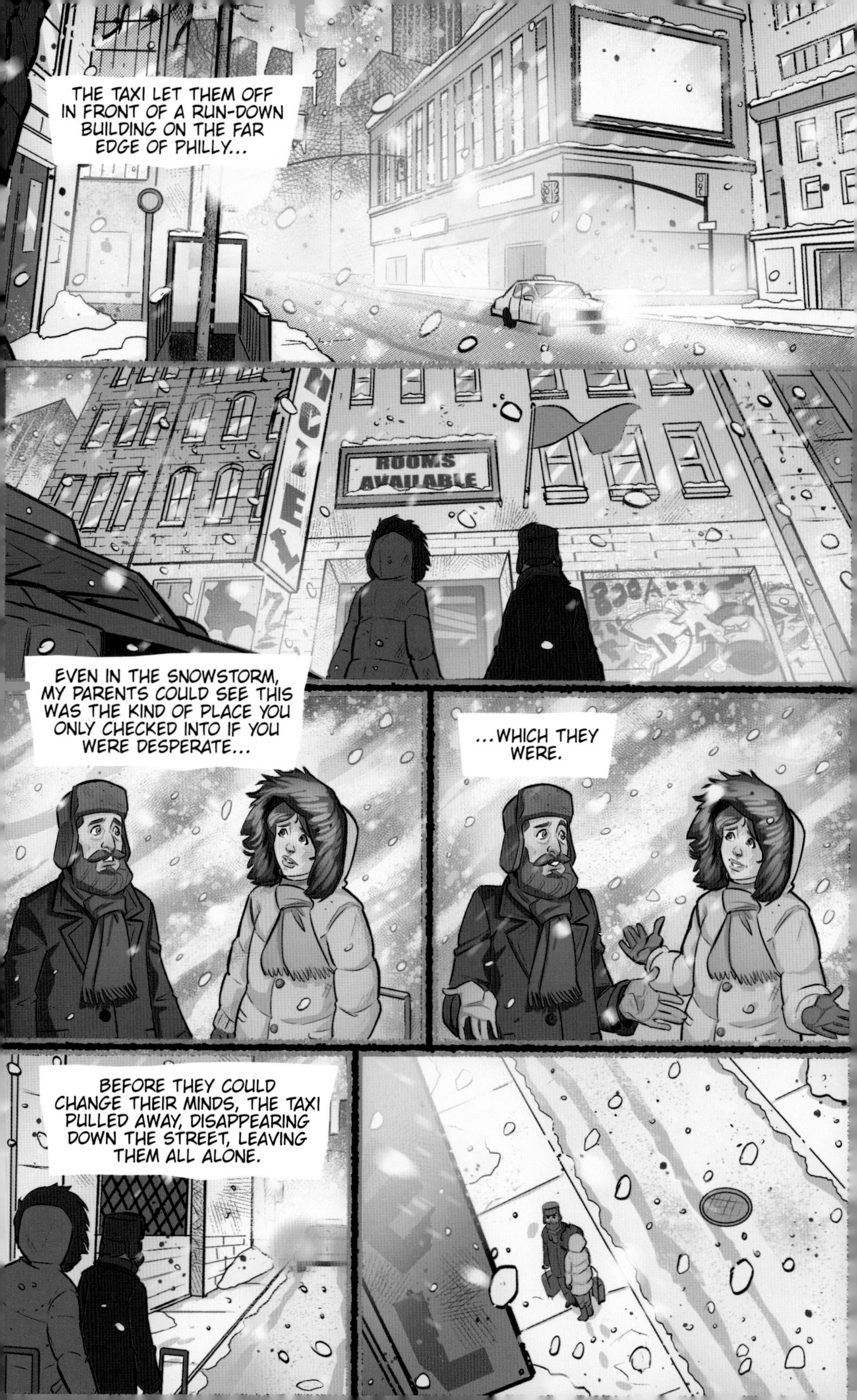
THE TAXI LET THEM OFF IN FRONT OF A RUN-DOWN BUILDING ON THE FAR EDGE OF PHILLY...
ROOMS AVAILABLE
EVEN IN THE SNOWSTORM, MY PARENTS COULD SEE THIS WAS THE KIND OF PLACE YOU ONLY CHECKED INTO IF YOU WERE DESPERATE...
...WHICH THEY WERE.
BEFORE THEY COULD CHANGE THEIR MINDS, THE TAXI PULLED AWAY, DISAPPEARING DOWN THE STREET, LEAVING THEM ALL ALONE.

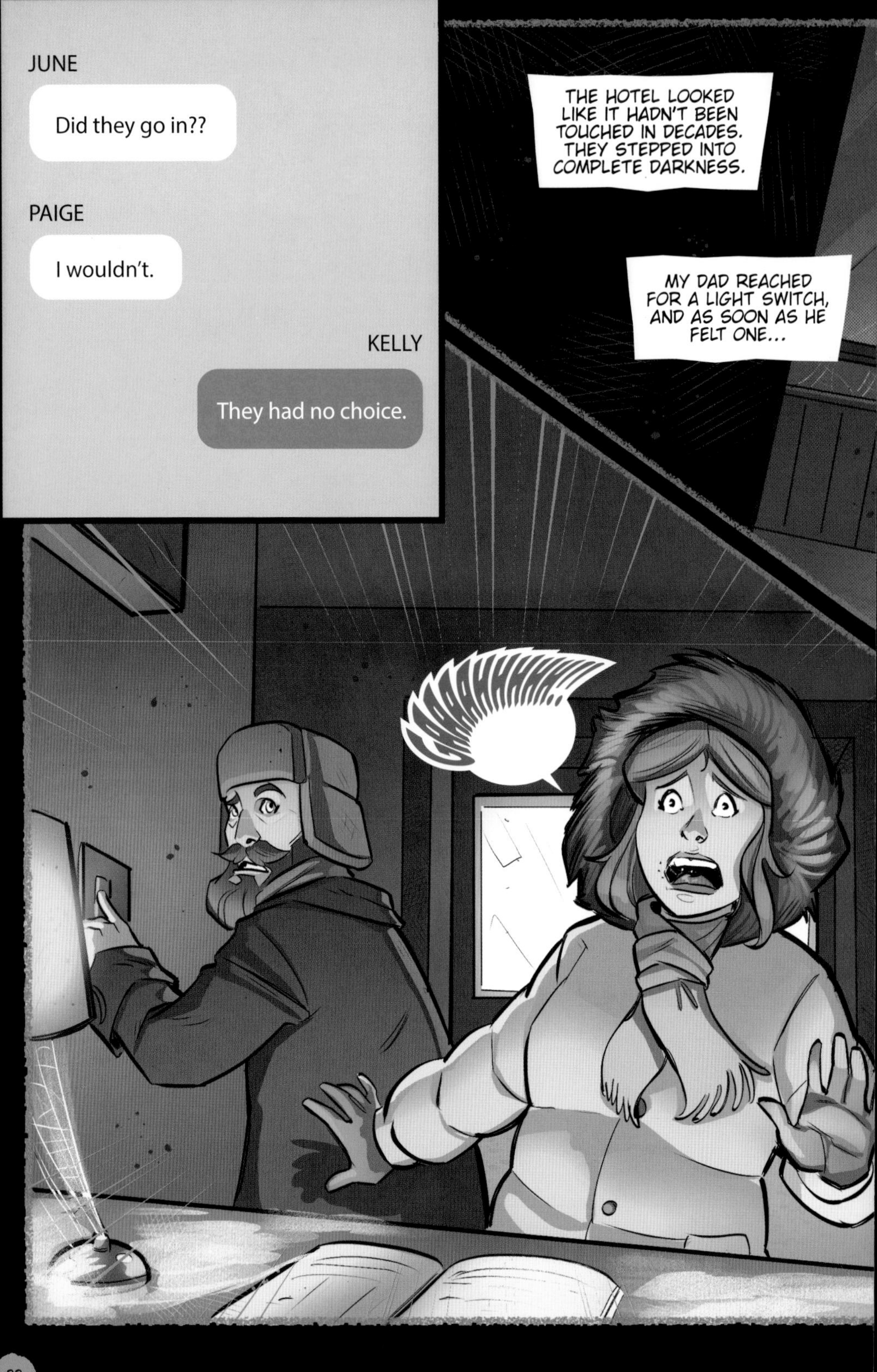
JUNE
Did they go in??
PAIGE
I wouldn't.
KELLY
They had no choice.
THE HOTEL LOOKED LIKE IT HADN'T BEEN TOUCHED IN DECADES. THEY STEPPED INTO COMPLETE DARKNESS.
MY DAD REACHED FOR A LIGHT SWITCH, AND AS SOON AS HE FELT ONE...

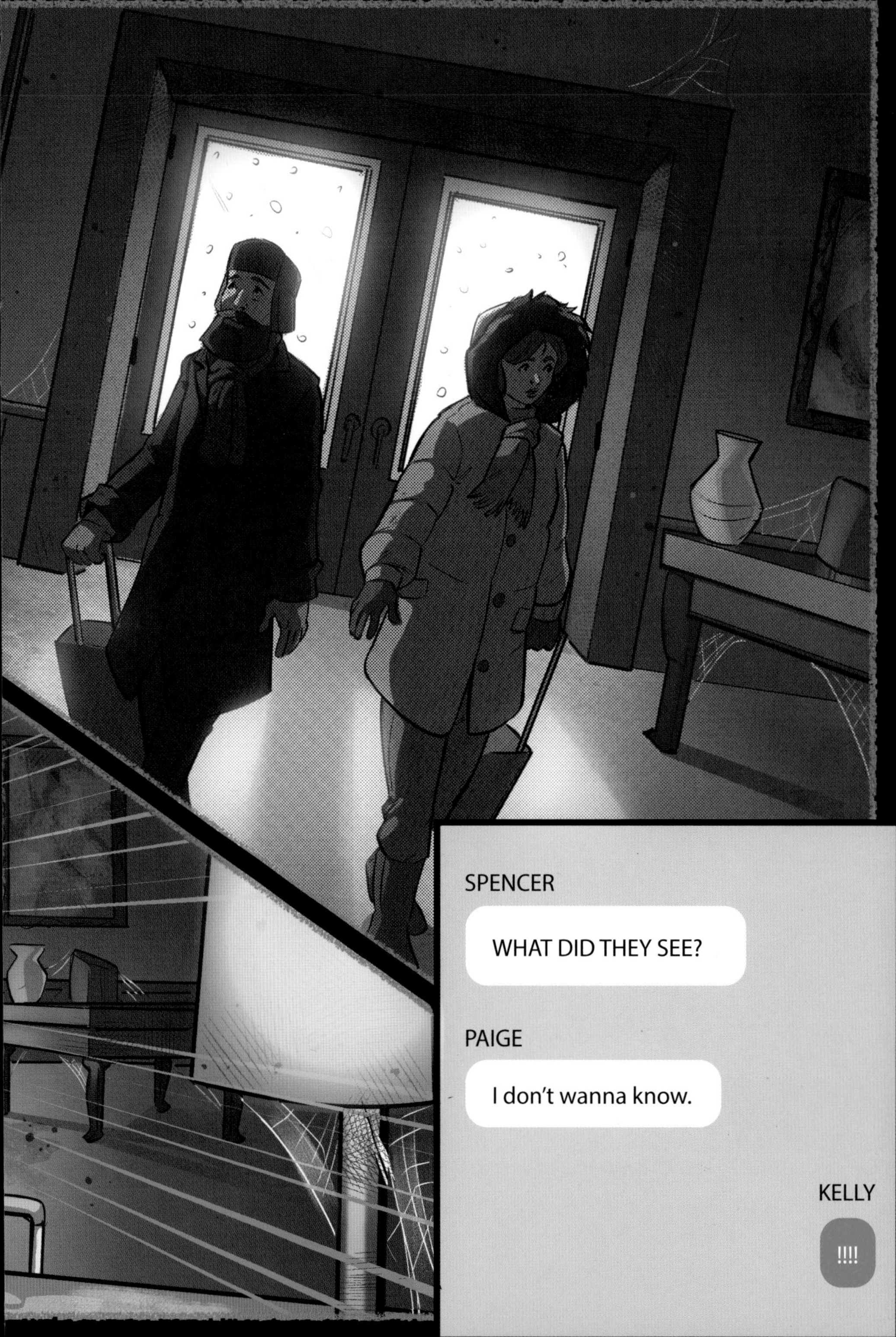
SPENCER
WHAT DID THEY SEE?
PAIGE
I don't wanna know.
KELLY
!!!!

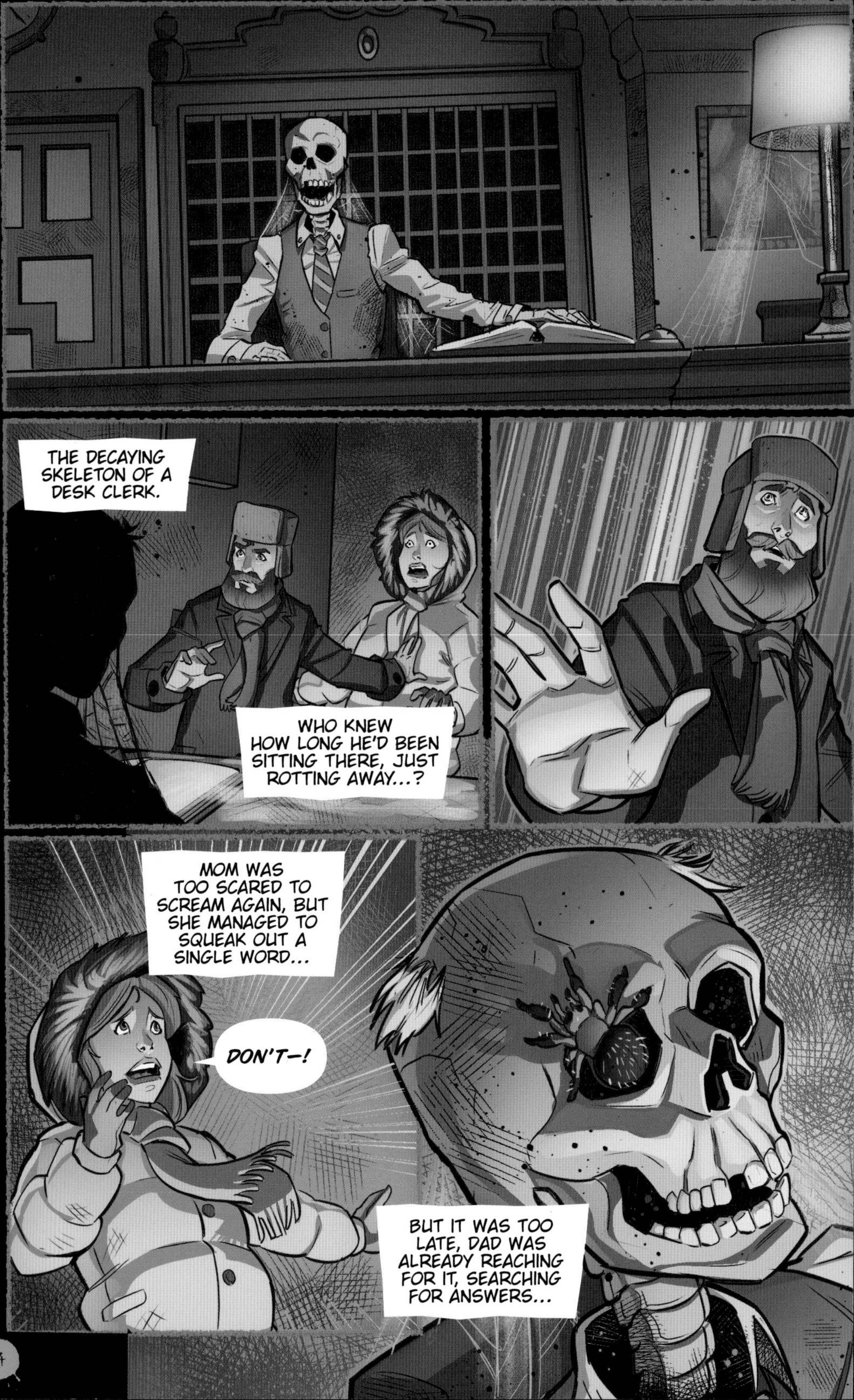
THE DECAYING SKELETON OF A DESK CLERK.
WHO KNEW HOW LONG HE'D BEEN SITTING THERE, JUST ROTTING AWAY...?
MOM WAS TOO SCARED TO SCREAM AGAIN, BUT SHE MANAGED TO SQUEAK OUT A SINGLE WORD...
DON'T—!
BUT IT WAS TOO LATE, DAD WAS ALREADY REACHING FOR IT, SEARCHING FOR ANSWERS...

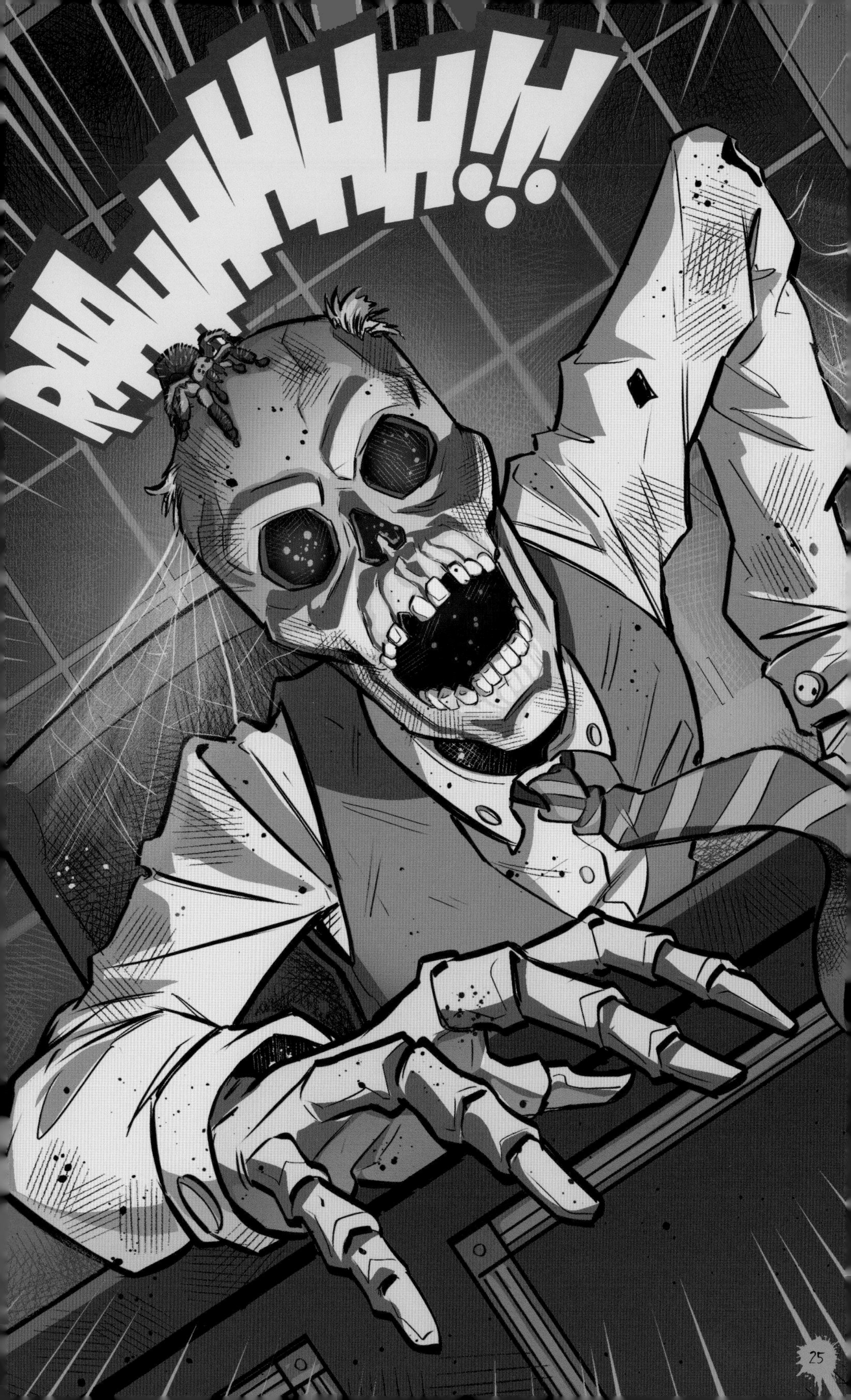
RAAAHHHH!!!

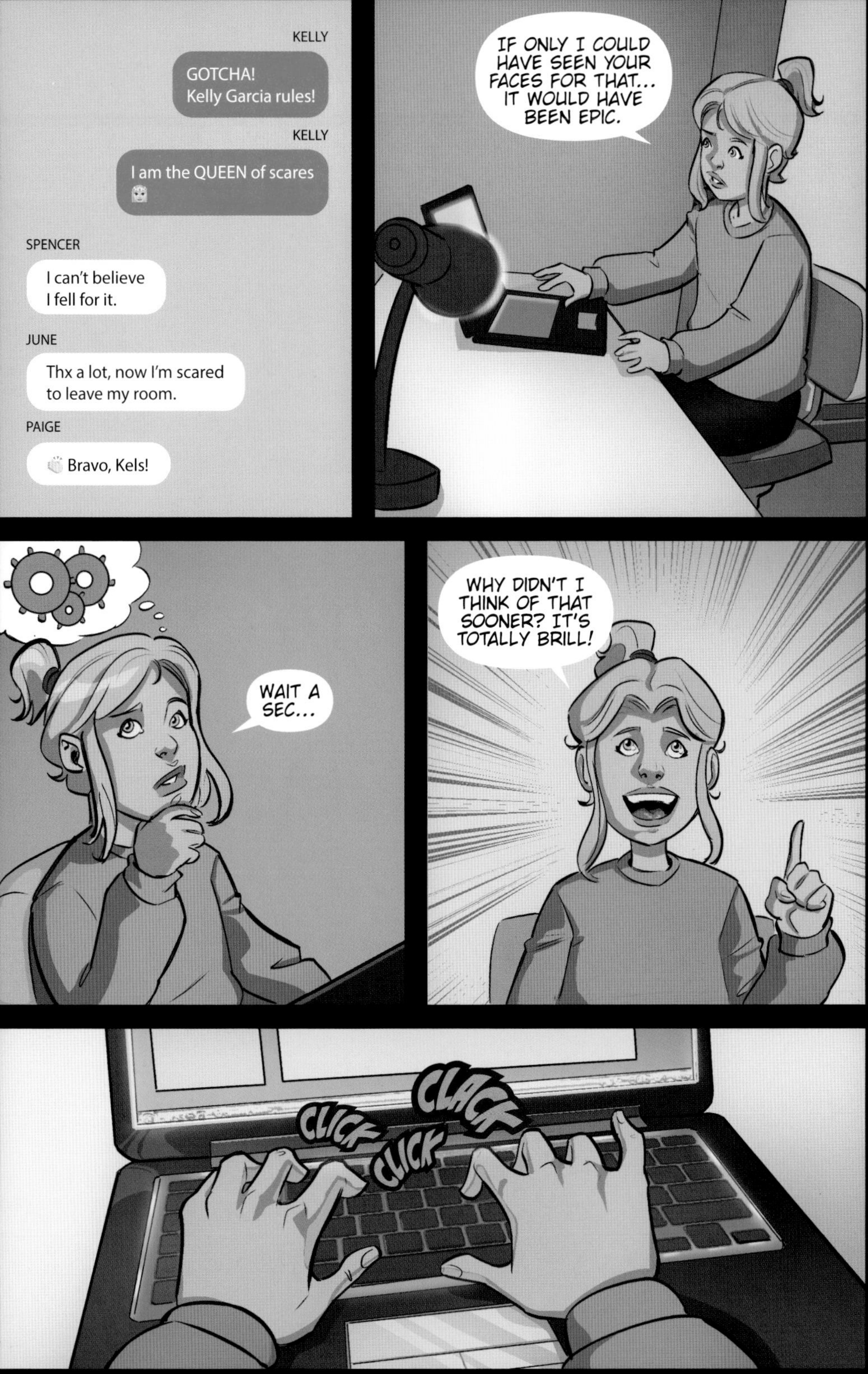
KELLY
GOTCHA! Kelly Garcia rules!
KELLY
I am the QUEEN of scares
SPENCER
I can't believe I fell for it.
JUNE
Thx a lot, now I'm scared to leave my room.
PAIGE
Bravo, Kels!
IF ONLY I COULD HAVE SEEN YOUR FACES FOR THAT... IT WOULD HAVE BEEN EPIC.
WAIT A SEC...
WHY DIDN'T I THINK OF THAT SOONER? IT'S TOTALLY BRILL!
CLICK
CLICK
CLACK

KELLY

Let's have a VIRTUAL SLEEPOVER tonight! All of us.

PAIGE

How's that gonna work?

KELLY

Just like we did for classes at home! Go to your CAMERA TIME app, put on your camera, and then we can all see each other and hang out all night, like we would if we were together. Spencer can come too since it'll be virtual!

SPENCER

Woohoo!

KELLY

8 o'clock. Wear pj's.

PAIGE

Love this!

JUNE

C u then!

KELLY

Before then, I have to warn u about something…

PAIGE

Oh great, now what?

KELLY

It's SERIOUS!

SPENCER

Spit it out!

KELLY

Get ready to be SCARED! VERY SCARED!

28

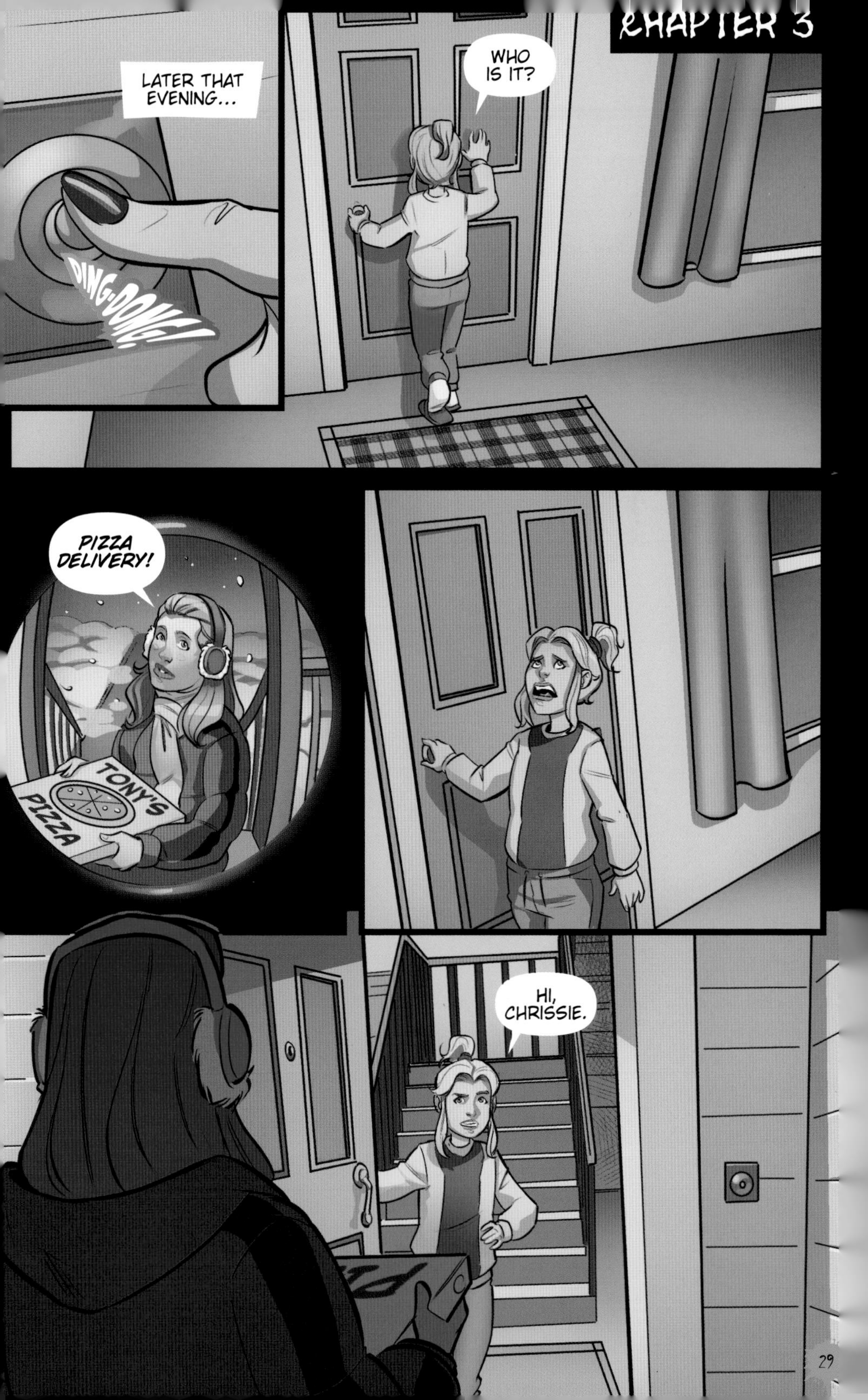
CHAPTER 3
LATER THAT EVENING...
DING-DONG!
WHO IS IT?
PIZZA DELIVERY!
TONY'S PIZZA
HI, CHRISSIE.

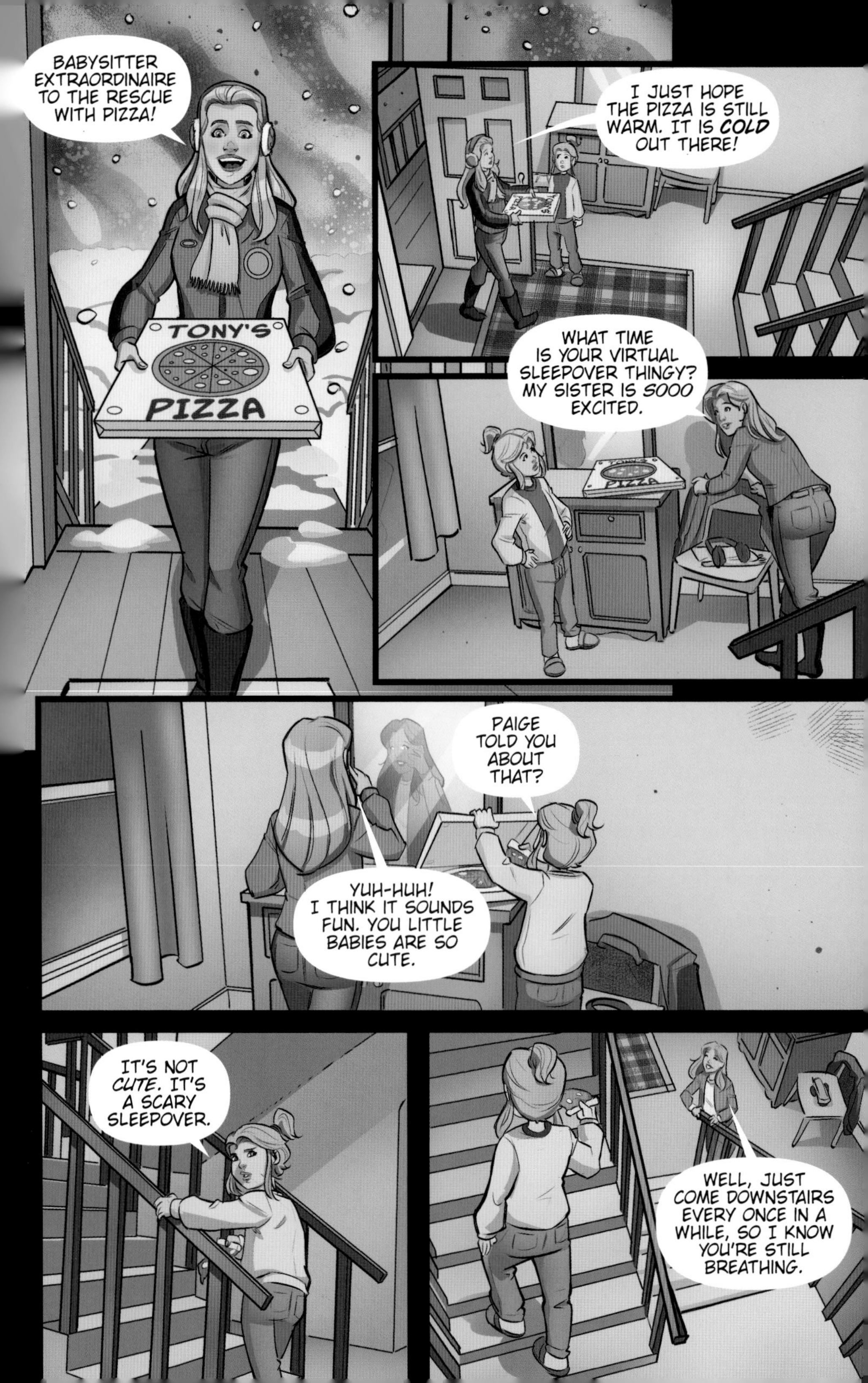
BABYSITTER EXTRAORDINAIRE TO THE RESCUE WITH PIZZA!
TONY'S PIZZA
I JUST HOPE THE PIZZA IS STILL WARM. IT IS COLD OUT THERE!
WHAT TIME IS YOUR VIRTUAL SLEEPOVER THINGY? MY SISTER IS SOOO EXCITED.
PAIGE TOLD YOU ABOUT THAT?
YUH-HUH! I THINK IT SOUNDS FUN. YOU LITTLE BABIES ARE SO CUTE.
IT'S NOT CUTE. IT'S A SCARY SLEEPOVER.
WELL, JUST COME DOWNSTAIRS EVERY ONCE IN A WHILE, SO I KNOW YOU'RE STILL BREATHING.

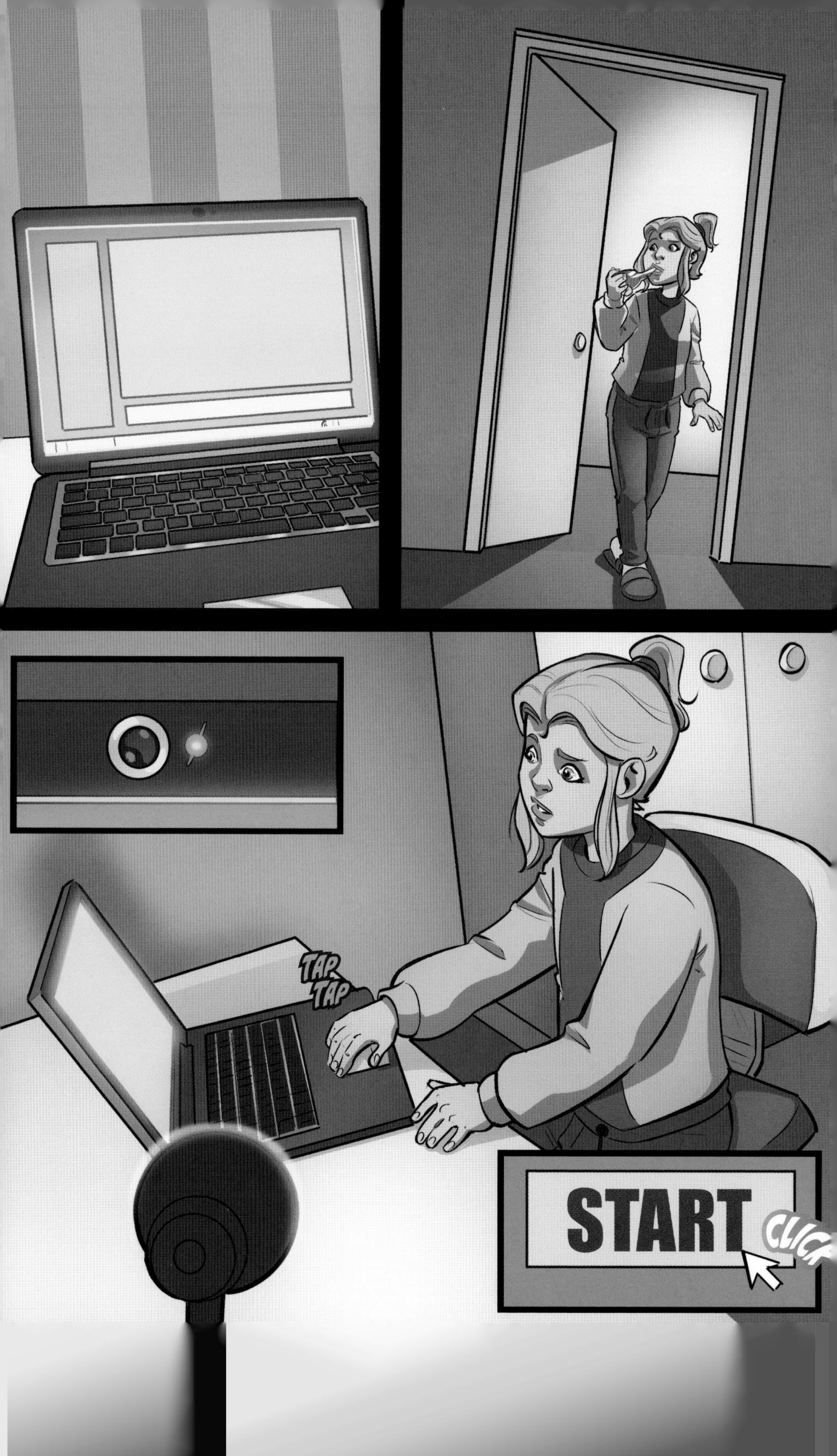
TAP
TAP
START
CLICK

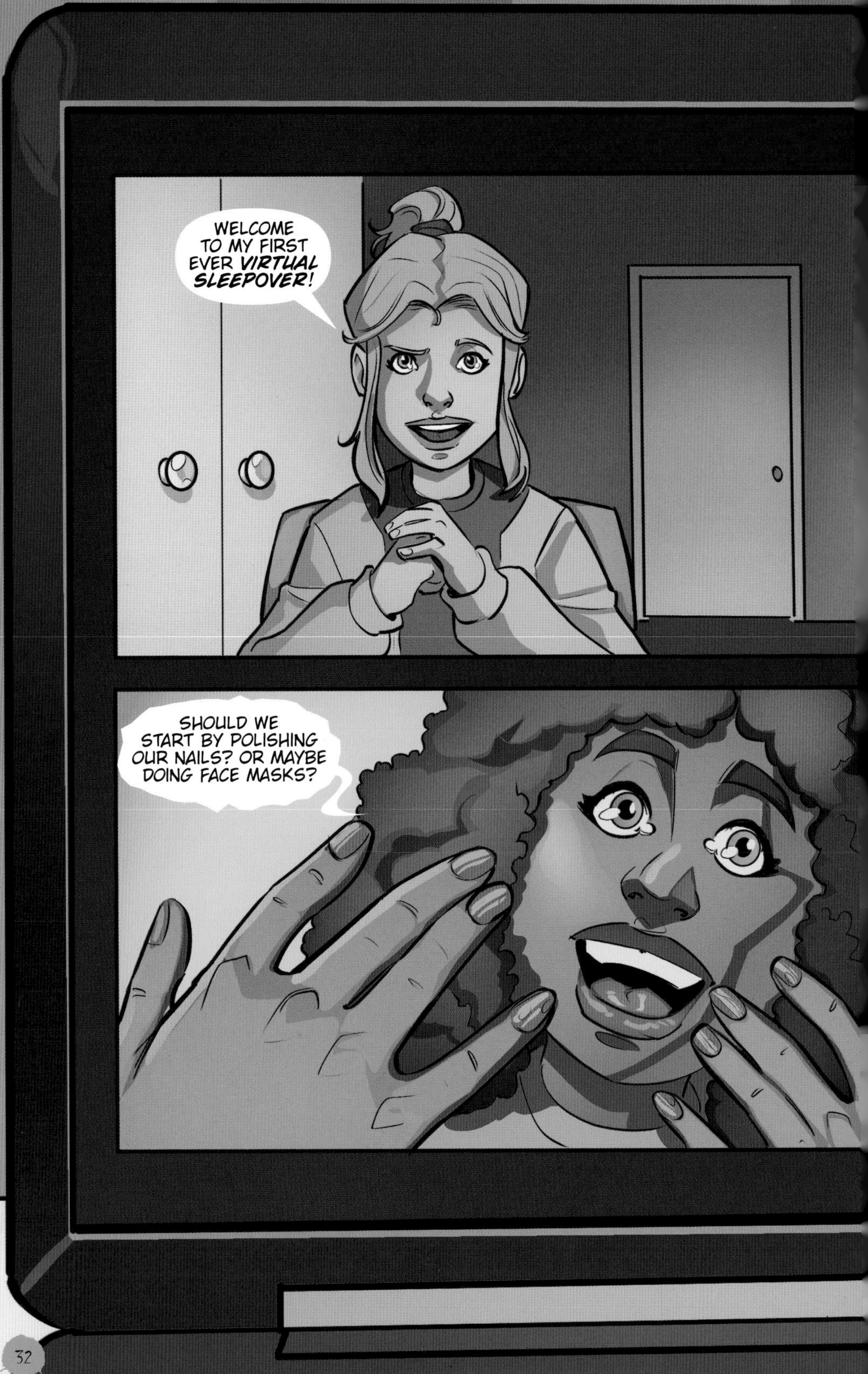
WELCOME TO MY FIRST EVER *VIRTUAL SLEEPOVER*!
SHOULD WE START BY POLISHING OUR NAILS? OR MAYBE DOING FACE MASKS?

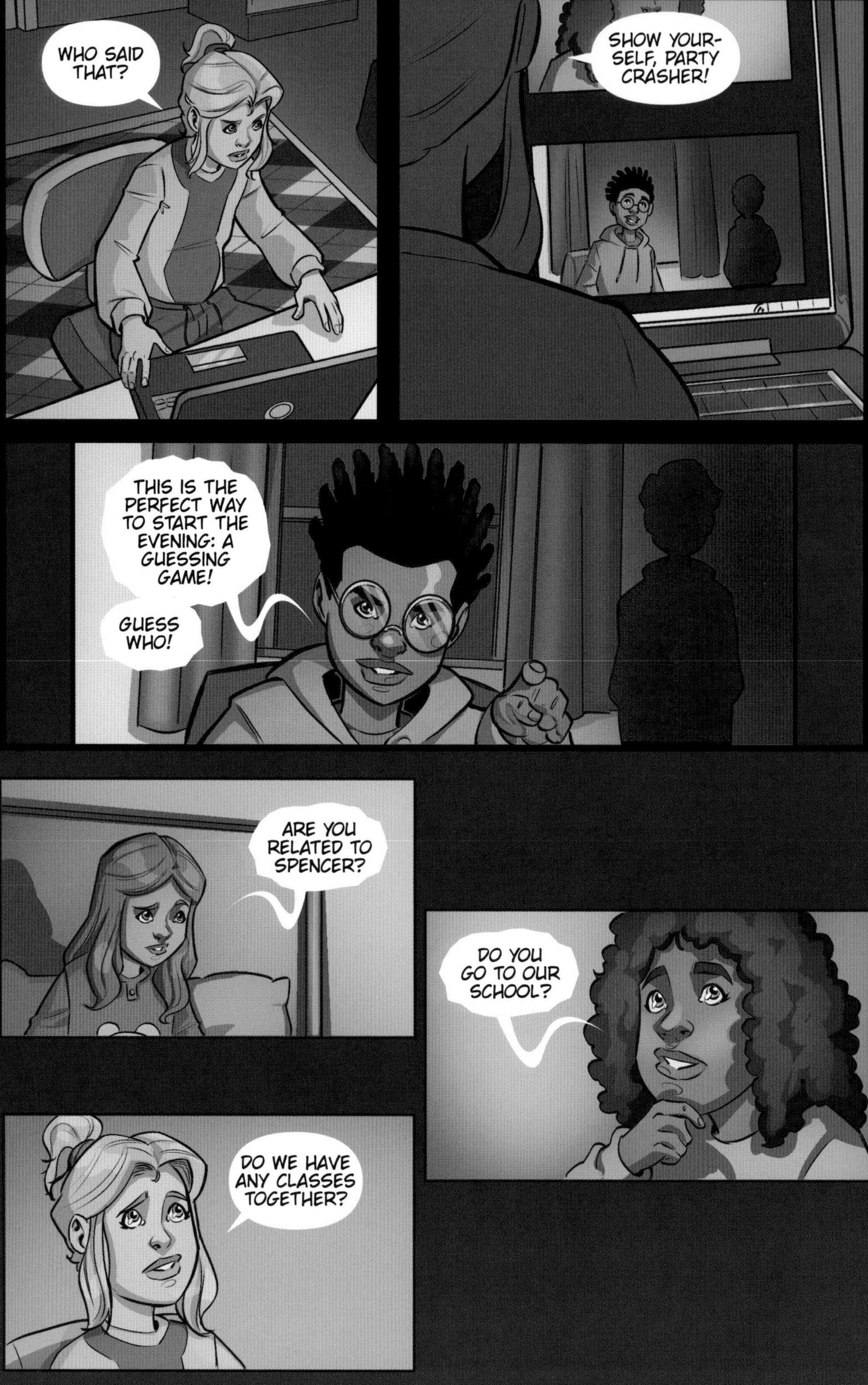
WHO SAID THAT?
SHOW YOURSELF, PARTY CRASHER!
THIS IS THE PERFECT WAY TO START THE EVENING: A GUESSING GAME!
GUESS WHO!
ARE YOU RELATED TO SPENCER?
DO YOU GO TO OUR SCHOOL?
DO WE HAVE ANY CLASSES TOGETHER?

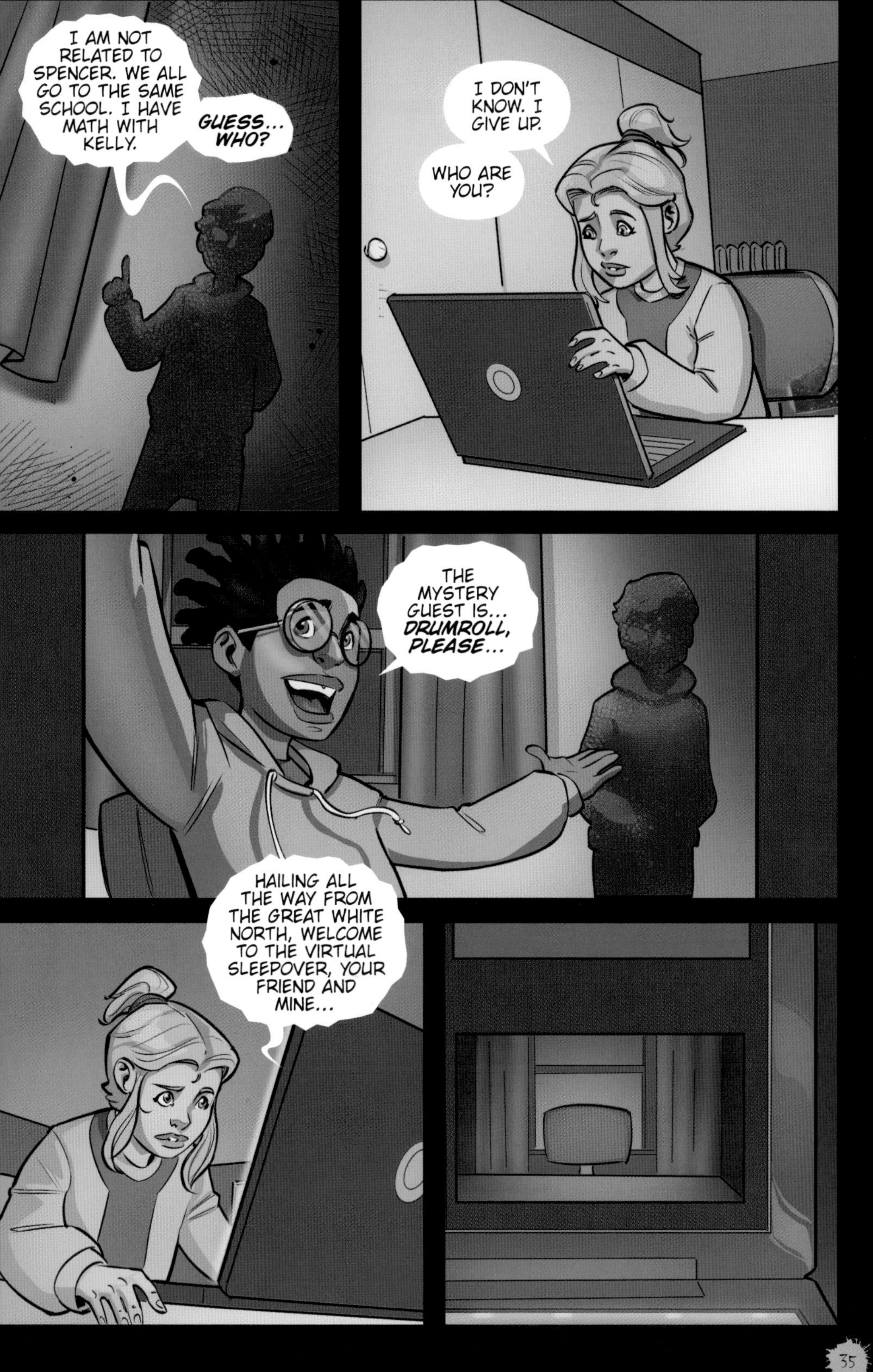
I AM NOT RELATED TO SPENCER. WE ALL GO TO THE SAME SCHOOL. I HAVE MATH WITH KELLY.
GUESS... WHO?
I DON'T KNOW. I GIVE UP.
WHO ARE YOU?
THE MYSTERY GUEST IS... DRUMROLL, PLEASE...
HAILING ALL THE WAY FROM THE GREAT WHITE NORTH, WELCOME TO THE VIRTUAL SLEEPOVER, YOUR FRIEND AND MINE...

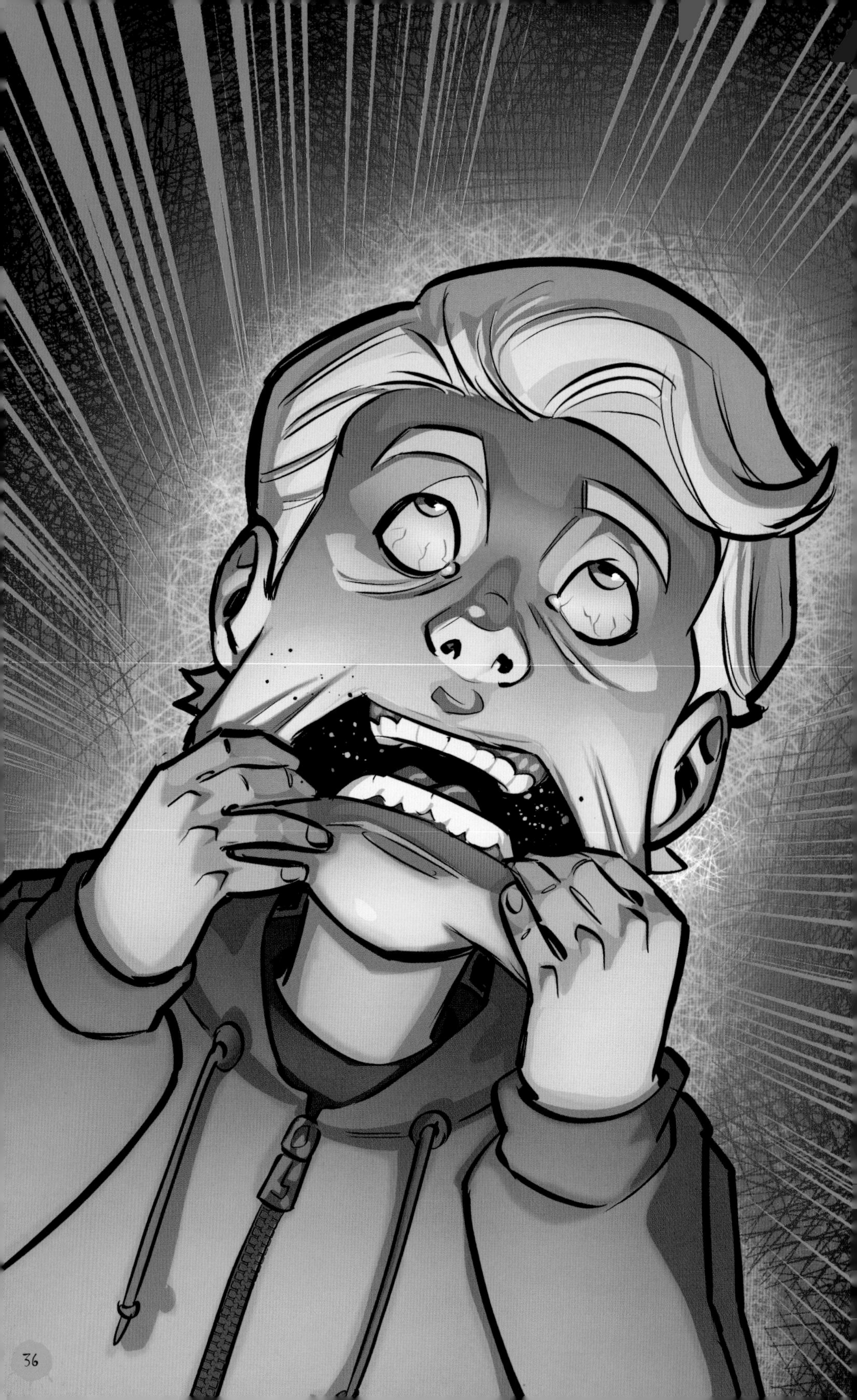

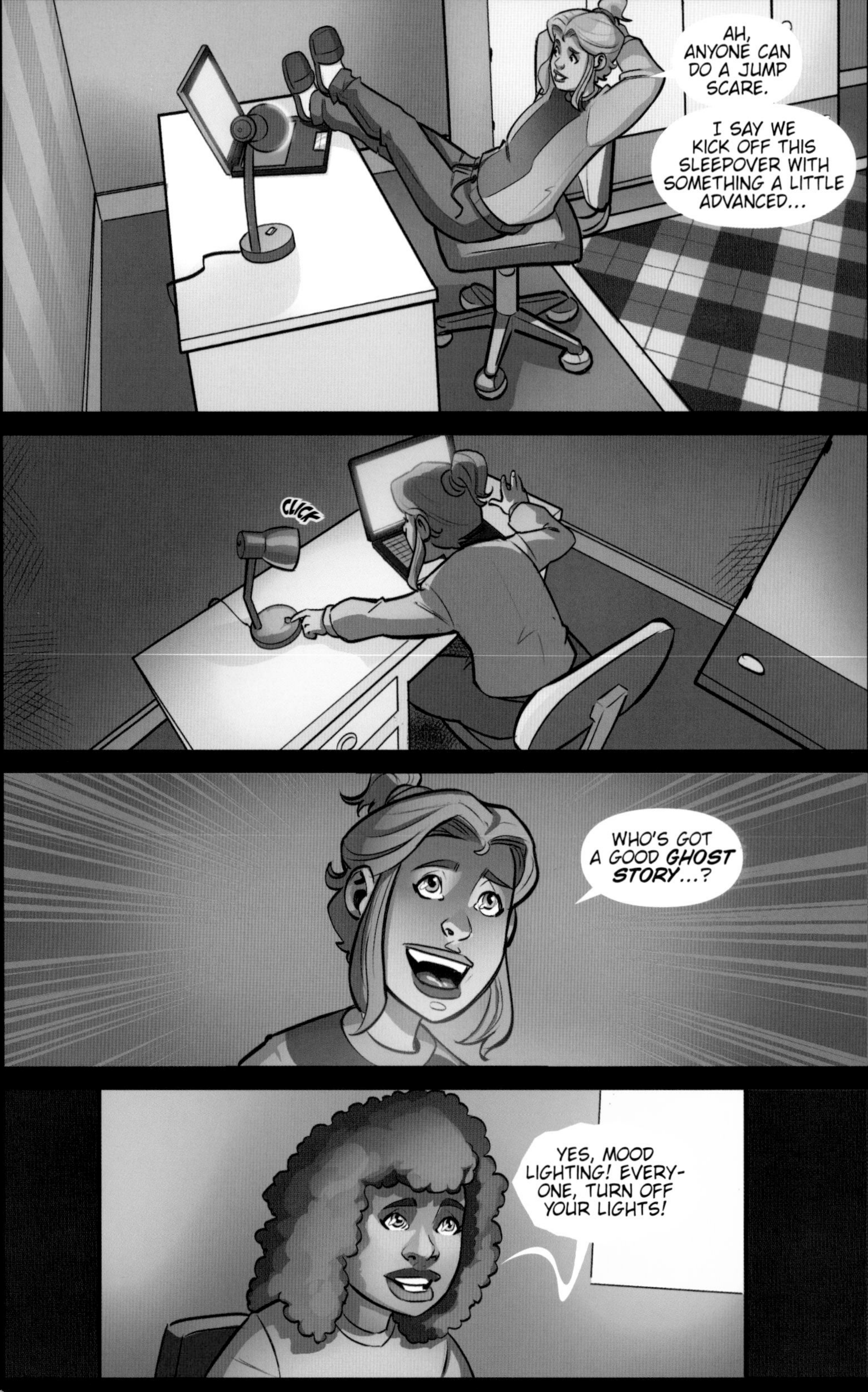
AH, ANYONE CAN DO A JUMP SCARE.
I SAY WE KICK OFF THIS SLEEPOVER WITH SOMETHING A LITTLE ADVANCED...
CLICK
WHO'S GOT A GOOD **GHOST STORY**...?
YES, MOOD LIGHTING! EVERY-ONE, TURN OFF YOUR LIGHTS!

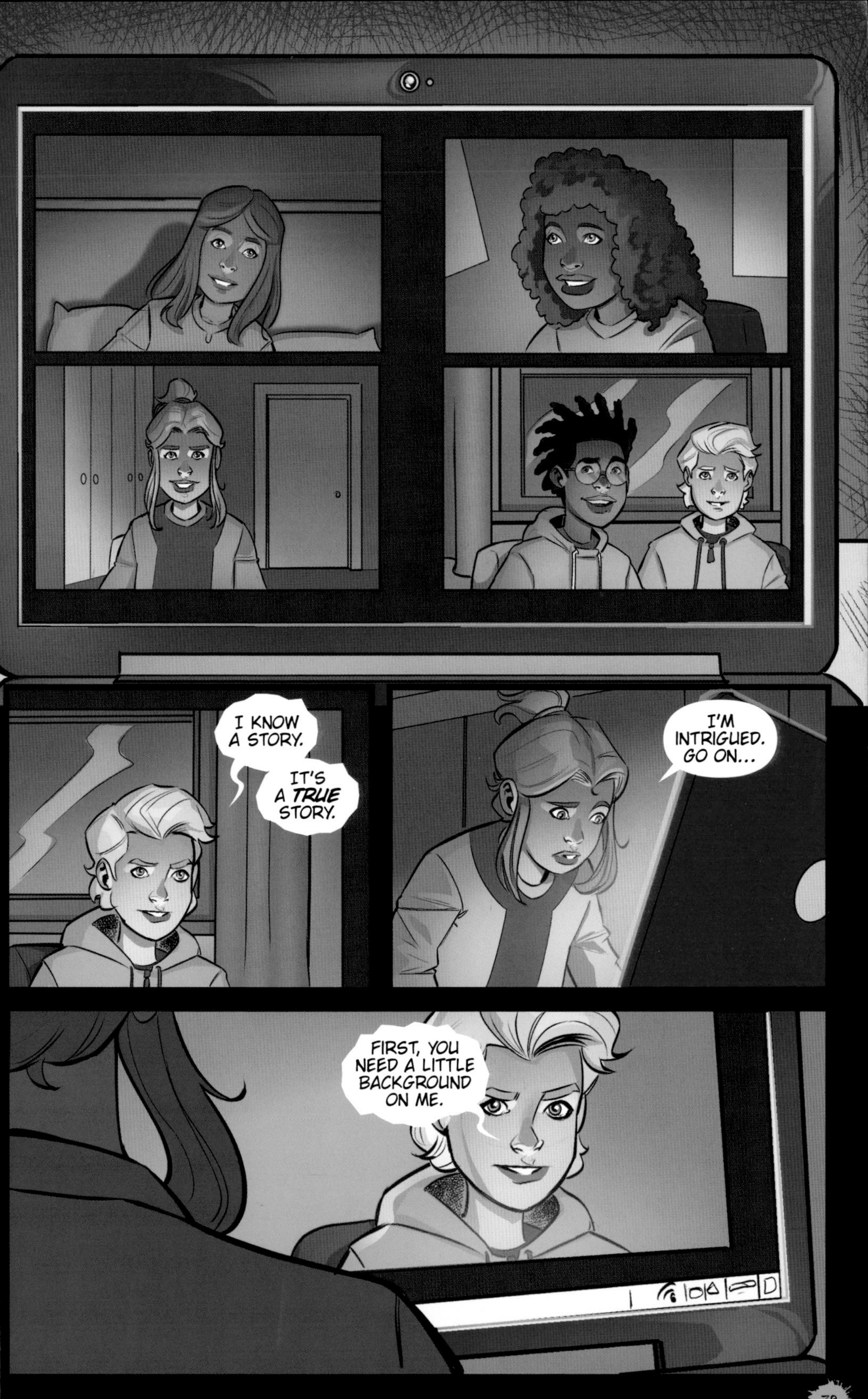
I KNOW A STORY.
IT'S A **TRUE** STORY.
I'M INTRIGUED. GO ON...
FIRST, YOU NEED A LITTLE BACKGROUND ON ME.

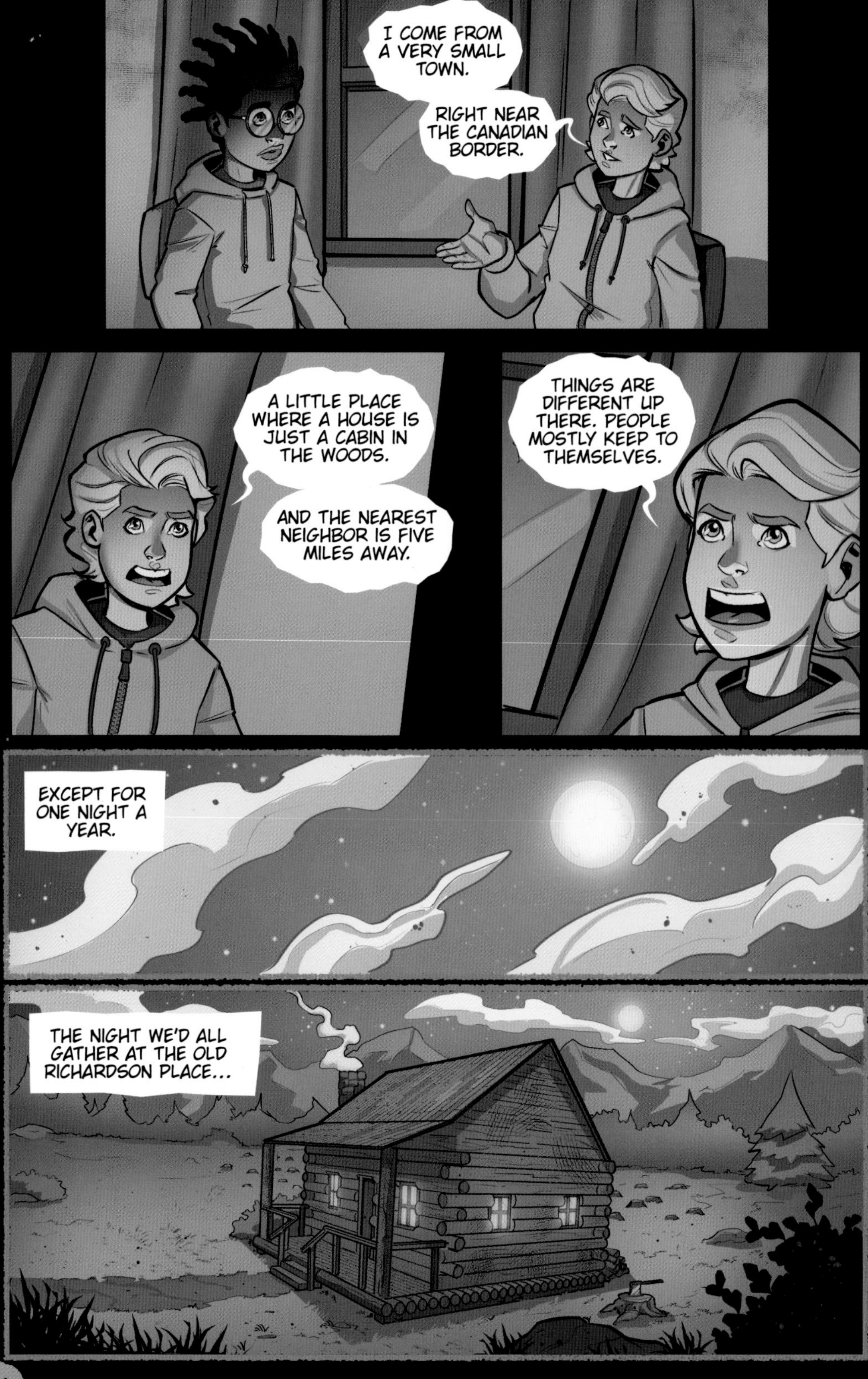
I COME FROM A VERY SMALL TOWN.
RIGHT NEAR THE CANADIAN BORDER.
A LITTLE PLACE WHERE A HOUSE IS JUST A CABIN IN THE WOODS.
AND THE NEAREST NEIGHBOR IS FIVE MILES AWAY.
THINGS ARE DIFFERENT UP THERE. PEOPLE MOSTLY KEEP TO THEMSELVES.
EXCEPT FOR ONE NIGHT A YEAR.
THE NIGHT WE'D ALL GATHER AT THE OLD RICHARDSON PLACE...

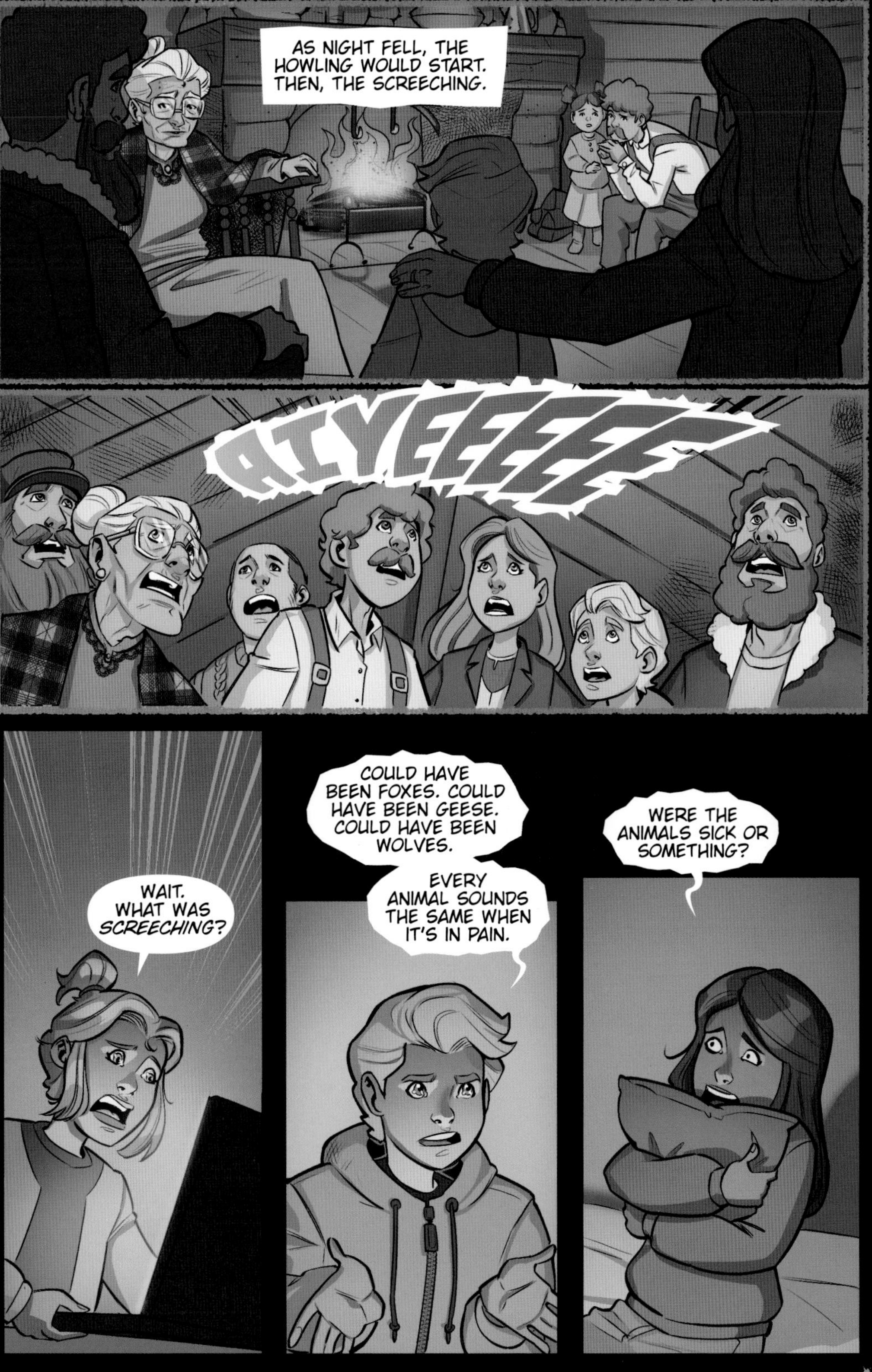
AS NIGHT FELL, THE HOWLING WOULD START. THEN, THE SCREECHING.
AIYEEEEE
WAIT. WHAT WAS SCREECHING?
COULD HAVE BEEN FOXES. COULD HAVE BEEN GEESE. COULD HAVE BEEN WOLVES.
EVERY ANIMAL SOUNDS THE SAME WHEN IT'S IN PAIN.
WERE THE ANIMALS SICK OR SOMETHING?

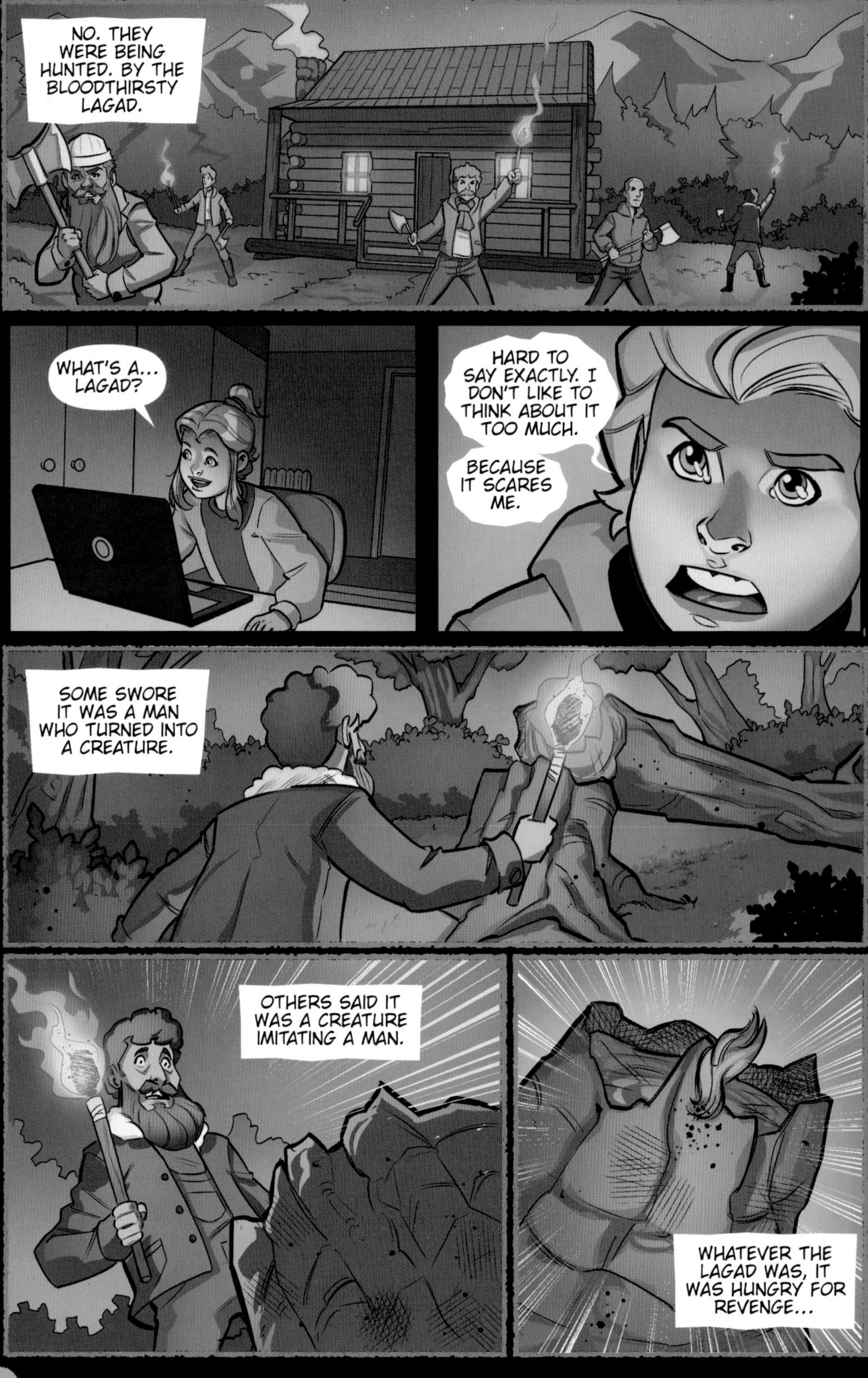
NO. THEY WERE BEING HUNTED. BY THE BLOODTHIRSTY LAGAD.
WHAT'S A... LAGAD?
HARD TO SAY EXACTLY. I DON'T LIKE TO THINK ABOUT IT TOO MUCH.
BECAUSE IT SCARES ME.
SOME SWORE IT WAS A MAN WHO TURNED INTO A CREATURE.
OTHERS SAID IT WAS A CREATURE IMITATING A MAN.
WHATEVER THE LAGAD WAS, IT WAS HUNGRY FOR REVENGE...

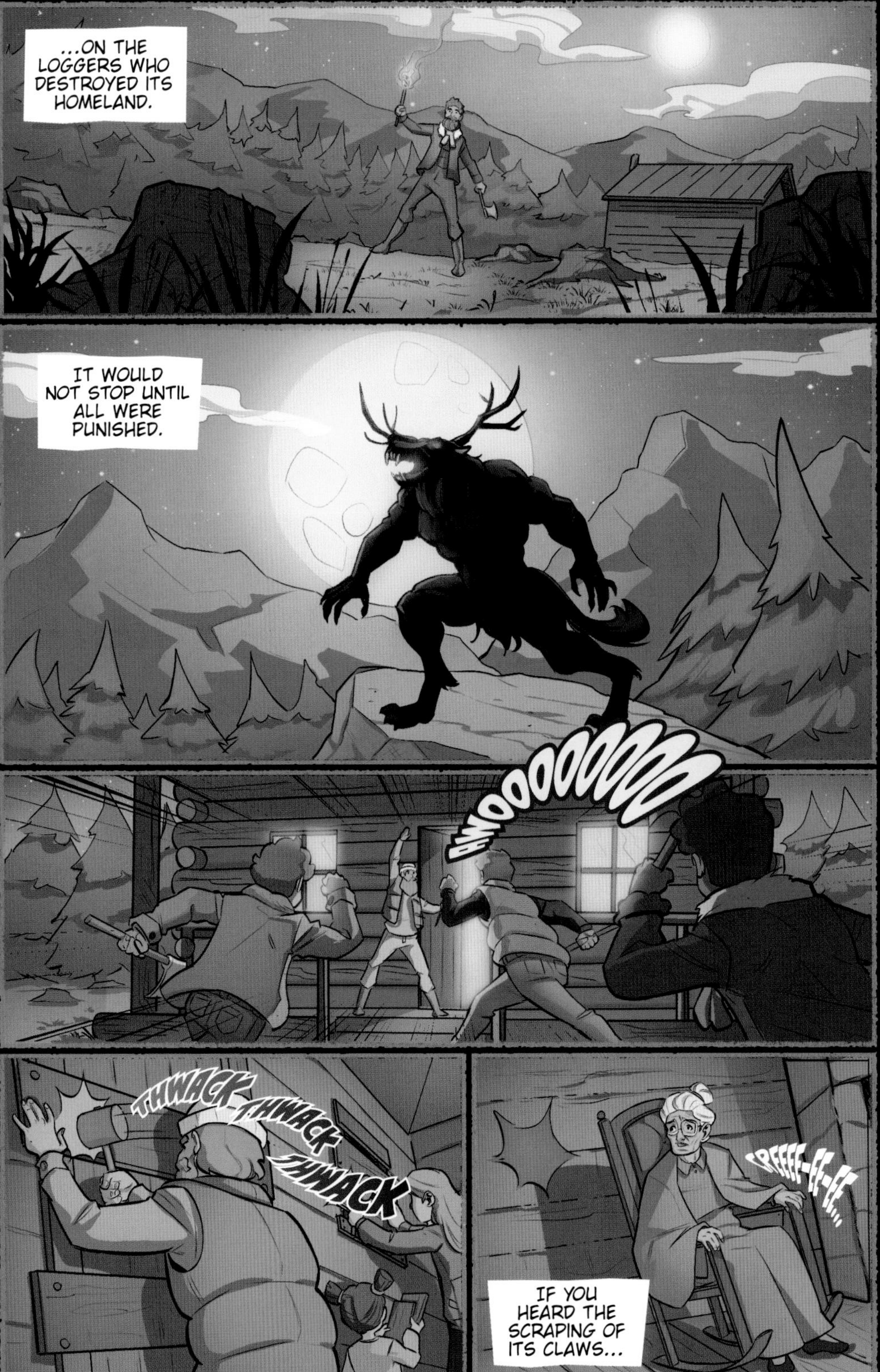
...ON THE LOGGERS WHO DESTROYED ITS HOMELAND.
IT WOULD NOT STOP UNTIL ALL WERE PUNISHED.
AWOOOOOOOO
THWACK
THWACK
THWACK
CREEEE-EE-EE...
IF YOU HEARD THE SCRAPING OF ITS CLAWS...

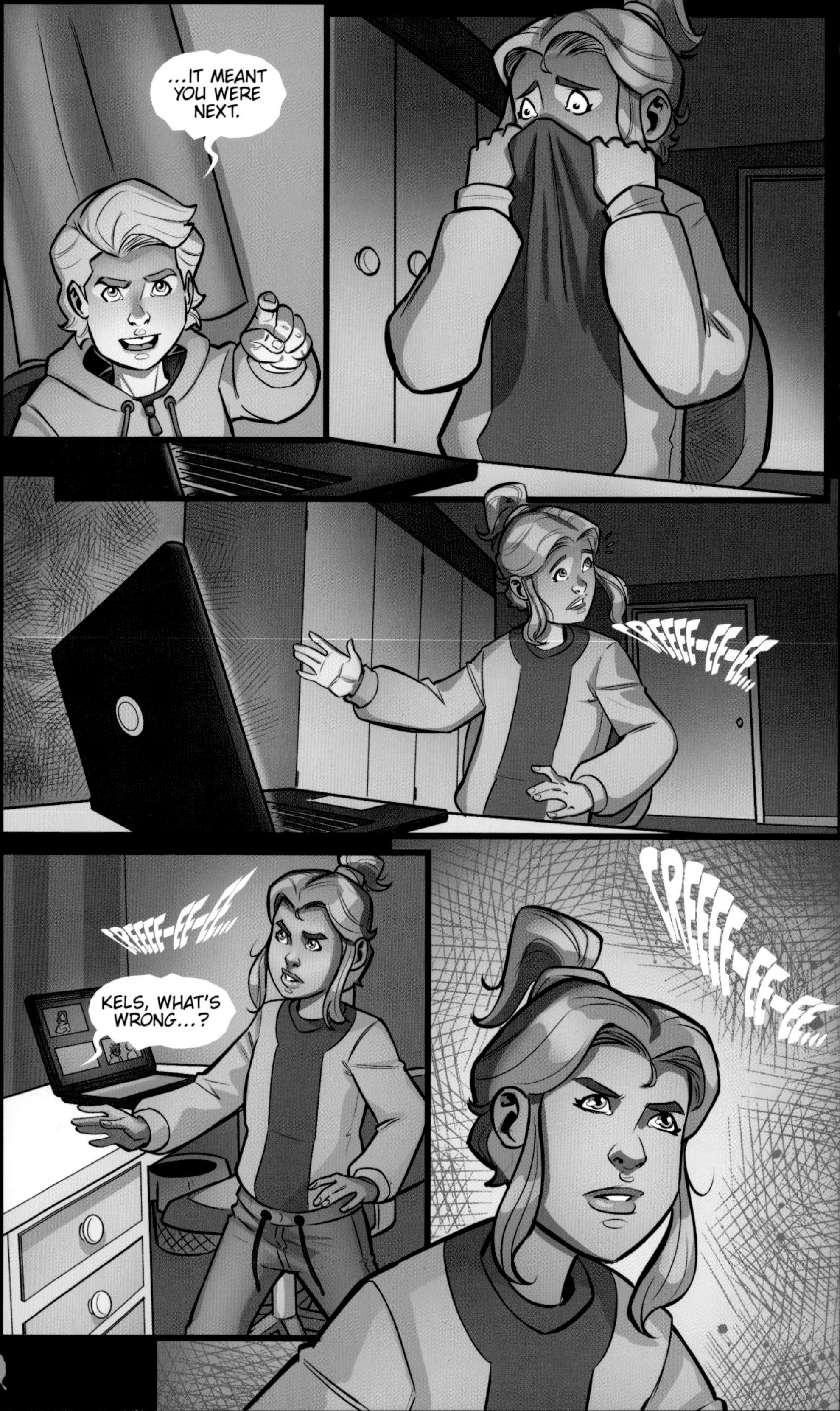
...IT MEANT YOU WERE NEXT.
CREEEE-EE-EE...
CREEEE-EE-EE...
KELS, WHAT'S WRONG...?
CREEEE-EE-EE...

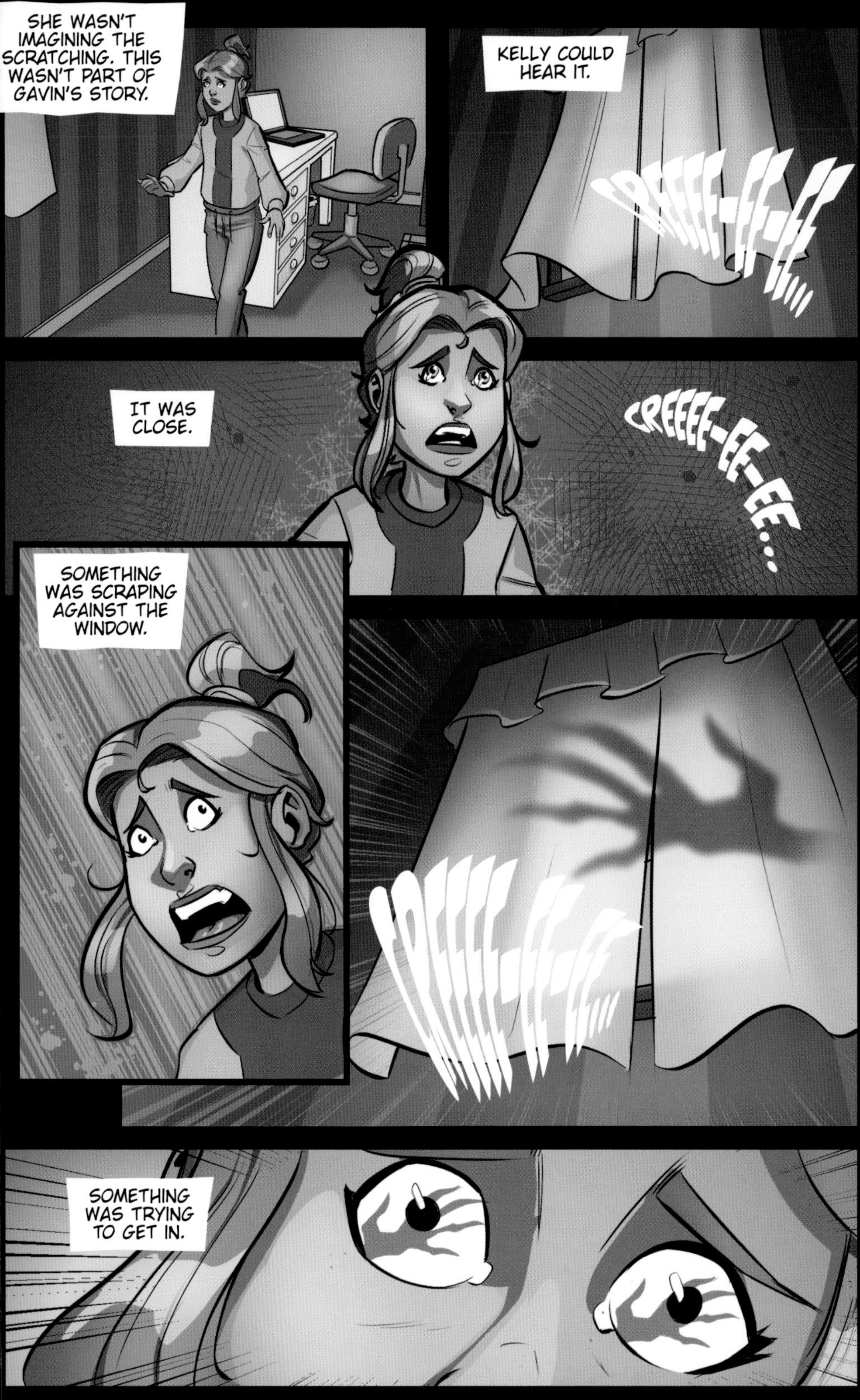
SHE WASN'T IMAGINING THE SCRATCHING. THIS WASN'T PART OF GAVIN'S STORY.
KELLY COULD HEAR IT.
CREEEE-EE-EE...
IT WAS CLOSE.
CREEEE-EE-EE...
SOMETHING WAS SCRAPING AGAINST THE WINDOW.
CREEEE-EE-EE...
SOMETHING WAS TRYING TO GET IN.

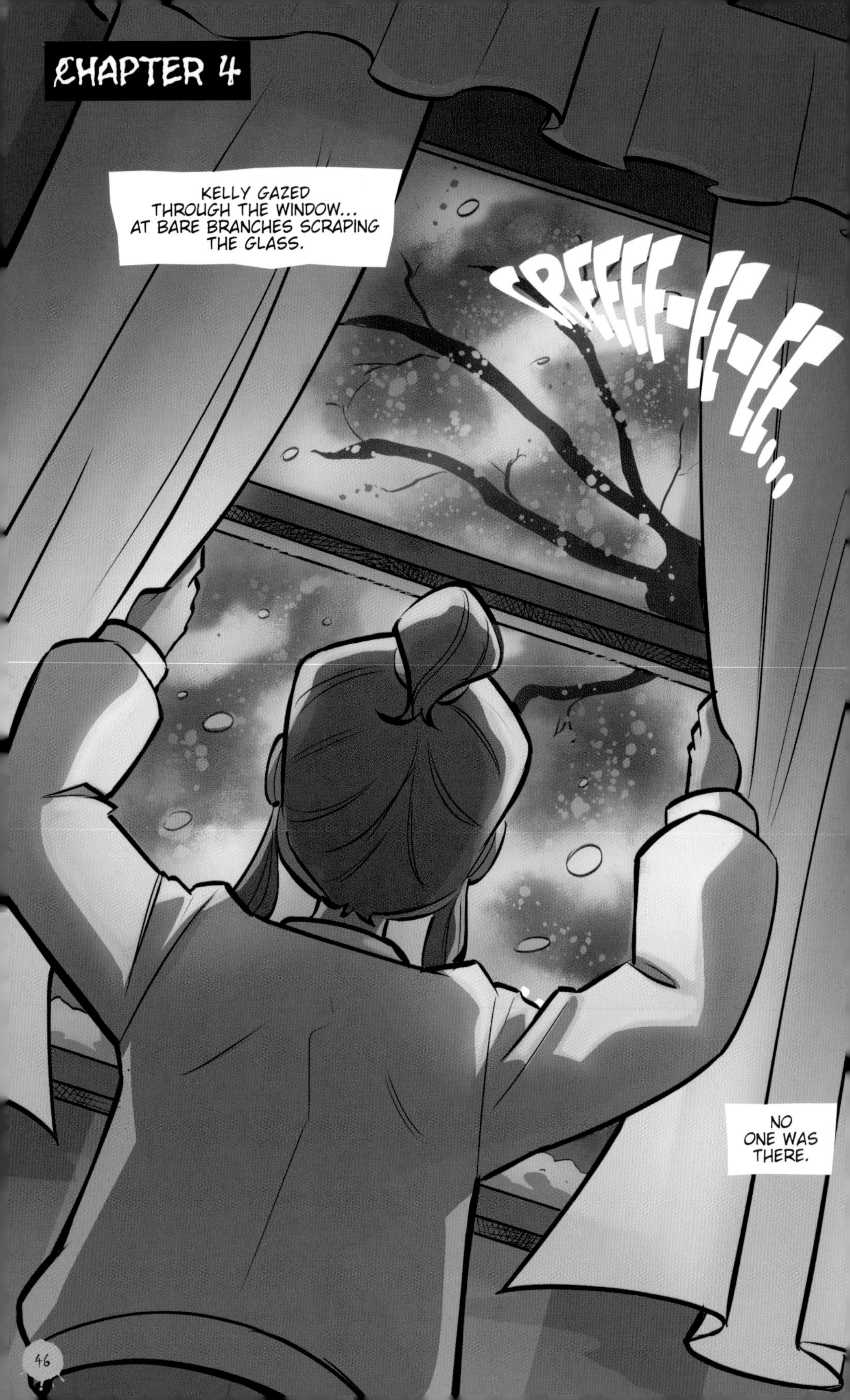
CHAPTER 4
KELLY GAZED THROUGH THE WINDOW... AT BARE BRANCHES SCRAPING THE GLASS.
CREEEE-EE-EE...
NO ONE WAS THERE.

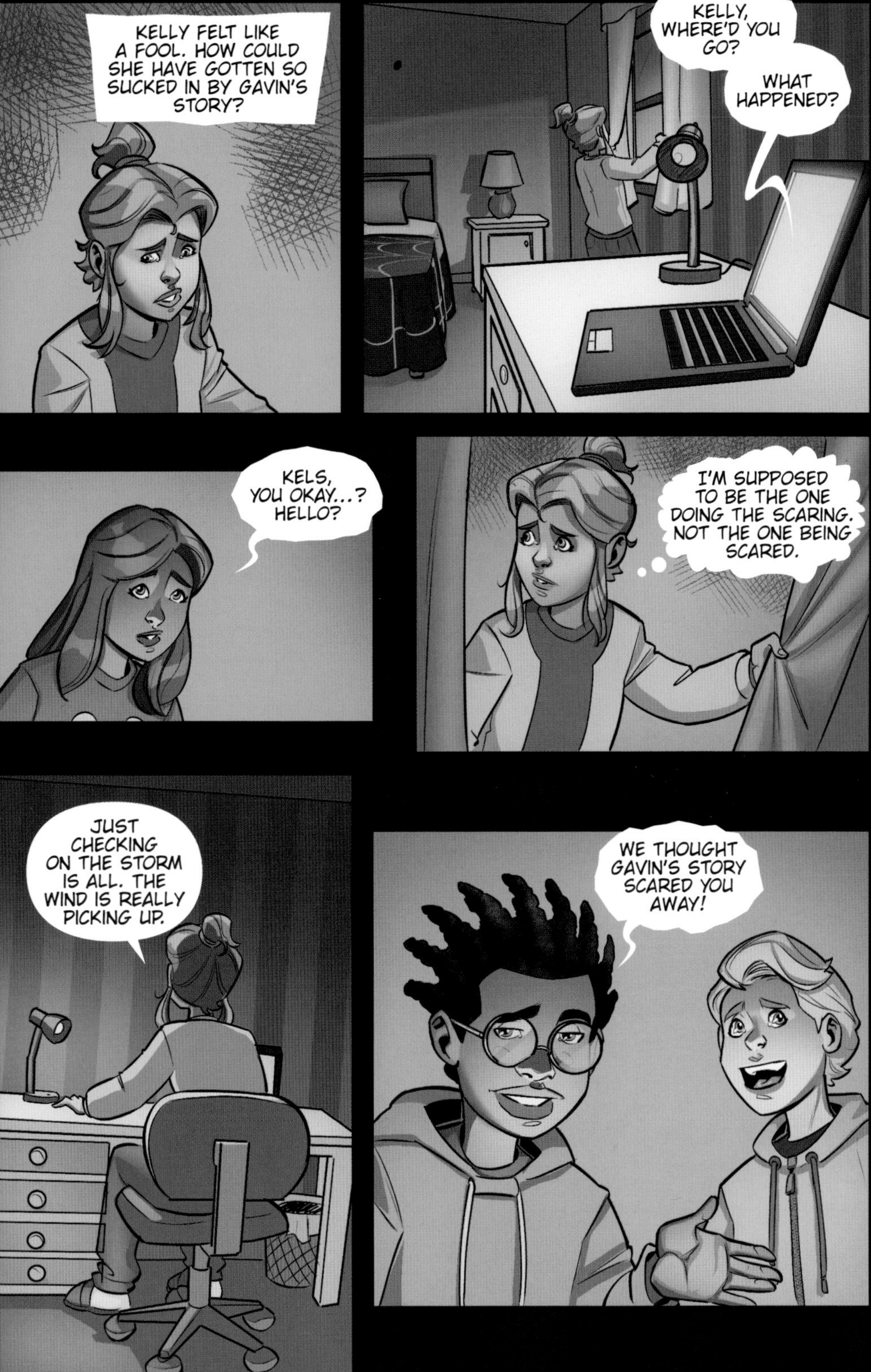
KELLY FELT LIKE A FOOL. HOW COULD SHE HAVE GOTTEN SO SUCKED IN BY GAVIN'S STORY?
KELLY, WHERE'D YOU GO?
WHAT HAPPENED?
KELS, YOU OKAY...? HELLO?
I'M SUPPOSED TO BE THE ONE DOING THE SCARING. NOT THE ONE BEING SCARED.
JUST CHECKING ON THE STORM IS ALL. THE WIND IS REALLY PICKING UP.
WE THOUGHT GAVIN'S STORY SCARED YOU AWAY!

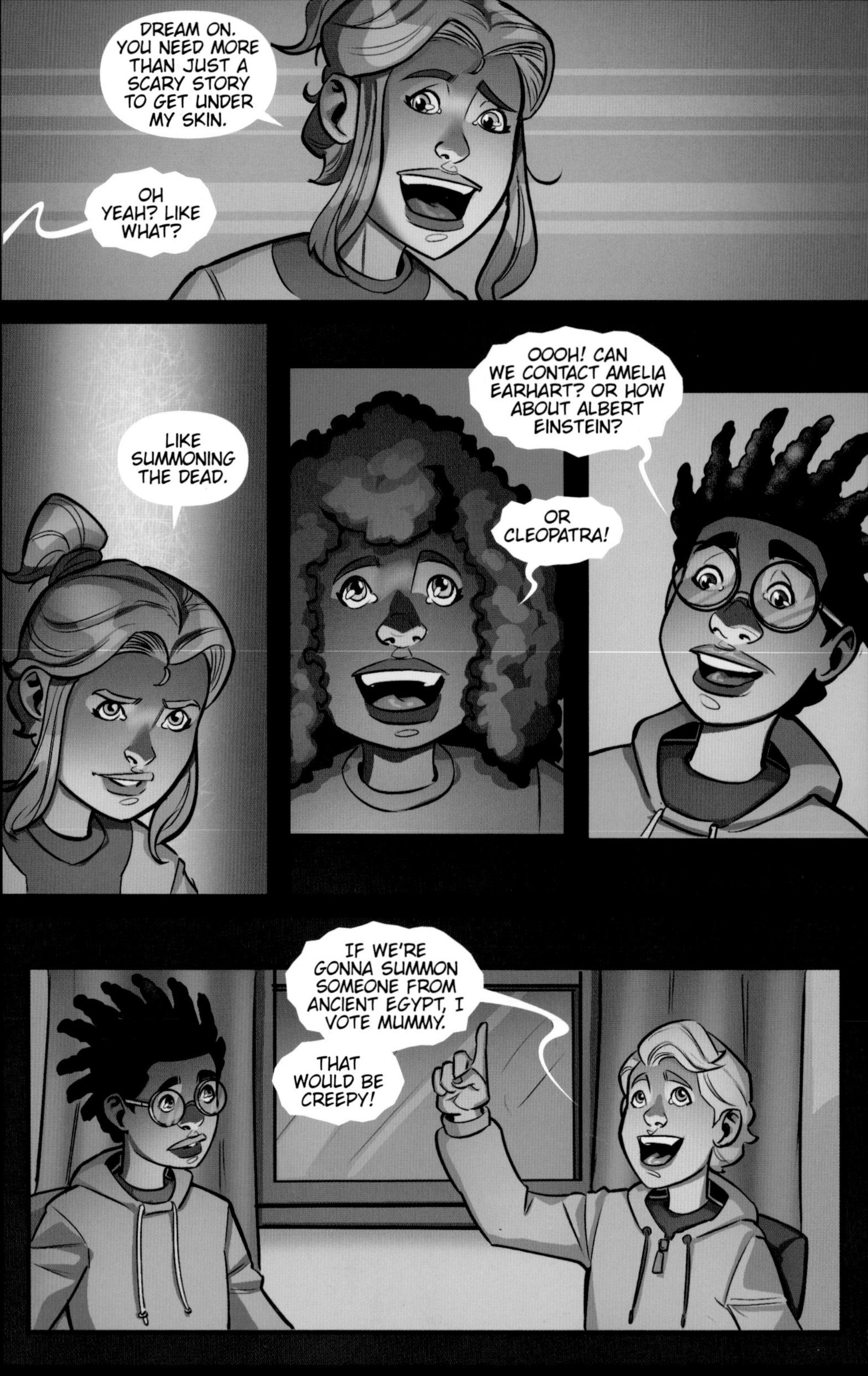
DREAM ON. YOU NEED MORE THAN JUST A SCARY STORY TO GET UNDER MY SKIN.
OH YEAH? LIKE WHAT?
LIKE SUMMONING THE DEAD.
OOOH! CAN WE CONTACT AMELIA EARHART? OR HOW ABOUT ALBERT EINSTEIN?
OR CLEOPATRA!
IF WE'RE GONNA SUMMON SOMEONE FROM ANCIENT EGYPT, I VOTE MUMMY.
THAT WOULD BE CREEPY!

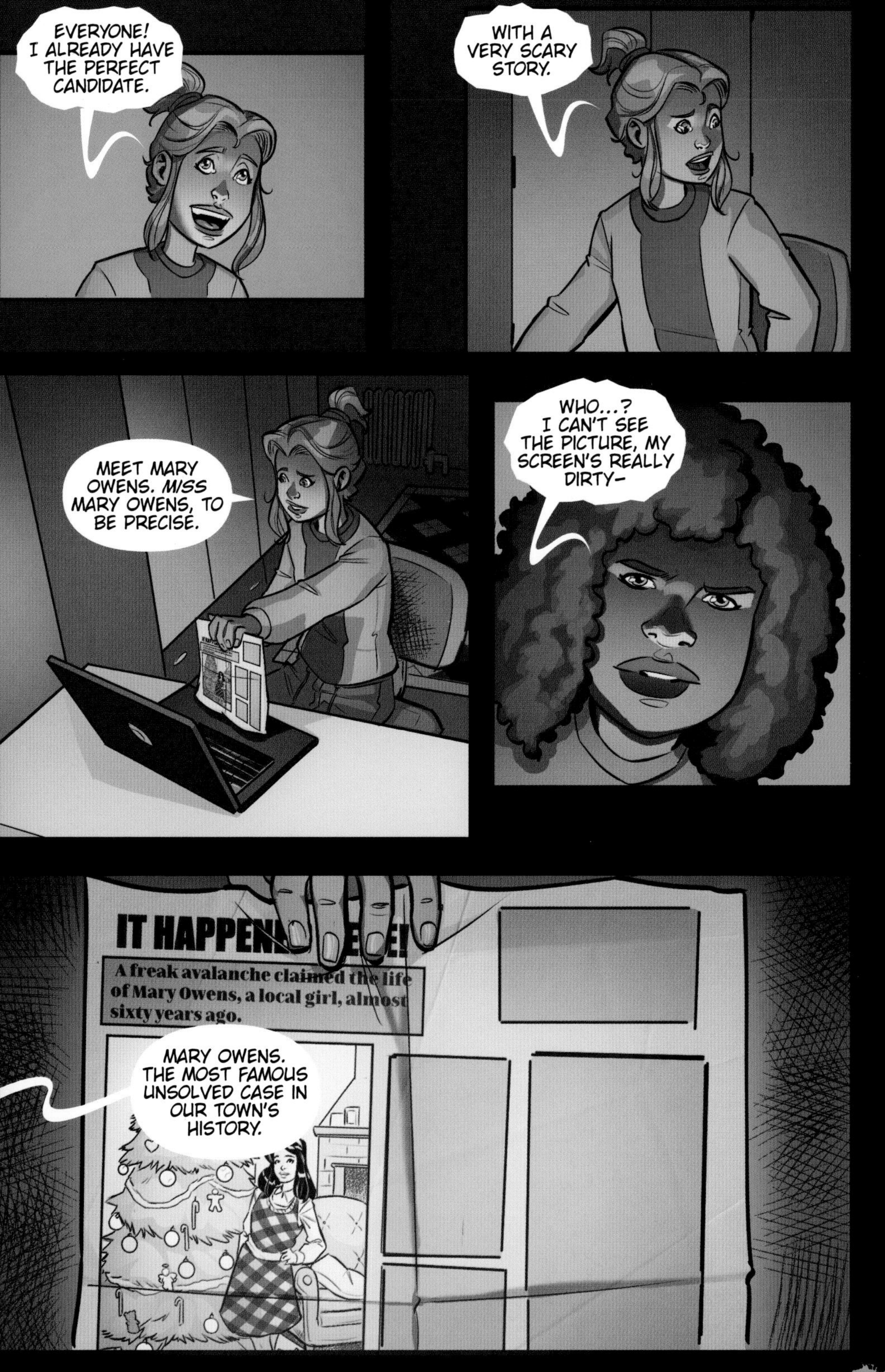
EVERYONE! I ALREADY HAVE THE PERFECT CANDIDATE.
WITH A VERY SCARY STORY.
MEET MARY OWENS. *MISS* MARY OWENS, TO BE PRECISE.
WHO...? I CAN'T SEE THE PICTURE, MY SCREEN'S REALLY DIRTY—
A freak avalanche claimed the life of Mary Owens, a local girl, almost sixty years ago.
MARY OWENS. THE MOST FAMOUS UNSOLVED CASE IN OUR TOWN'S HISTORY.

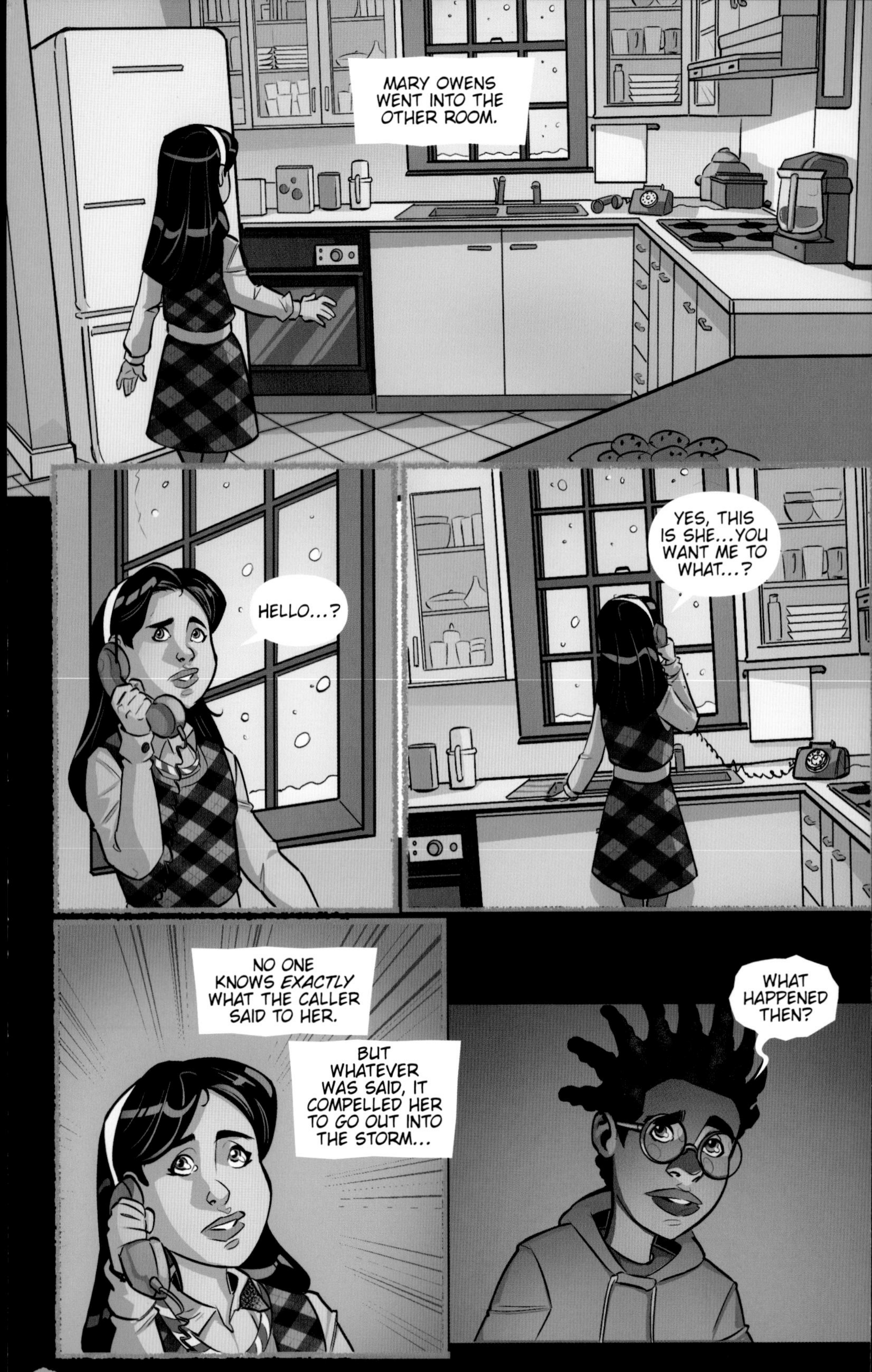

MARY OWENS WENT INTO THE OTHER ROOM.
HELLO...?
YES, THIS IS SHE...YOU WANT ME TO WHAT...?
NO ONE KNOWS *EXACTLY* WHAT THE CALLER SAID TO HER.
BUT WHATEVER WAS SAID, IT COMPELLED HER TO GO OUT INTO THE STORM...
WHAT HAPPENED THEN?

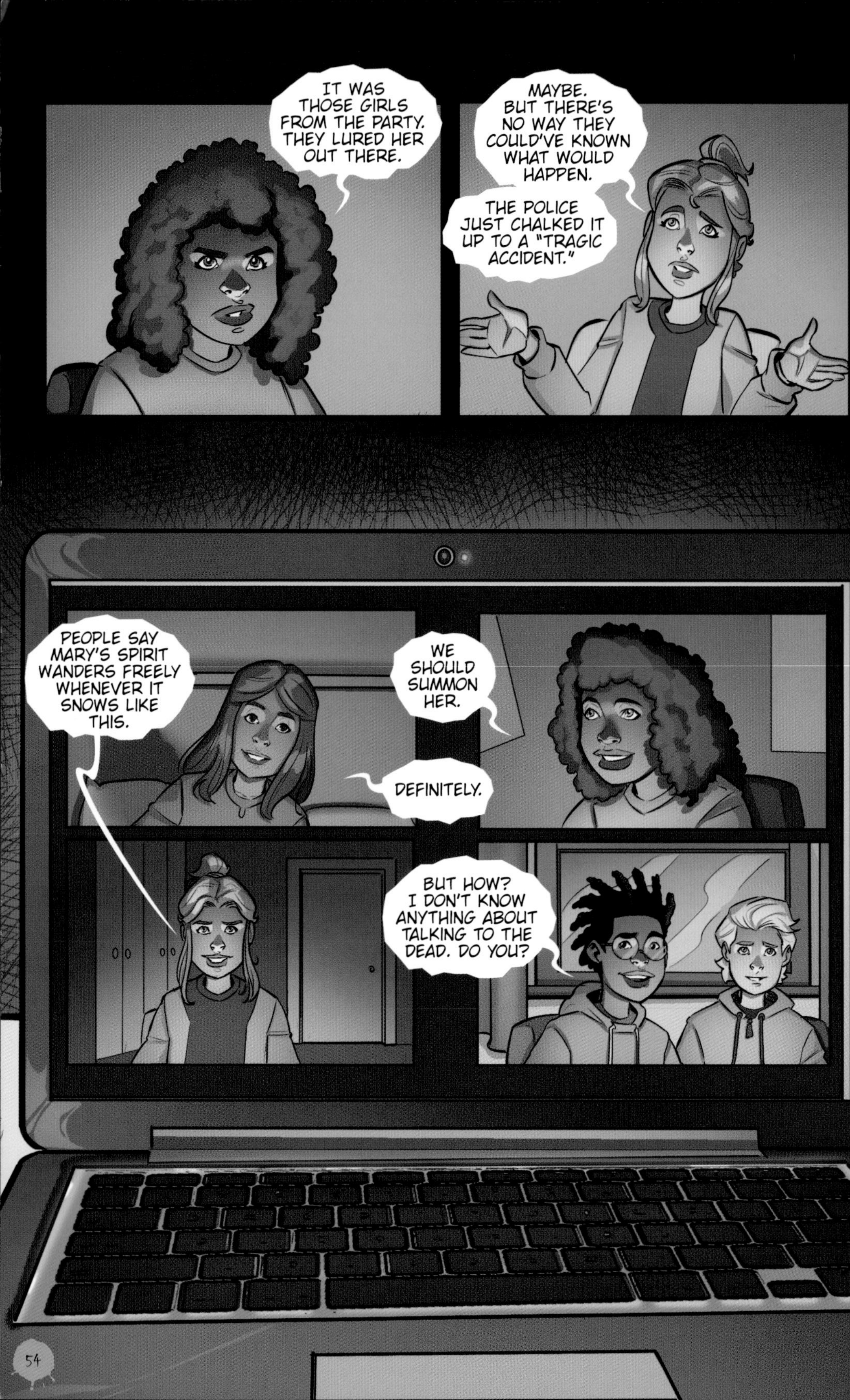
IT WAS THOSE GIRLS FROM THE PARTY. THEY LURED HER OUT THERE.
MAYBE. BUT THERE'S NO WAY THEY COULD'VE KNOWN WHAT WOULD HAPPEN.
THE POLICE JUST CHALKED IT UP TO A "TRAGIC ACCIDENT."
PEOPLE SAY MARY'S SPIRIT WANDERS FREELY WHENEVER IT SNOWS LIKE THIS.
WE SHOULD SUMMON HER.
DEFINITELY.
BUT HOW? I DON'T KNOW ANYTHING ABOUT TALKING TO THE DEAD. DO YOU?

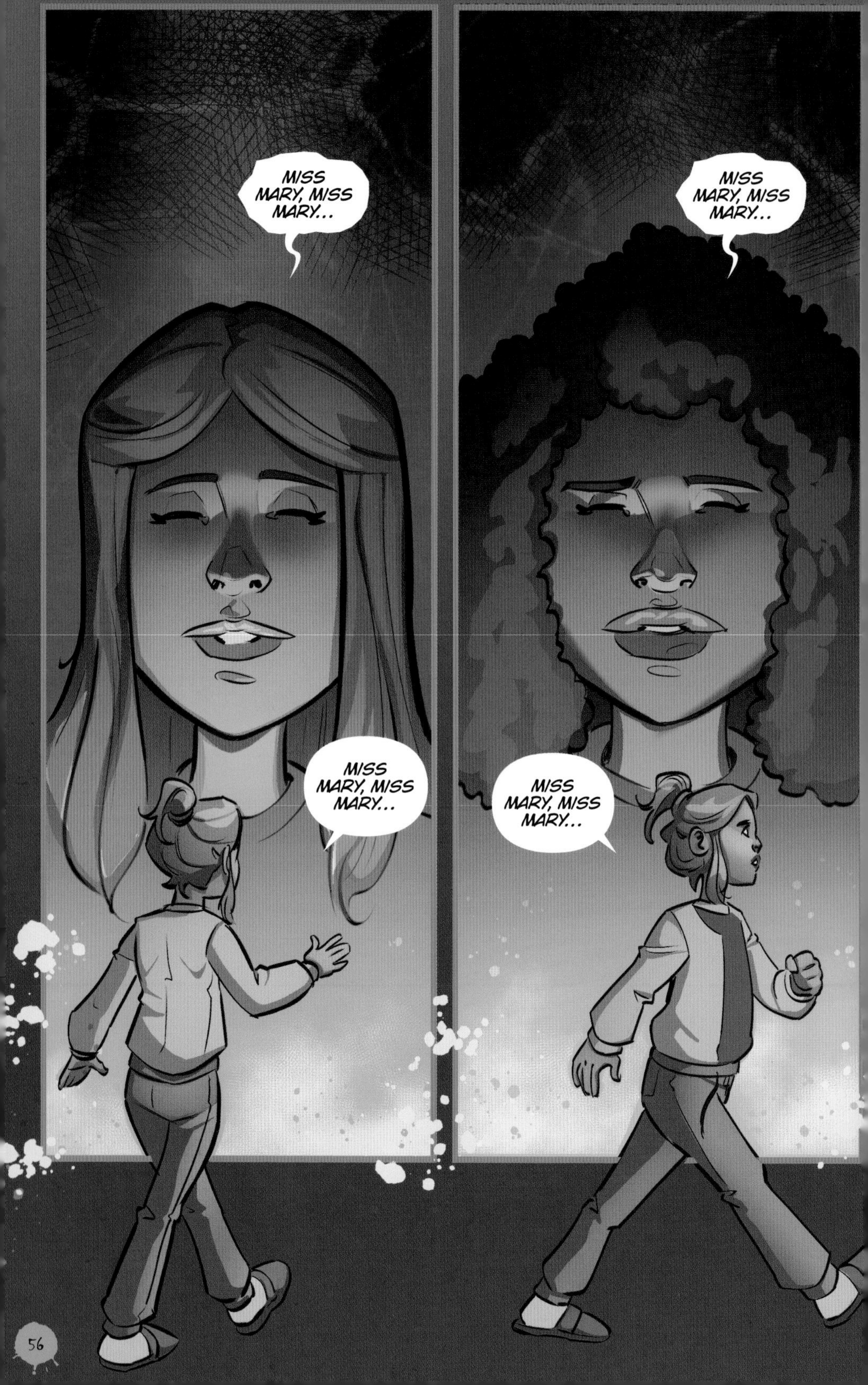
MISS MARY, MISS MARY...
MISS MARY, MISS MARY...
MISS MARY, MISS MARY...
MISS MARY, MISS MARY...

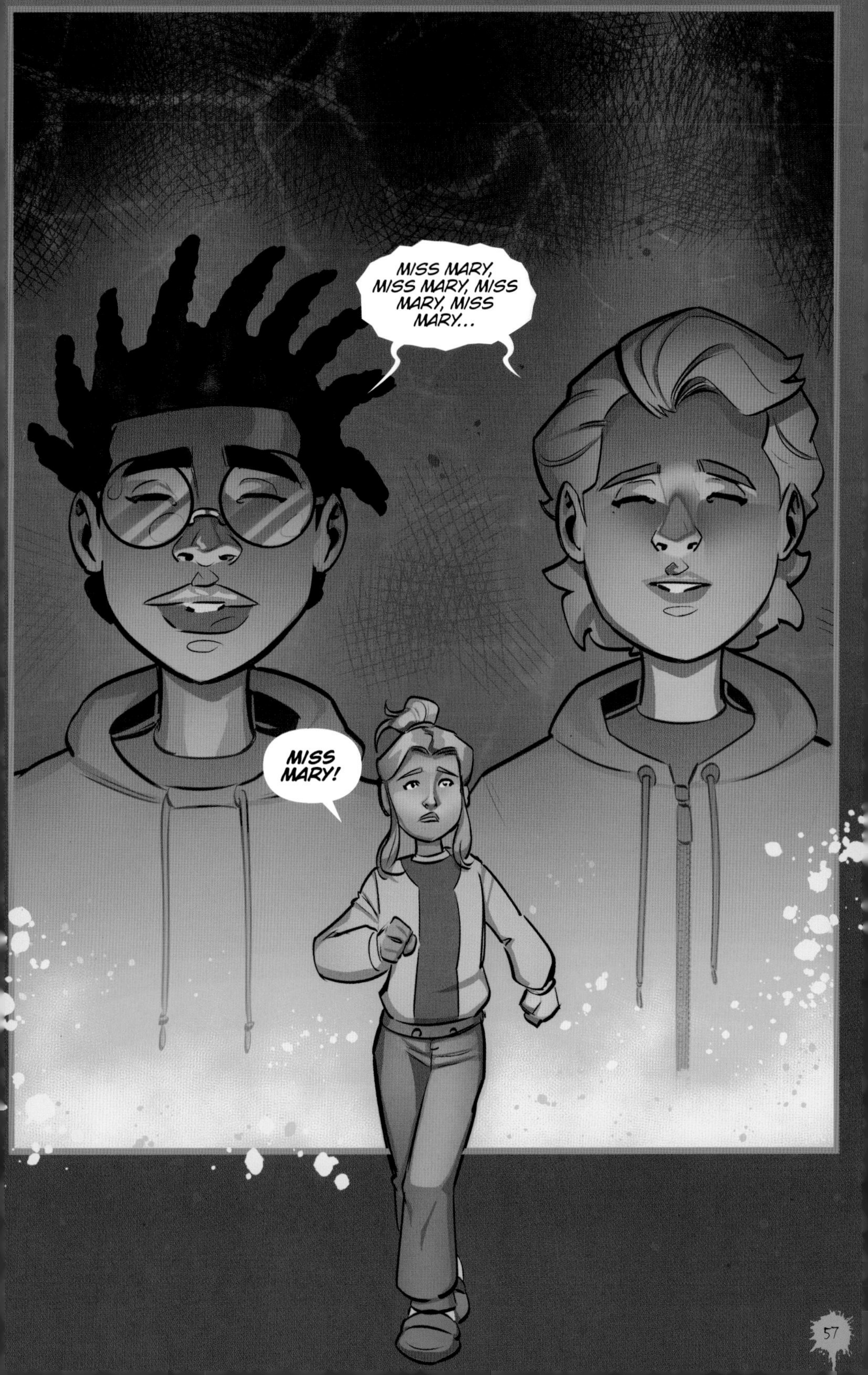
MISS MARY, MISS MARY, MISS MARY, MISS MARY...
MISS MARY!

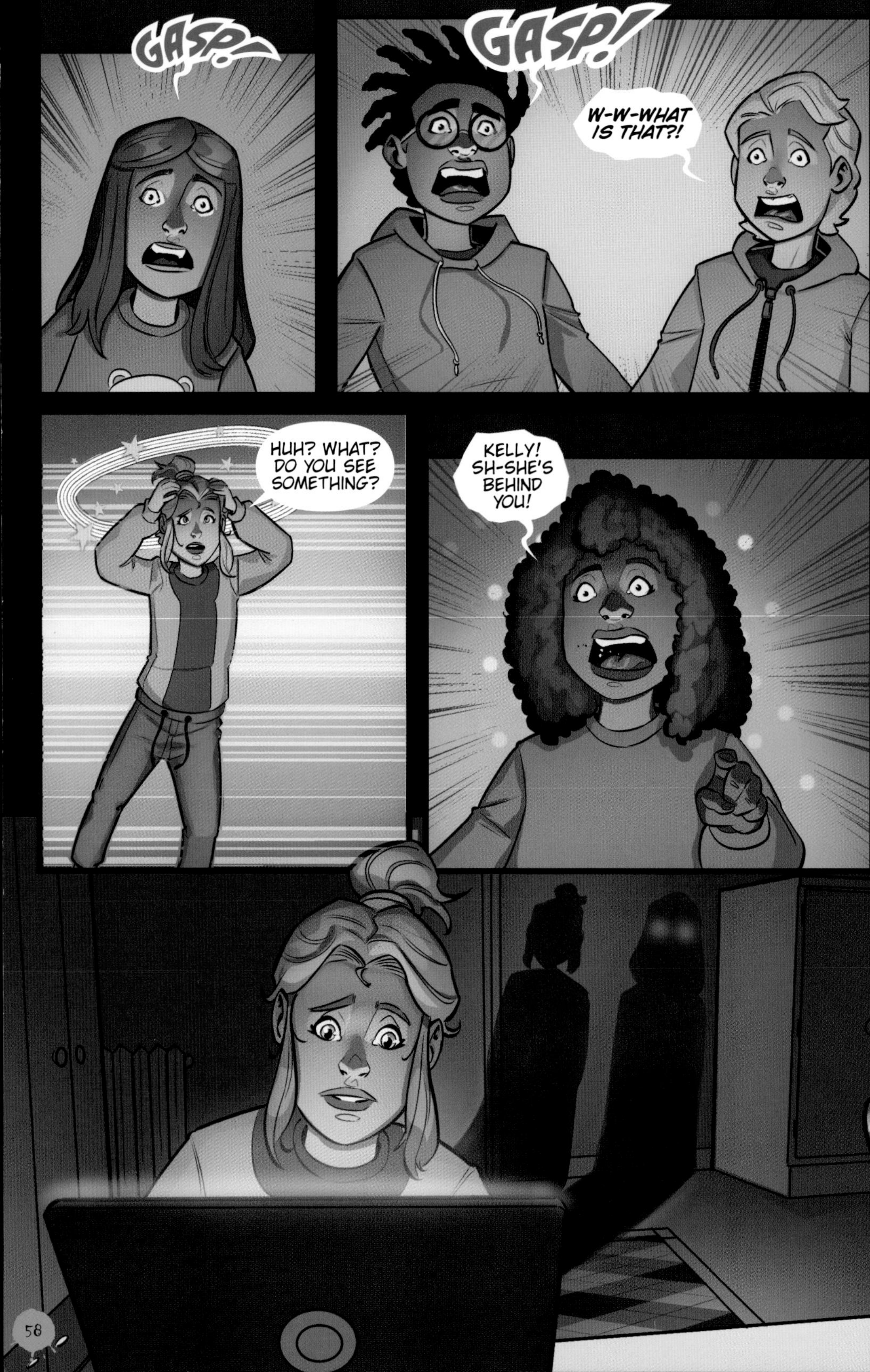
GASP!
GASP!
W-W-WHAT IS THAT?!
HUH? WHAT? DO YOU SEE SOMETHING?
KELLY! SH-SHE'S BEHIND YOU!

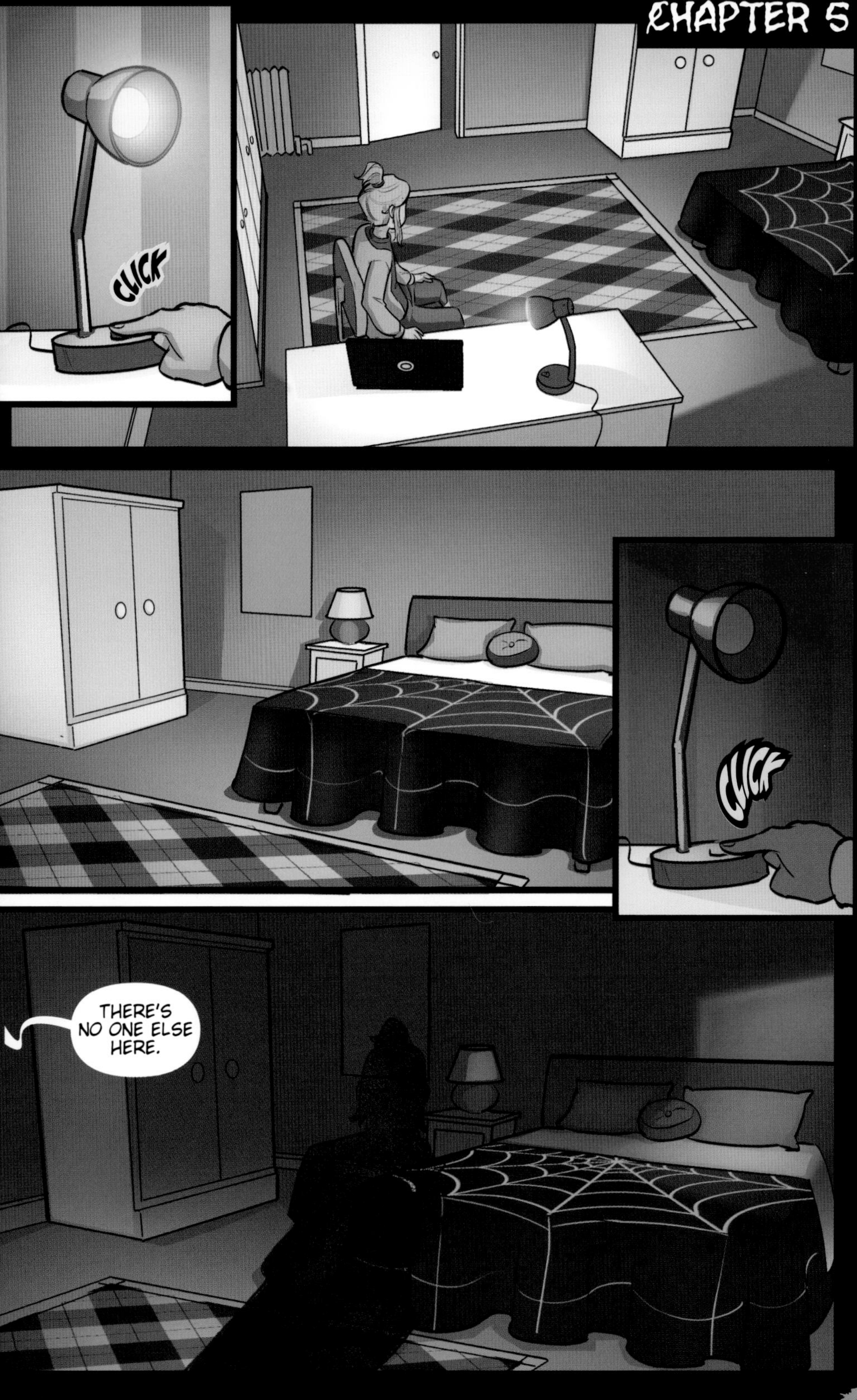
CHAPTER 5
CLICK
CLICK
THERE'S NO ONE ELSE HERE.

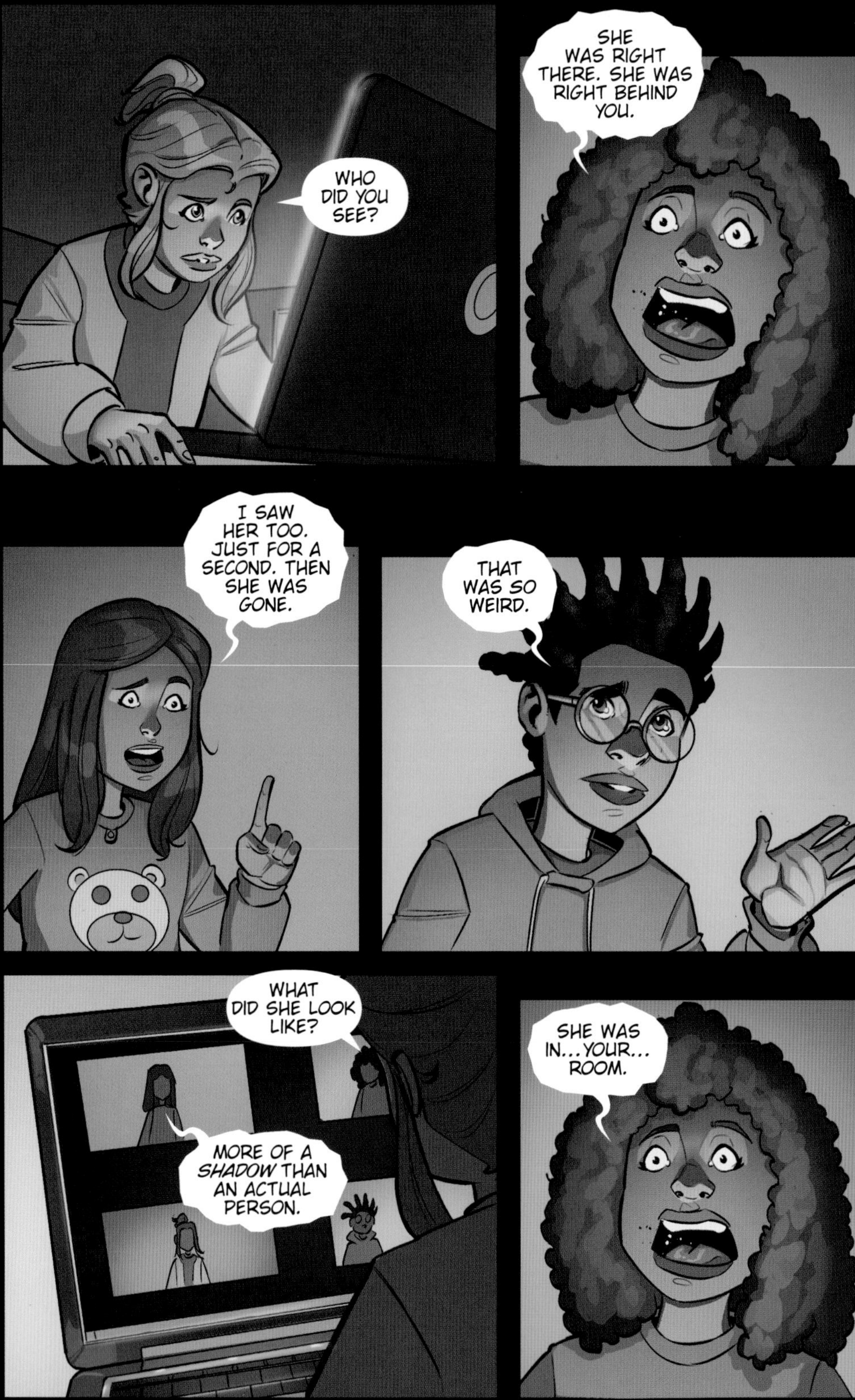
WHO DID YOU SEE?
SHE WAS RIGHT THERE. SHE WAS RIGHT BEHIND YOU.
I SAW HER TOO. JUST FOR A SECOND. THEN SHE WAS GONE.
THAT WAS SO WEIRD.
WHAT DID SHE LOOK LIKE?
MORE OF A SHADOW THAN AN ACTUAL PERSON.
SHE WAS IN...YOUR... ROOM.

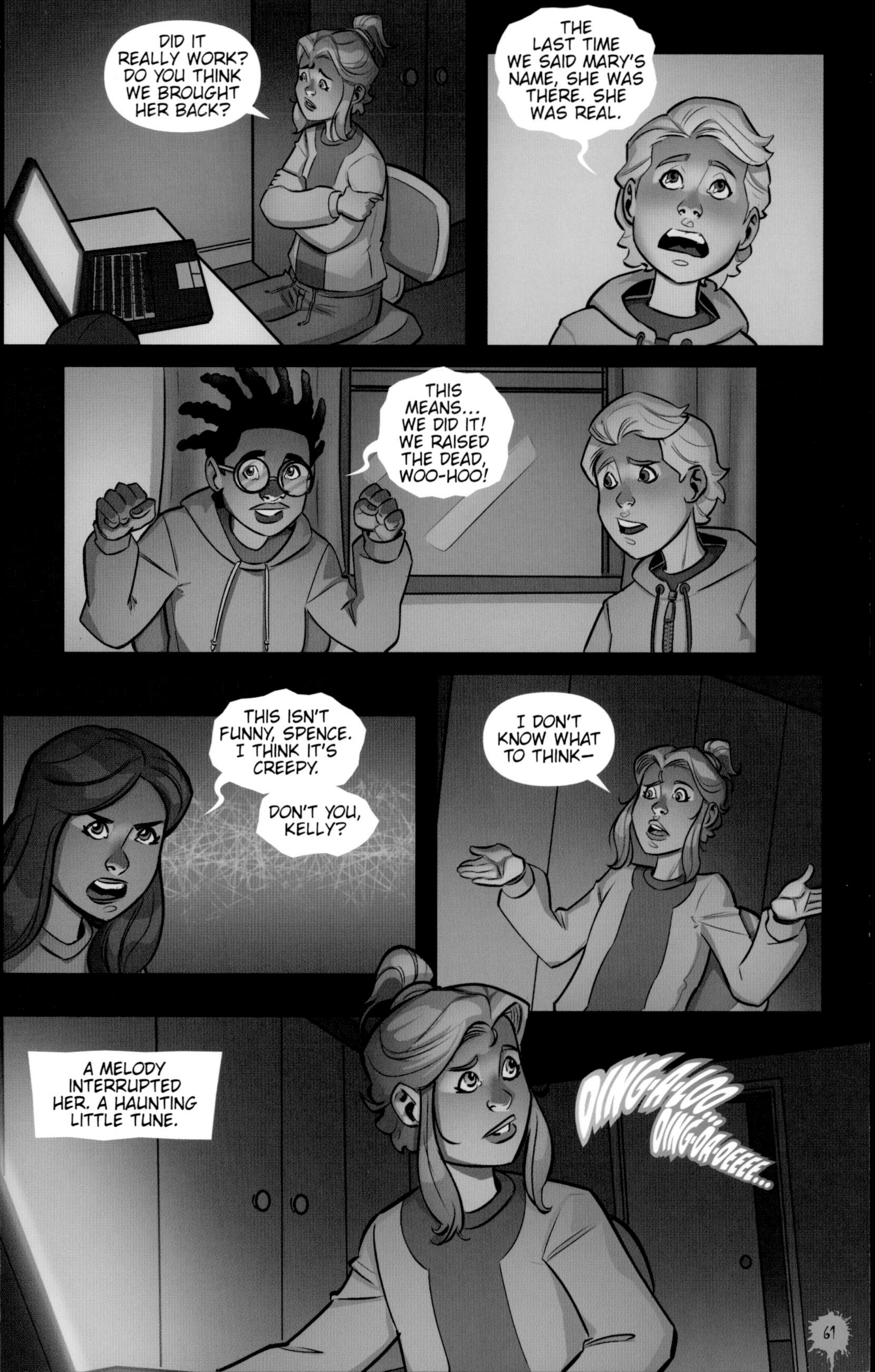
DID IT REALLY WORK? DO YOU THINK WE BROUGHT HER BACK?
THE LAST TIME WE SAID MARY'S NAME, SHE WAS THERE. SHE WAS REAL.
THIS MEANS... WE DID IT! WE RAISED THE DEAD, WOO-HOO!
THIS ISN'T FUNNY, SPENCE. I THINK IT'S CREEPY.
DON'T YOU, KELLY?
I DON'T KNOW WHAT TO THINK—
A MELODY INTERRUPTED HER. A HAUNTING LITTLE TUNE.
DING-A-LOO...
DING-OA-OEEEE...

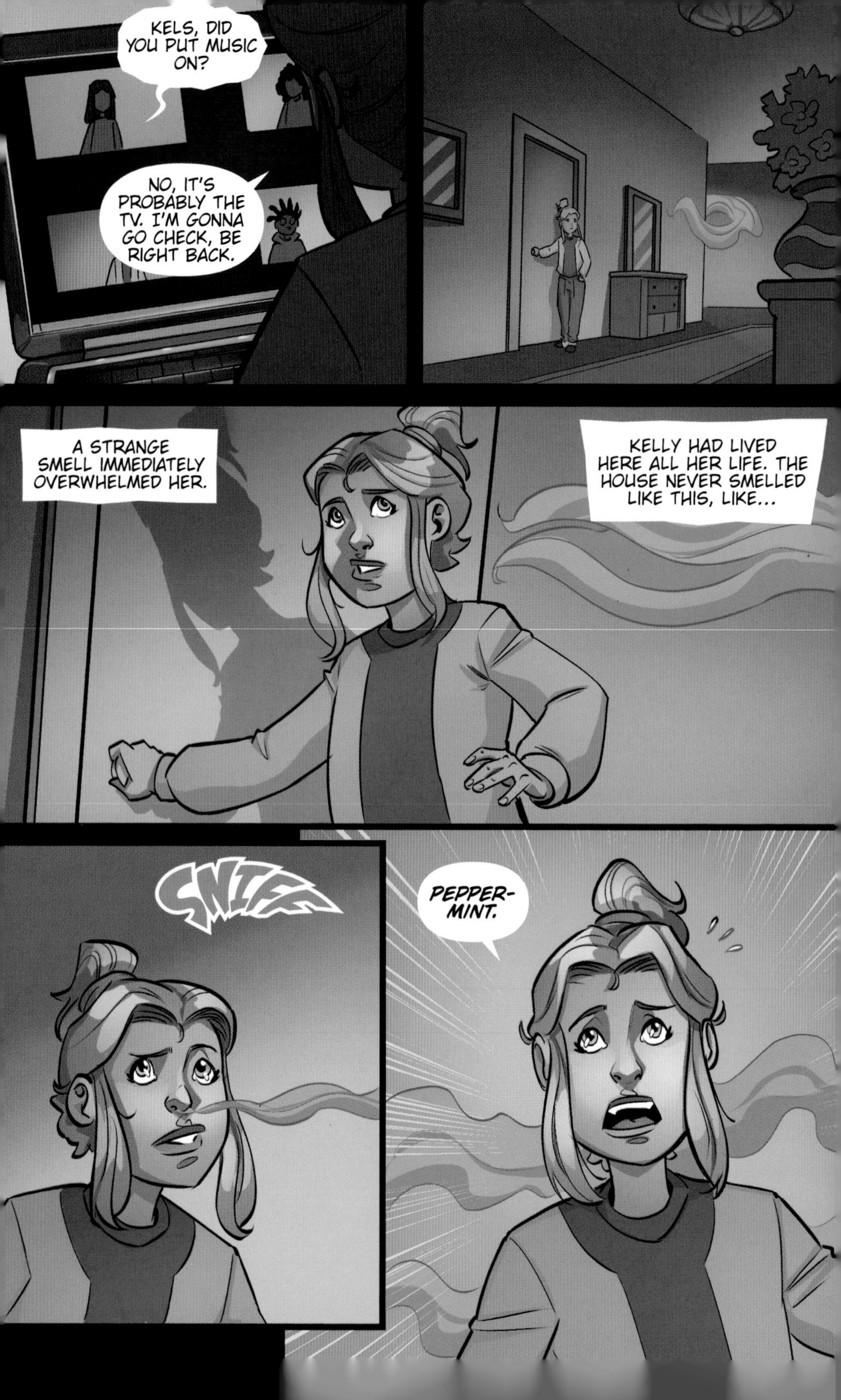
KELS, DID YOU PUT MUSIC ON?
NO, IT'S PROBABLY THE TV. I'M GONNA GO CHECK, BE RIGHT BACK.
A STRANGE SMELL IMMEDIATELY OVERWHELMED HER.
KELLY HAD LIVED HERE ALL HER LIFE. THE HOUSE NEVER SMELLED LIKE THIS, LIKE...
SNIFF
PEPPER-MINT.

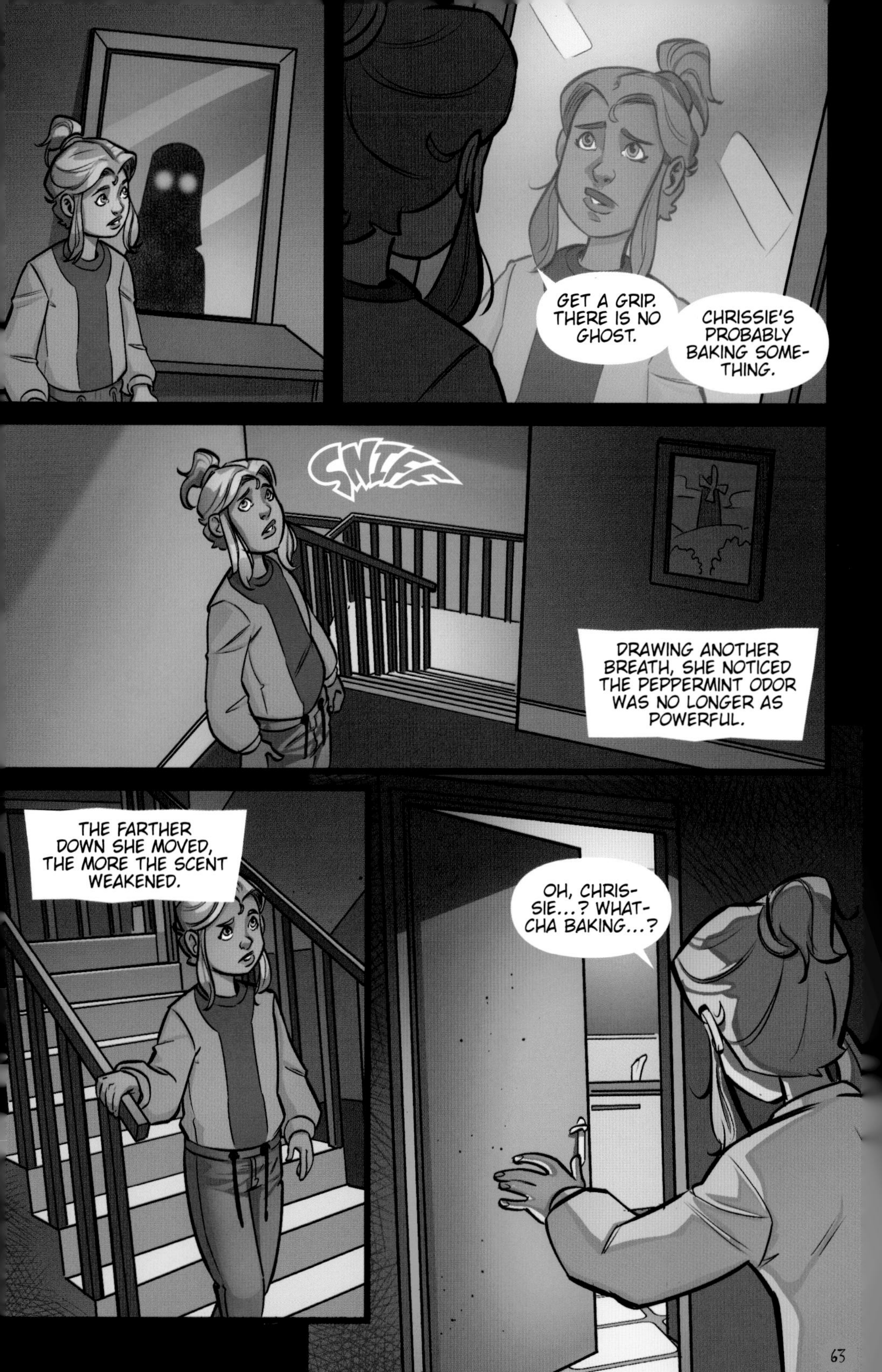
GET A GRIP. THERE IS NO GHOST.
CHRISSIE'S PROBABLY BAKING SOME-THING.
SNIFF
DRAWING ANOTHER BREATH, SHE NOTICED THE PEPPERMINT ODOR WAS NO LONGER AS POWERFUL.
THE FARTHER DOWN SHE MOVED, THE MORE THE SCENT WEAKENED.
OH, CHRIS-SIE...? WHAT-CHA BAKING...?

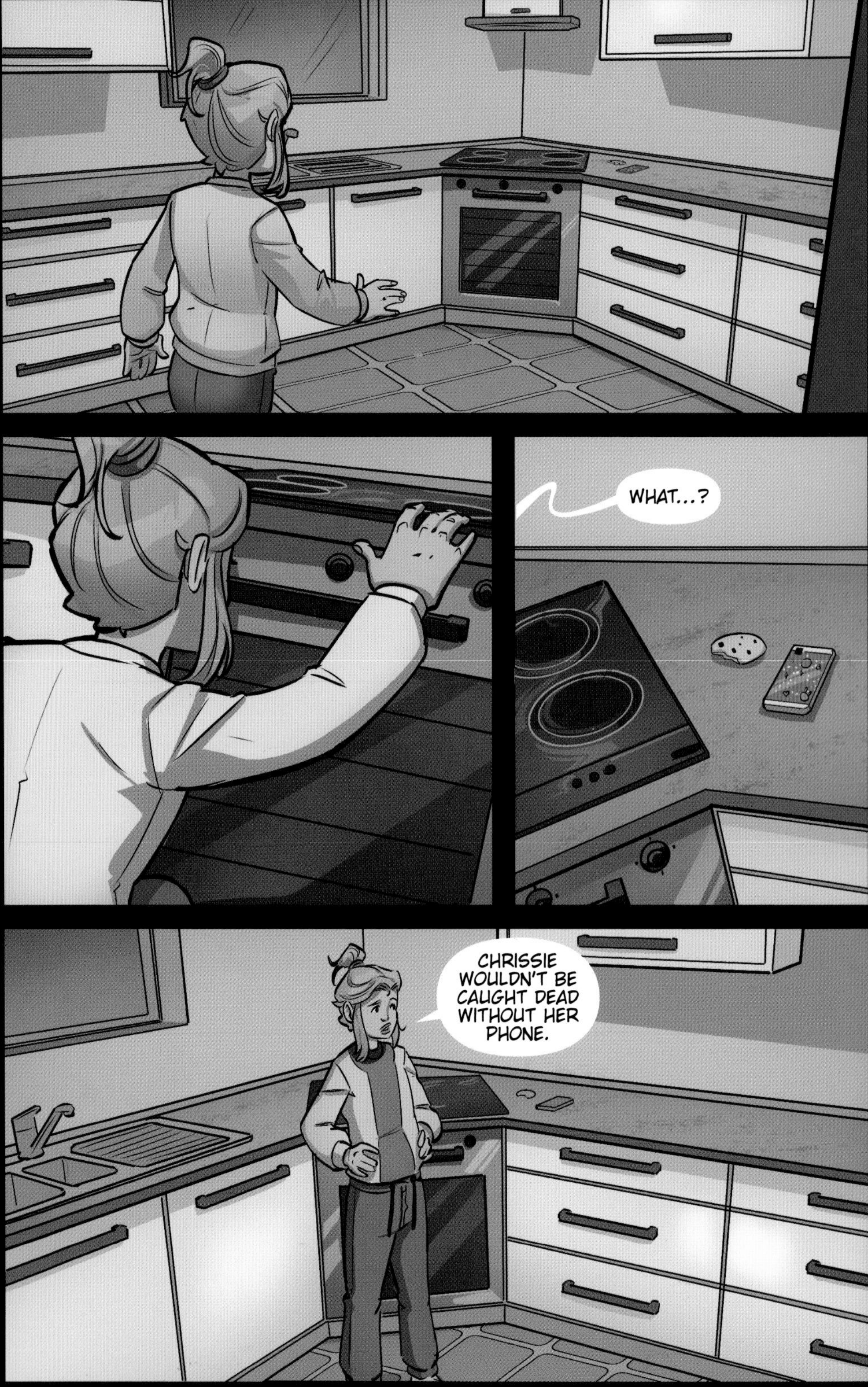
WHAT...?
CHRISSIE WOULDN'T BE CAUGHT DEAD WITHOUT HER PHONE.

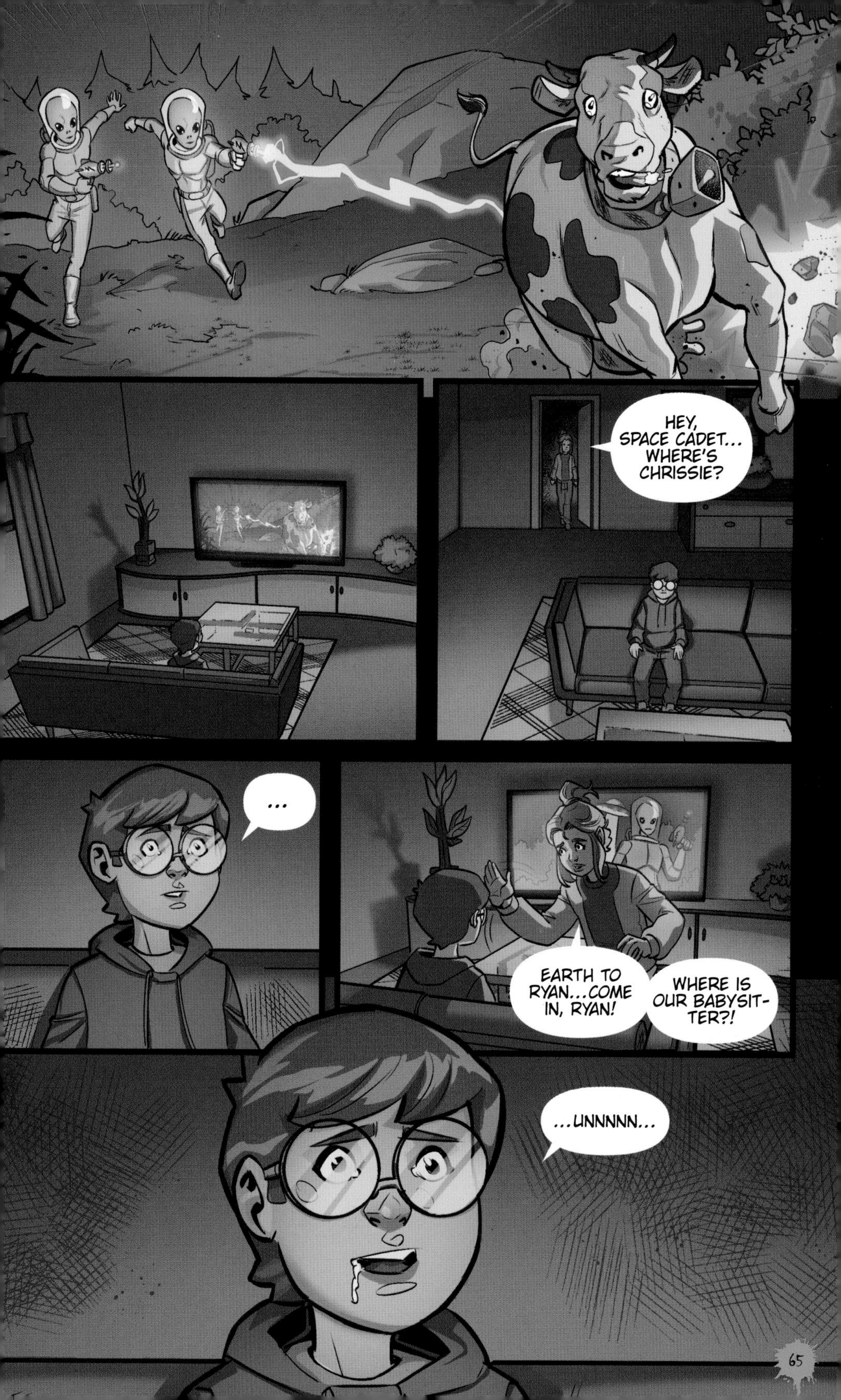

HEY, SPACE CADET... WHERE'S CHRISSIE?
...
EARTH TO RYAN...COME IN, RYAN!
WHERE IS OUR BABYSIT-TER?!
...UNNNNN...

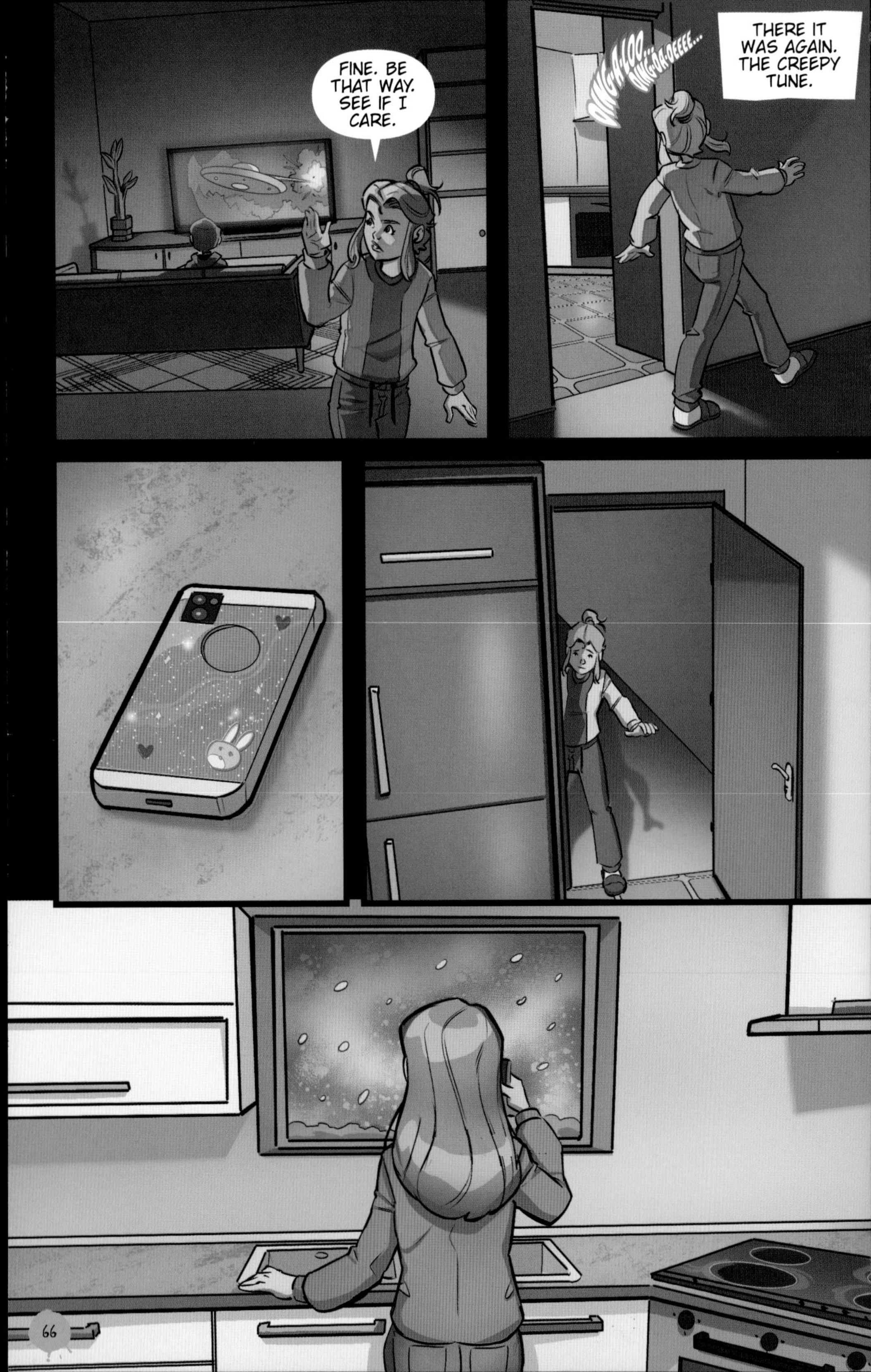
FINE. BE THAT WAY. SEE IF I CARE.
THERE IT WAS AGAIN. THE CREEPY TUNE.
DING-A-LOO... DING-DA-DEEEE...

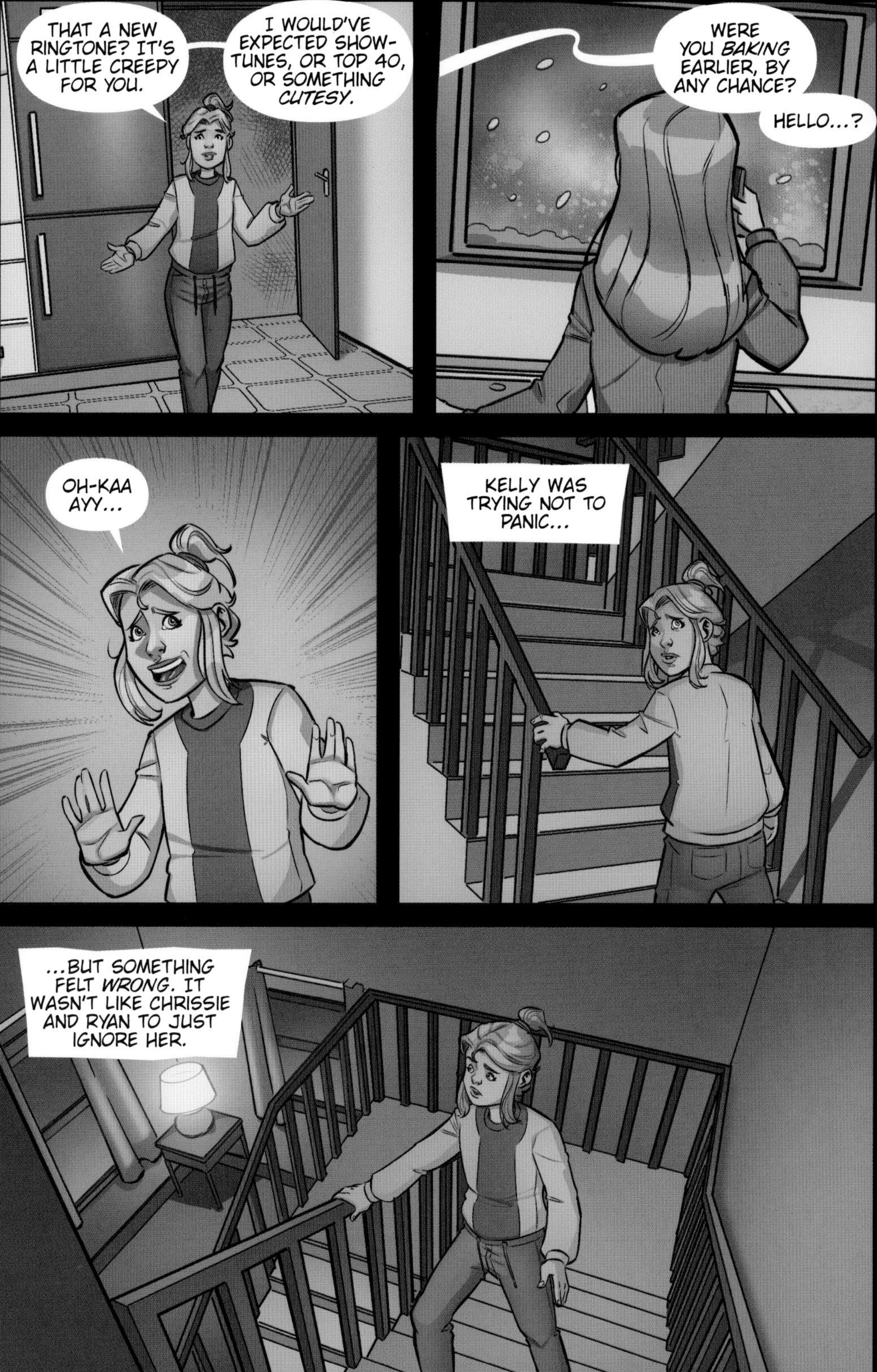
THAT A NEW RINGTONE? IT'S A LITTLE CREEPY FOR YOU.
I WOULD'VE EXPECTED SHOW-TUNES, OR TOP 40, OR SOMETHING *CUTESY*.
WERE YOU *BAKING* EARLIER, BY ANY CHANCE?
HELLO...?
OH-KAA AYY...
KELLY WAS TRYING NOT TO PANIC...
...BUT SOMETHING FELT *WRONG*. IT WASN'T LIKE CHRISSIE AND RYAN TO JUST IGNORE HER.

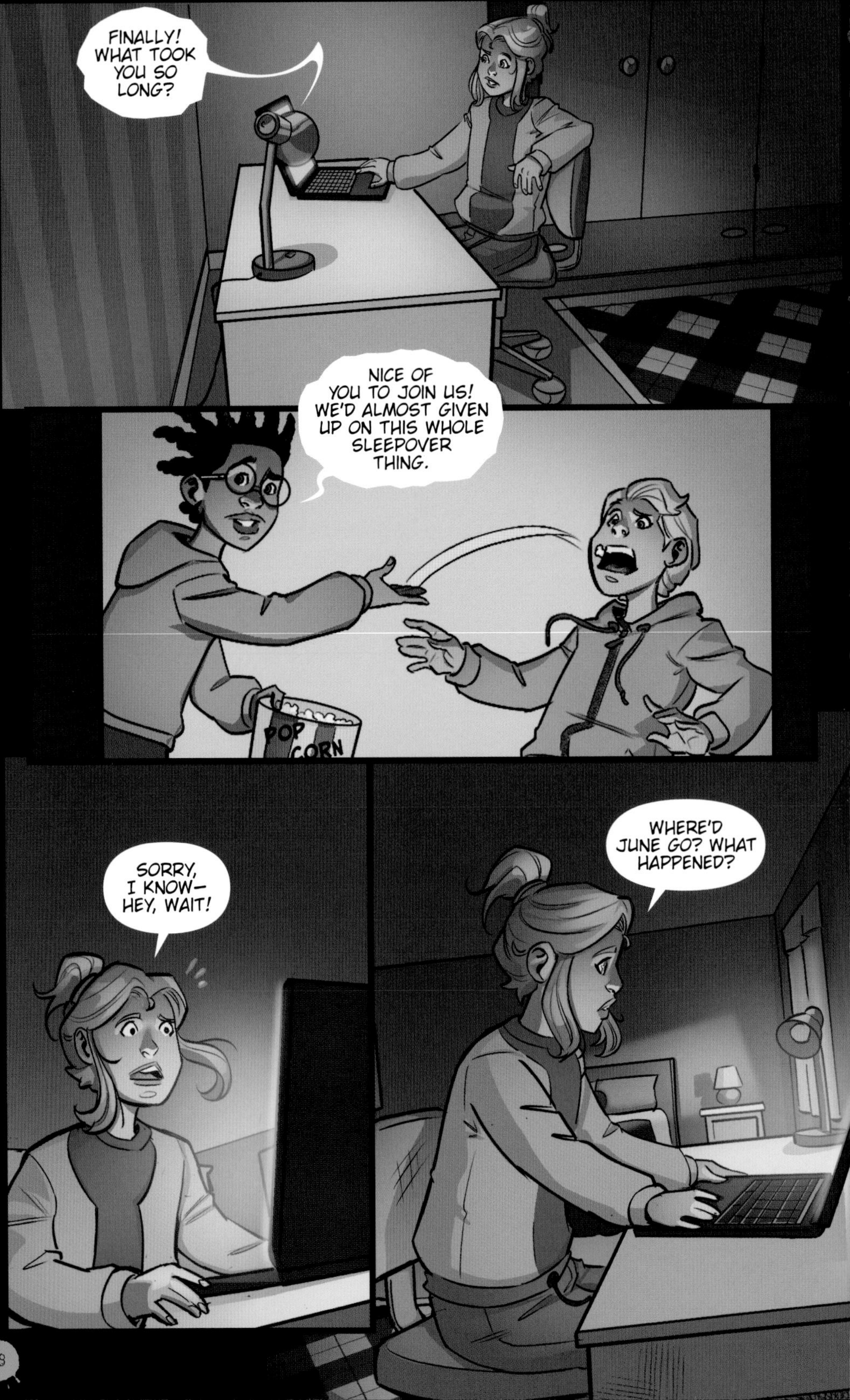
FINALLY! WHAT TOOK YOU SO LONG?
NICE OF YOU TO JOIN US! WE'D ALMOST GIVEN UP ON THIS WHOLE SLEEPOVER THING.
POP CORN
SORRY, I KNOW— HEY, WAIT!
WHERE'D JUNE GO? WHAT HAPPENED?

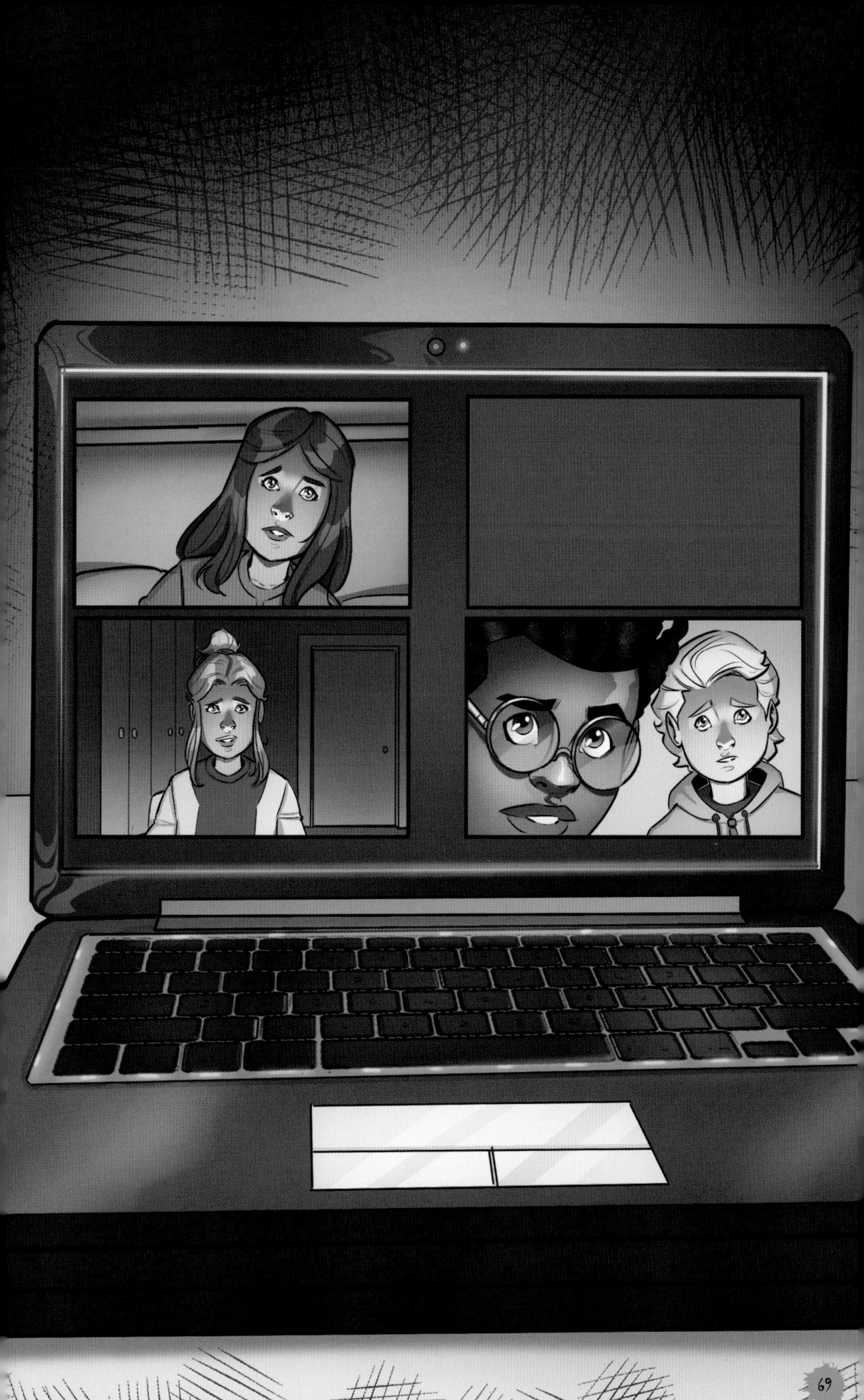

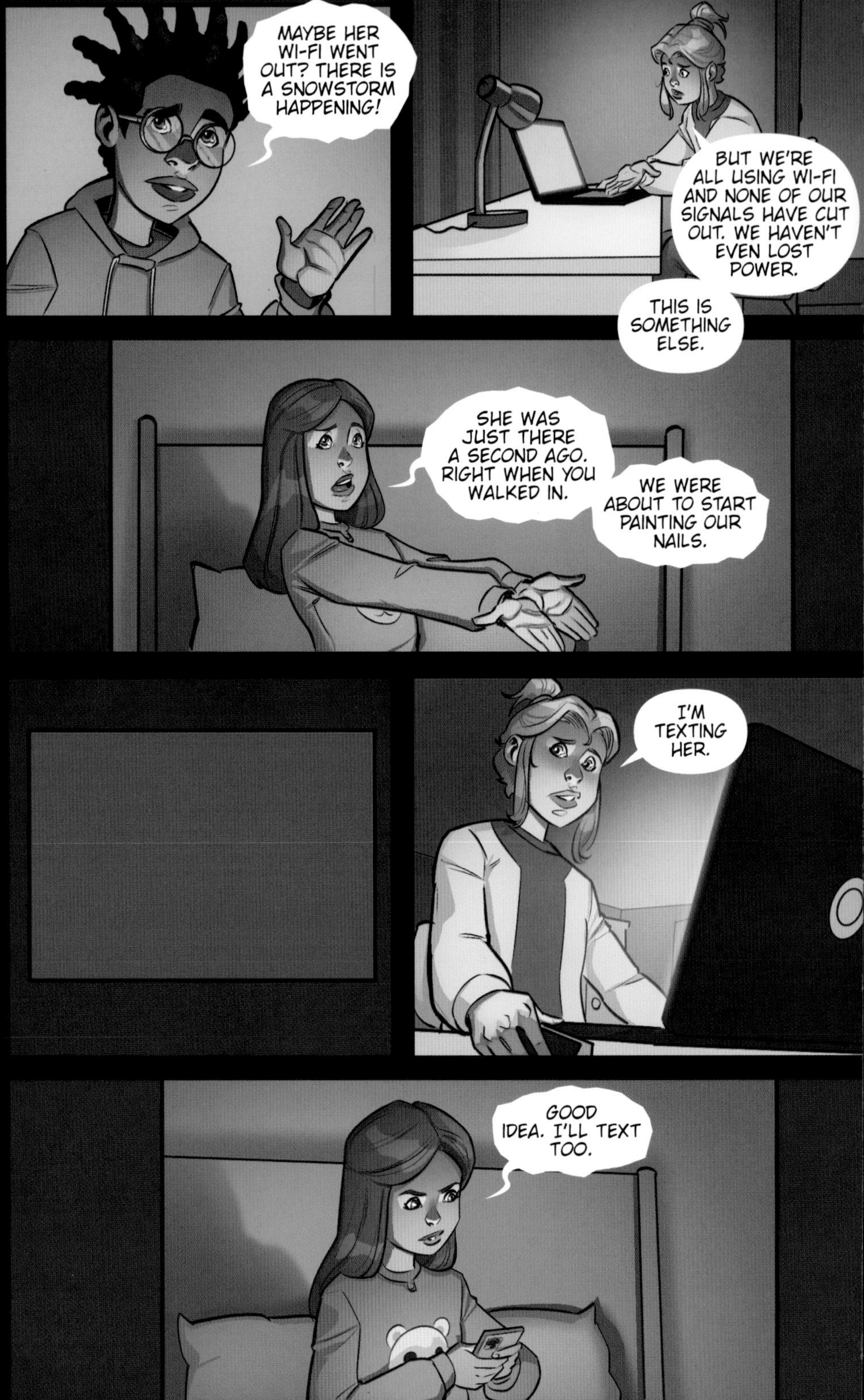
MAYBE HER WI-FI WENT OUT? THERE IS A SNOWSTORM HAPPENING!
BUT WE'RE ALL USING WI-FI AND NONE OF OUR SIGNALS HAVE CUT OUT. WE HAVEN'T EVEN LOST POWER.
THIS IS SOMETHING ELSE.
SHE WAS JUST THERE A SECOND AGO. RIGHT WHEN YOU WALKED IN.
WE WERE ABOUT TO START PAINTING OUR NAILS.
I'M TEXTING HER.
GOOD IDEA. I'LL TEXT TOO.

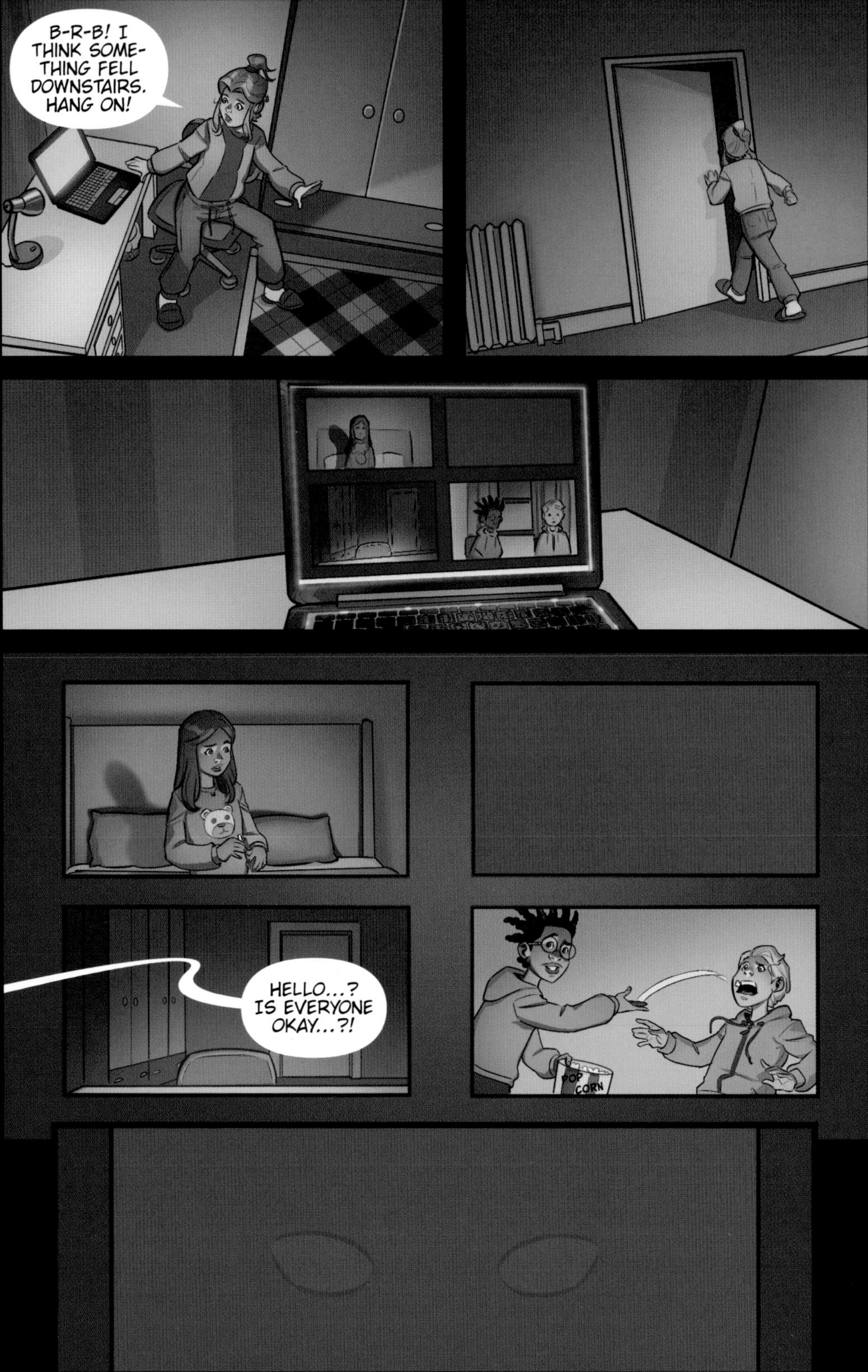

B-R-B! I THINK SOMETHING FELL DOWNSTAIRS. HANG ON!
HELLO...? IS EVERYONE OKAY...?!
POP CORN

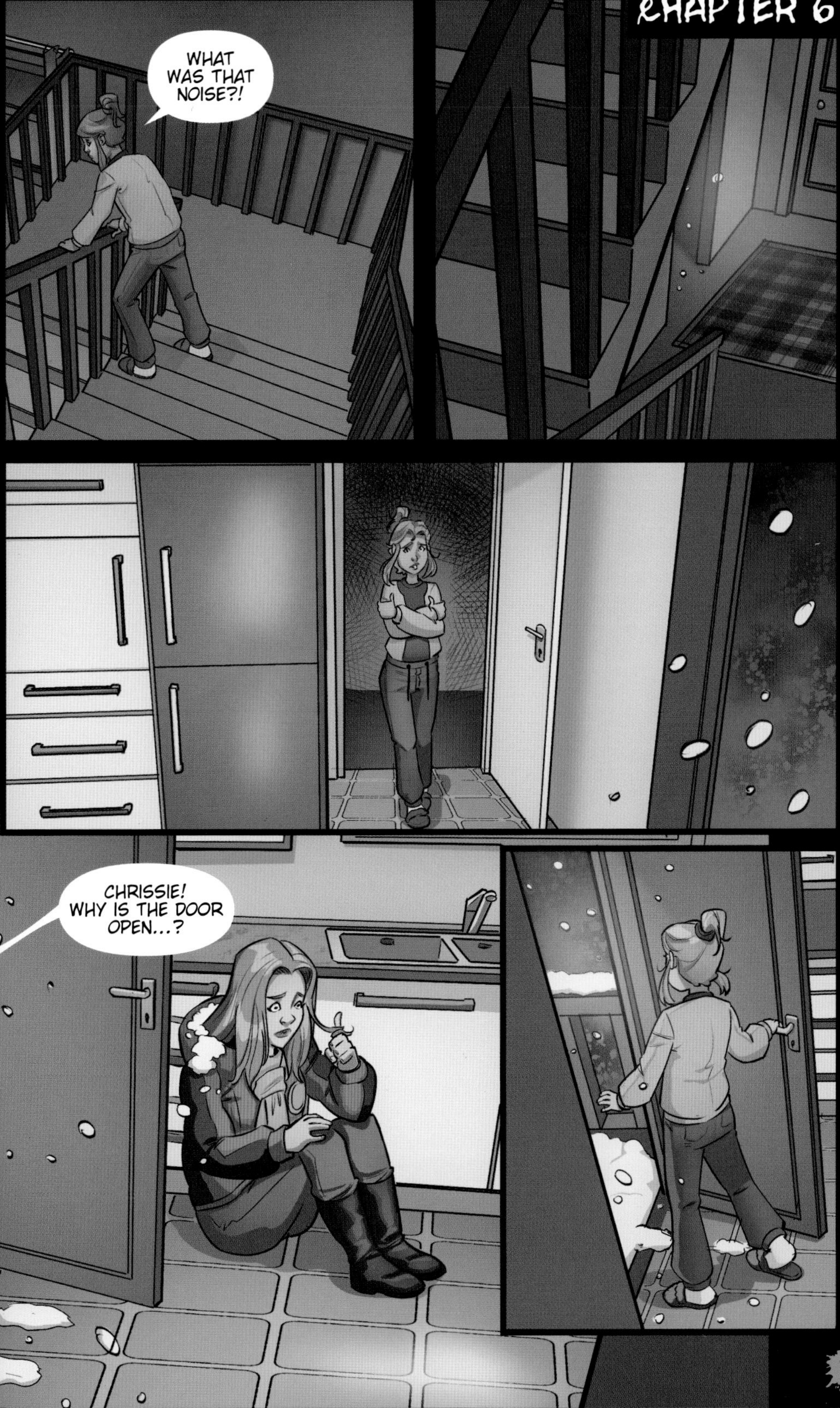
WHAT WAS THAT NOISE?!
CHRISSIE! WHY IS THE DOOR OPEN...?

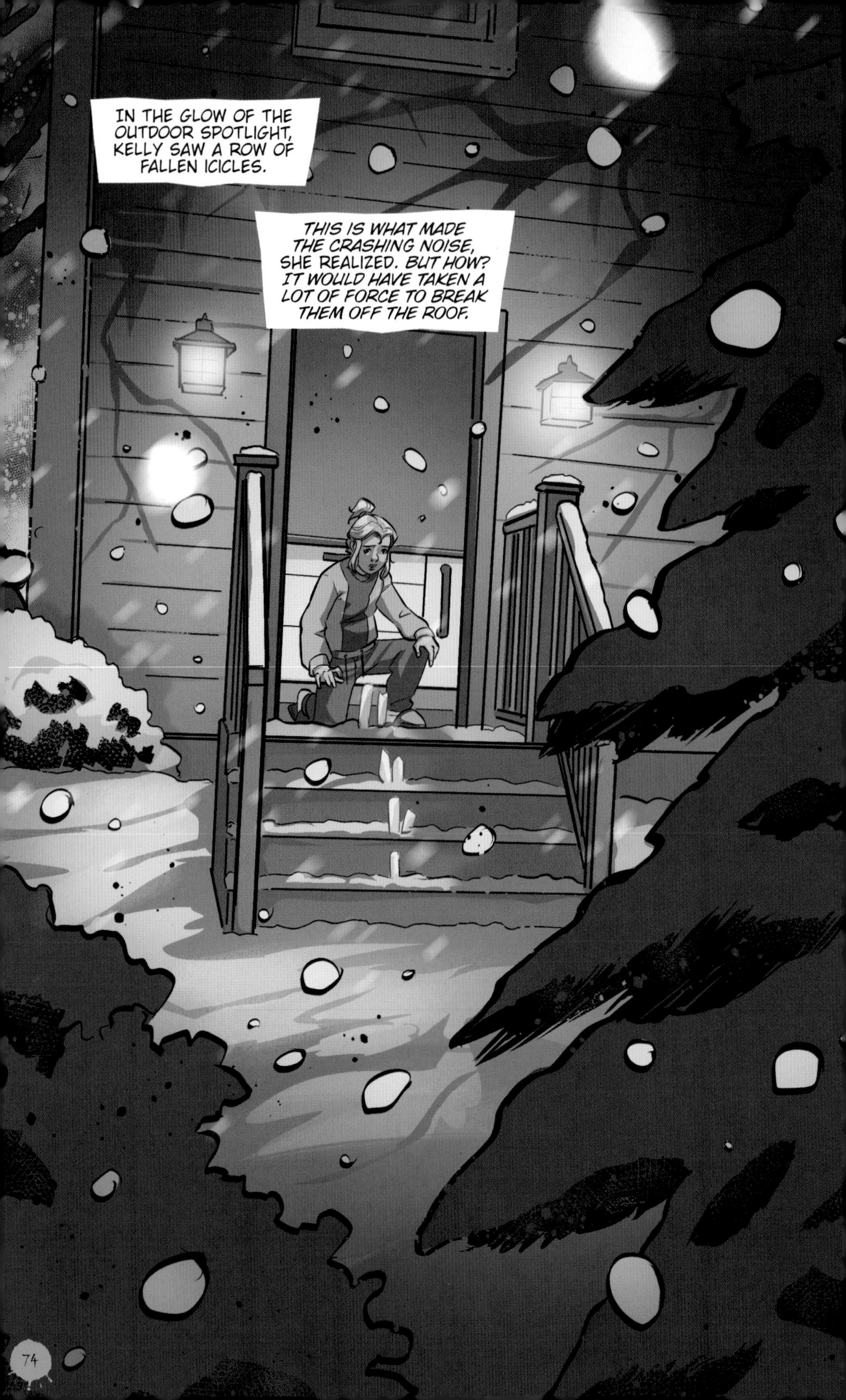
IN THE GLOW OF THE OUTDOOR SPOTLIGHT, KELLY SAW A ROW OF FALLEN ICICLES.
THIS IS WHAT MADE THE CRASHING NOISE, SHE REALIZED. BUT HOW? IT WOULD HAVE TAKEN A LOT OF FORCE TO BREAK THEM OFF THE ROOF.

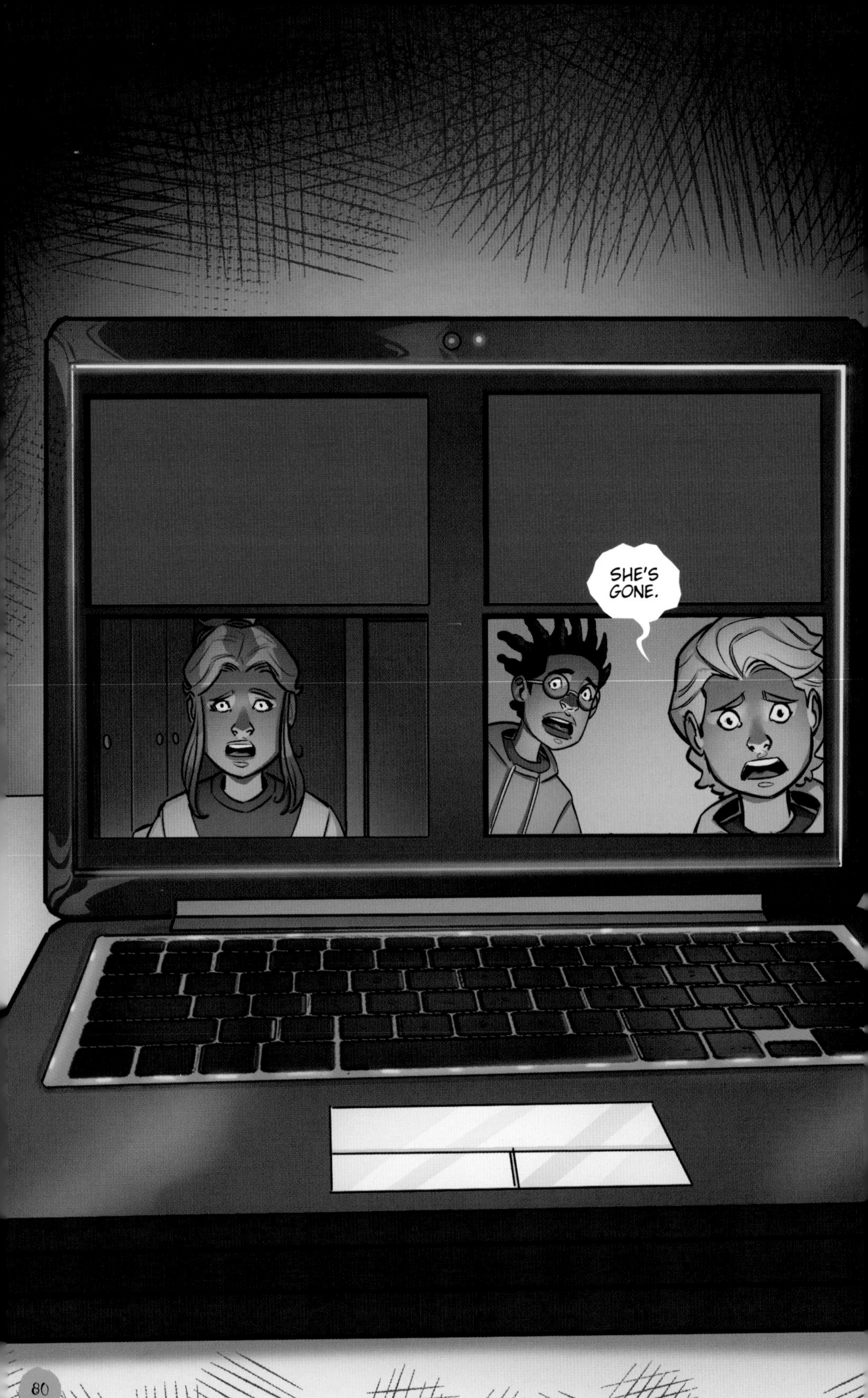
SHE'S GONE.

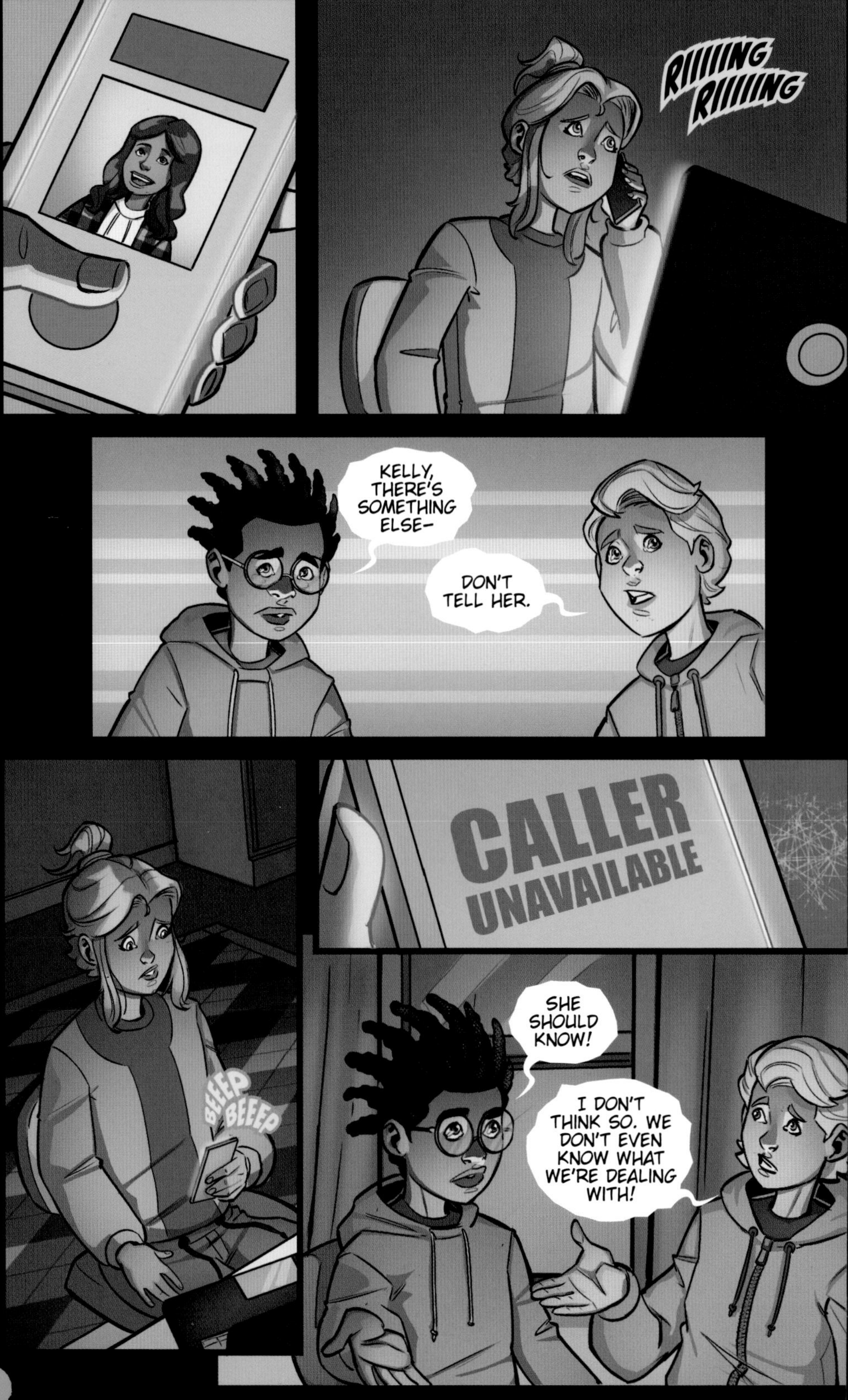
RIIIIING
RIIIIING
KELLY, THERE'S SOMETHING ELSE-
DON'T TELL HER.
CALLER UNAVAILABLE
BEEEP BEEEP
SHE SHOULD KNOW!
I DON'T THINK SO. WE DON'T EVEN KNOW WHAT WE'RE DEALING WITH!

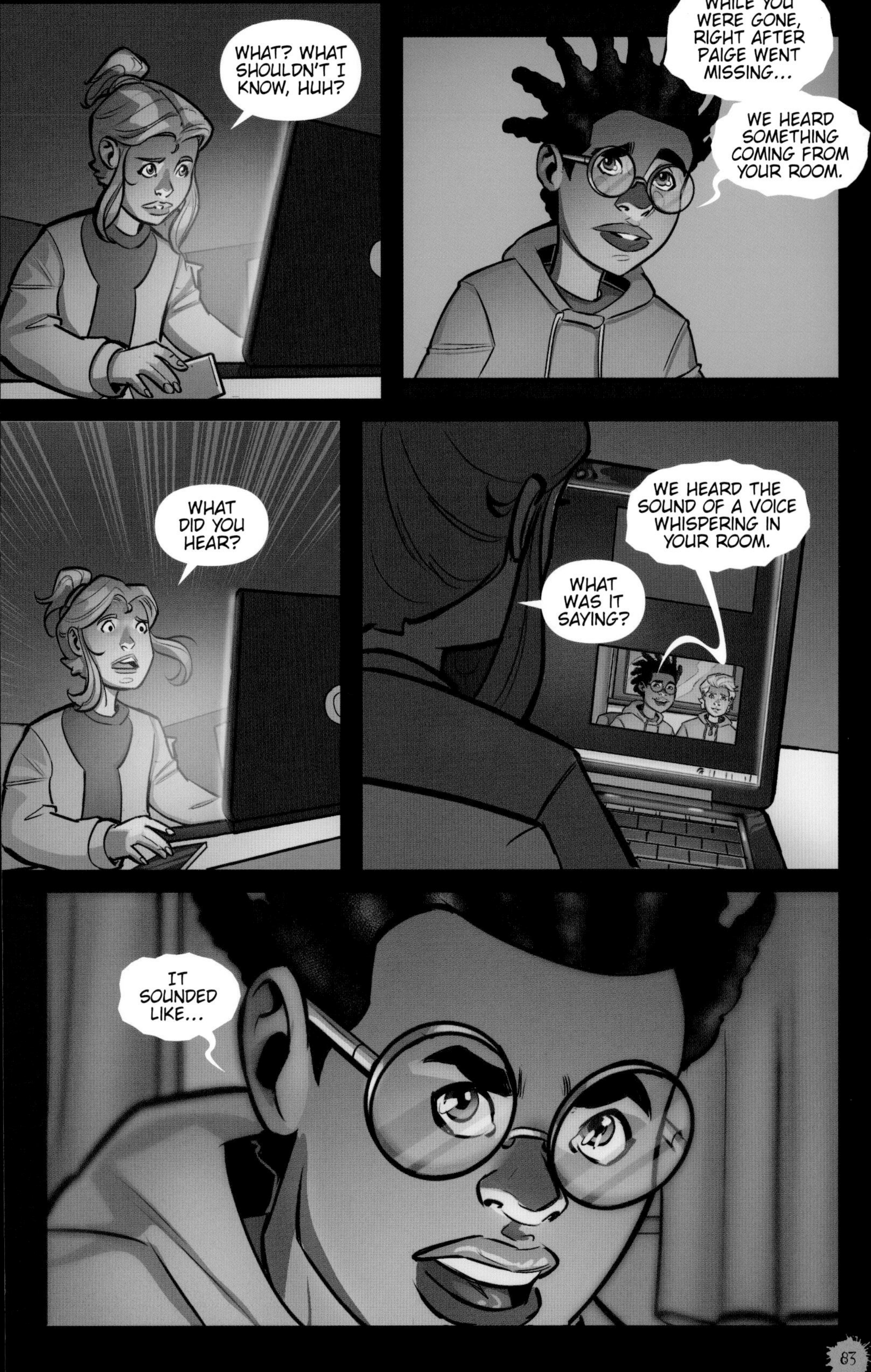
WHAT? WHAT SHOULDN'T I KNOW, HUH?
WHILE YOU WERE GONE, RIGHT AFTER PAIGE WENT MISSING...
WE HEARD SOMETHING COMING FROM YOUR ROOM.
WHAT DID YOU HEAR?
WE HEARD THE SOUND OF A VOICE WHISPERING IN YOUR ROOM.
WHAT WAS IT SAYING?
IT SOUNDED LIKE...

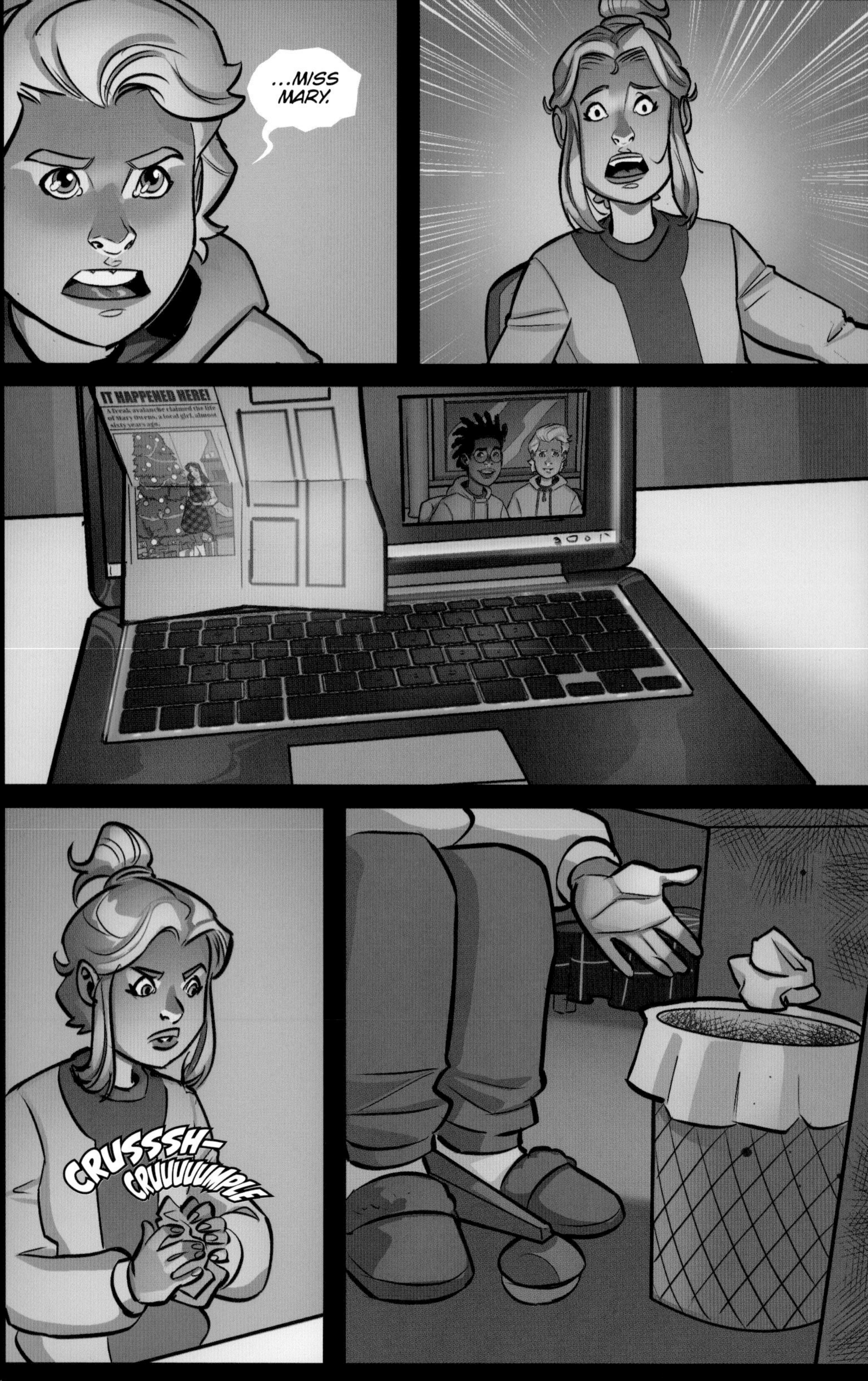
...MISS MARY.
IT HAPPENED HERE!
A freak avalanche claimed the life of Mary Owens, a local girl, almost sixty years ago.
CRUSSSH–CRUUUUUMPLE

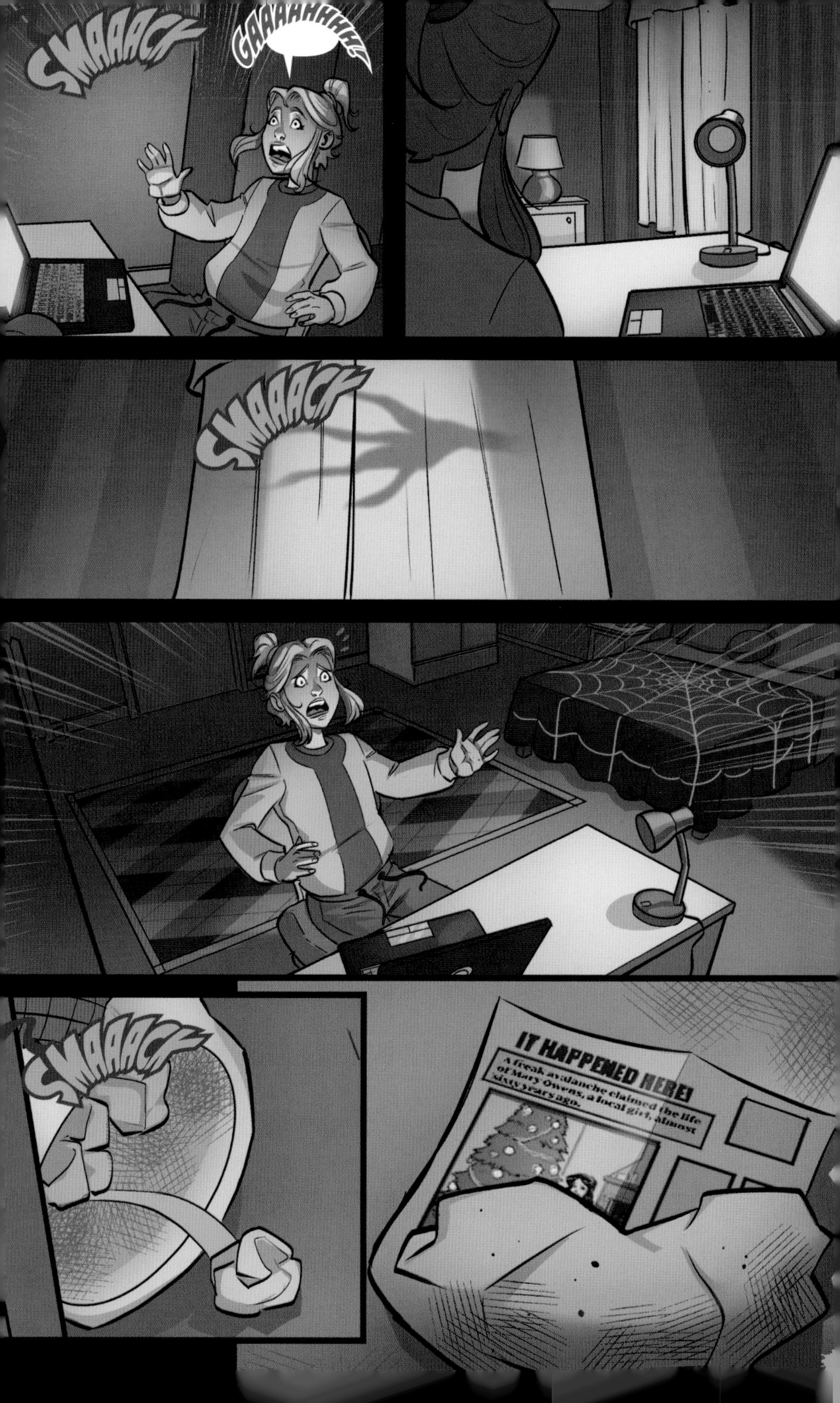
SMAAACK
GAAAAHHHH!
SMAAACK
SMAAACK
IT HAPPENED HERE!
A freak avalanche claimed the life of Mary Owens, a local girl, almost sixty years ago.

CHAPTER 7

HEY, YOU LEFT YOUR CAMERA. WE CAN'T SEE YOU.

WHAT IS IT...?

I'M HERE. JUST FREAKING OUT A LITTLE.

I'M NERVOUS ABOUT JUNE AND PAIGE.

I'M CALLING PAIGE AGAIN.

I THOUGHT SHE WASN'T ANSWERING—

I'M TRYING HER LANDLINE.

PEOPLE STILL HAVE THOSE?

RIIIIING RIIIIING RIIIIING

ISN'T PAIGE'S BIG SISTER BABYSITTING YOU? WHY DON'T YOU JUST GO ASK HER IF SHE KNOWS WHAT'S UP WITH PAIGE?

YES, THAT'S A GREAT IDEA! GO ASK HER.

NO ANSWER.

BEEP

I DON'T THINK CHRISSIE IS GOING TO BE MUCH HELP. SHE'S ACTING VERY WEIRD TONIGHT.

LIKE MORE THAN USUAL. SHE'S SAYING THINGS I DON'T UNDERSTAND. LIKE SHE'S—

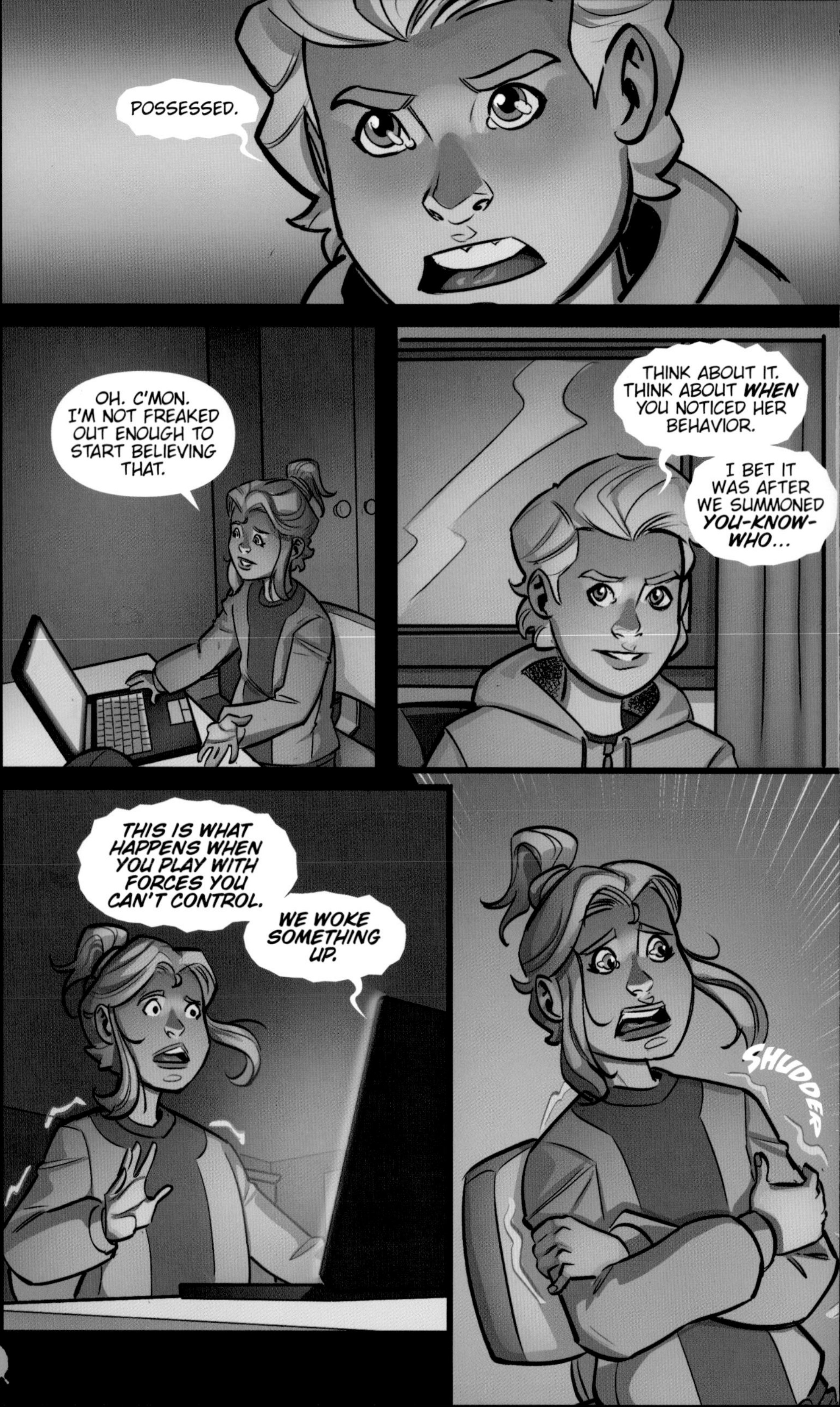
POSSESSED.
OH. C'MON. I'M NOT FREAKED OUT ENOUGH TO START BELIEVING THAT.
THINK ABOUT IT. THINK ABOUT WHEN YOU NOTICED HER BEHAVIOR.
I BET IT WAS AFTER WE SUMMONED YOU-KNOW-WHO...
THIS IS WHAT HAPPENS WHEN YOU PLAY WITH FORCES YOU CAN'T CONTROL.
WE WOKE SOMETHING UP.
SHUDDER

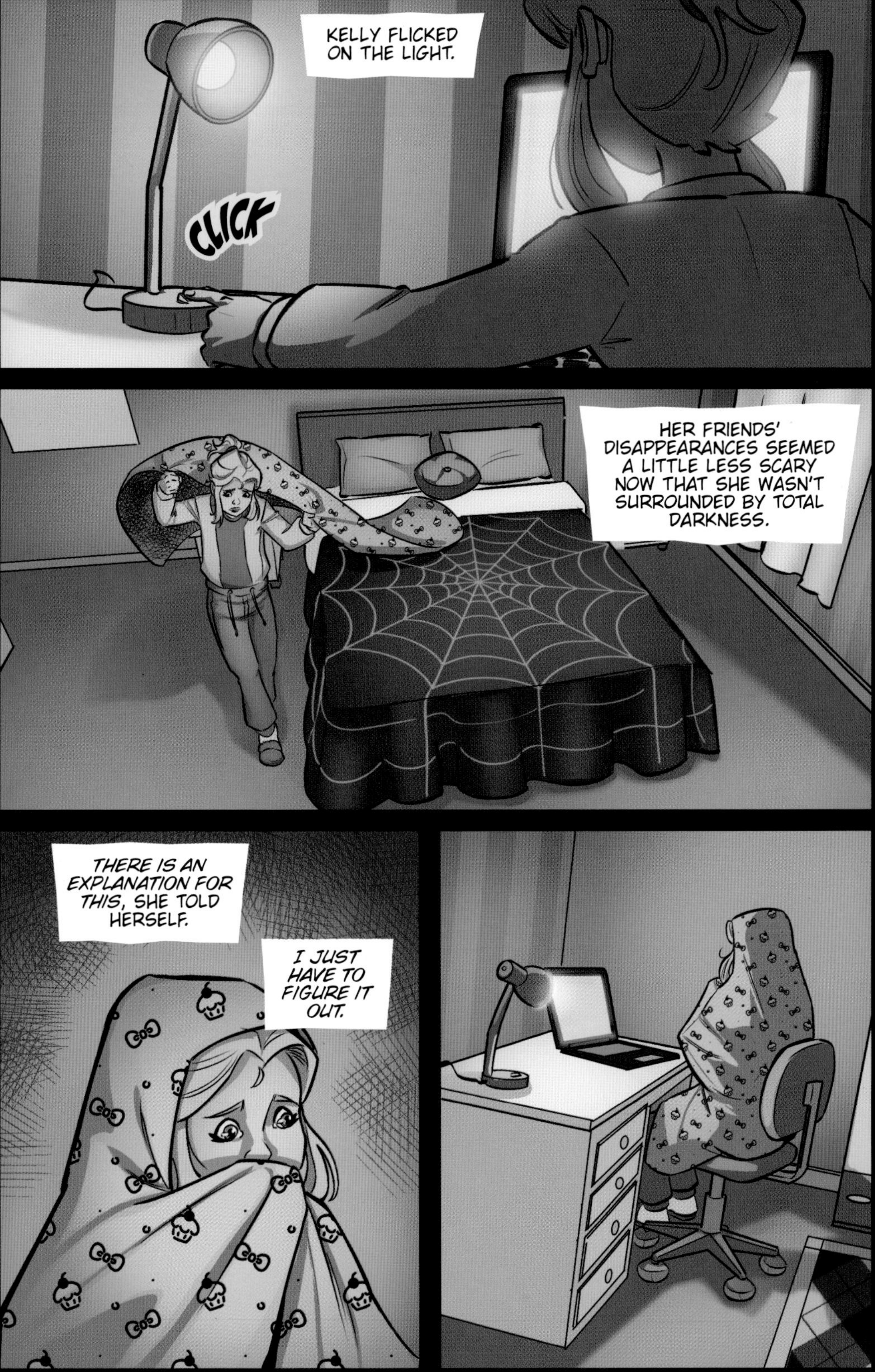
KELLY FLICKED ON THE LIGHT.
CLICK
HER FRIENDS' DISAPPEARANCES SEEMED A LITTLE LESS SCARY NOW THAT SHE WASN'T SURROUNDED BY TOTAL DARKNESS.
THERE IS AN EXPLANATION FOR THIS, SHE TOLD HERSELF.
I JUST HAVE TO FIGURE IT OUT.

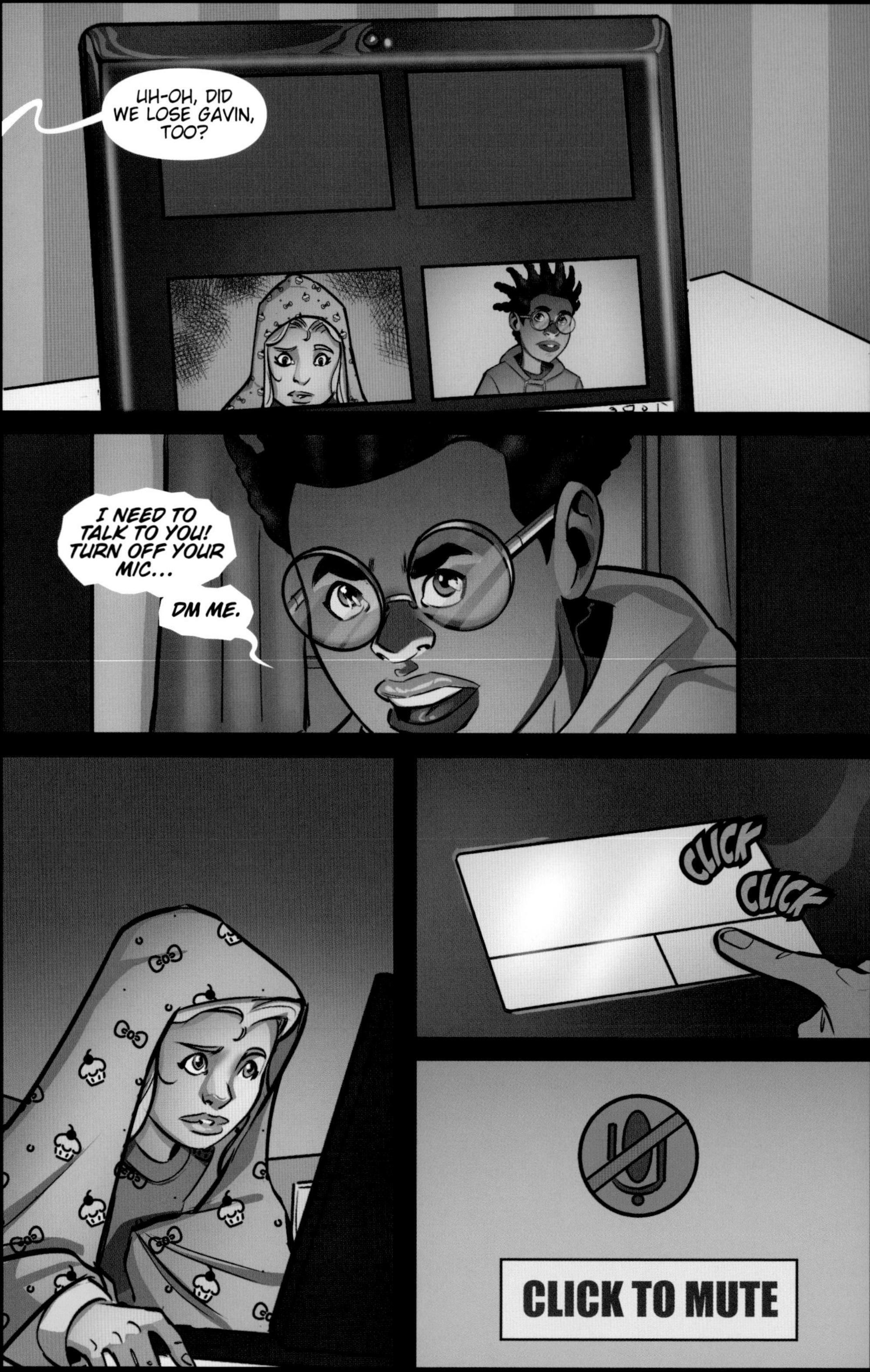
UH-OH, DID WE LOSE GAVIN, TOO?
I NEED TO TALK TO YOU! TURN OFF YOUR MIC...
DM ME.
CLICK
CLICK
CLICK TO MUTE

CHAT WITH SPENCER

KELLY

What's wrong?

SPENCER

Gavin is what's wrong.

KELLY

???

SPENCER

Don't have much time. I am freaking out over here.

KELLY

About Miss Mary?

SPENCER

Yes, but about Gavin too.

KELLY

Y?

SPENCER

He's been acting strange all night. Twitchy. Nervous. It started with the Miss Mary thing. He keeps mumbling stuff under his breath too. You can't hear it on your end, but I can.

KELLY

What is he saying?

SPENCER

Stuff that makes no sense. COLDNESS IS COMING and LAGAD IS LIFE and YOU CANNOT BE HERE.

He is NOT in control, IMO.

KELLY

That sounds EXACTLY like Chrissie!!!!

WAIT. Is it possible he's playing you?

SPENCER

Maybe? I barely know him. I don't want him to stay over anymore. I don't trust him.

I don't feel safe.

What do I do?

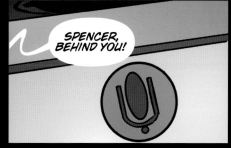

SPENCER, BEHIND YOU!

AGGGGHHH!!

NO! STOP! PLEASE!

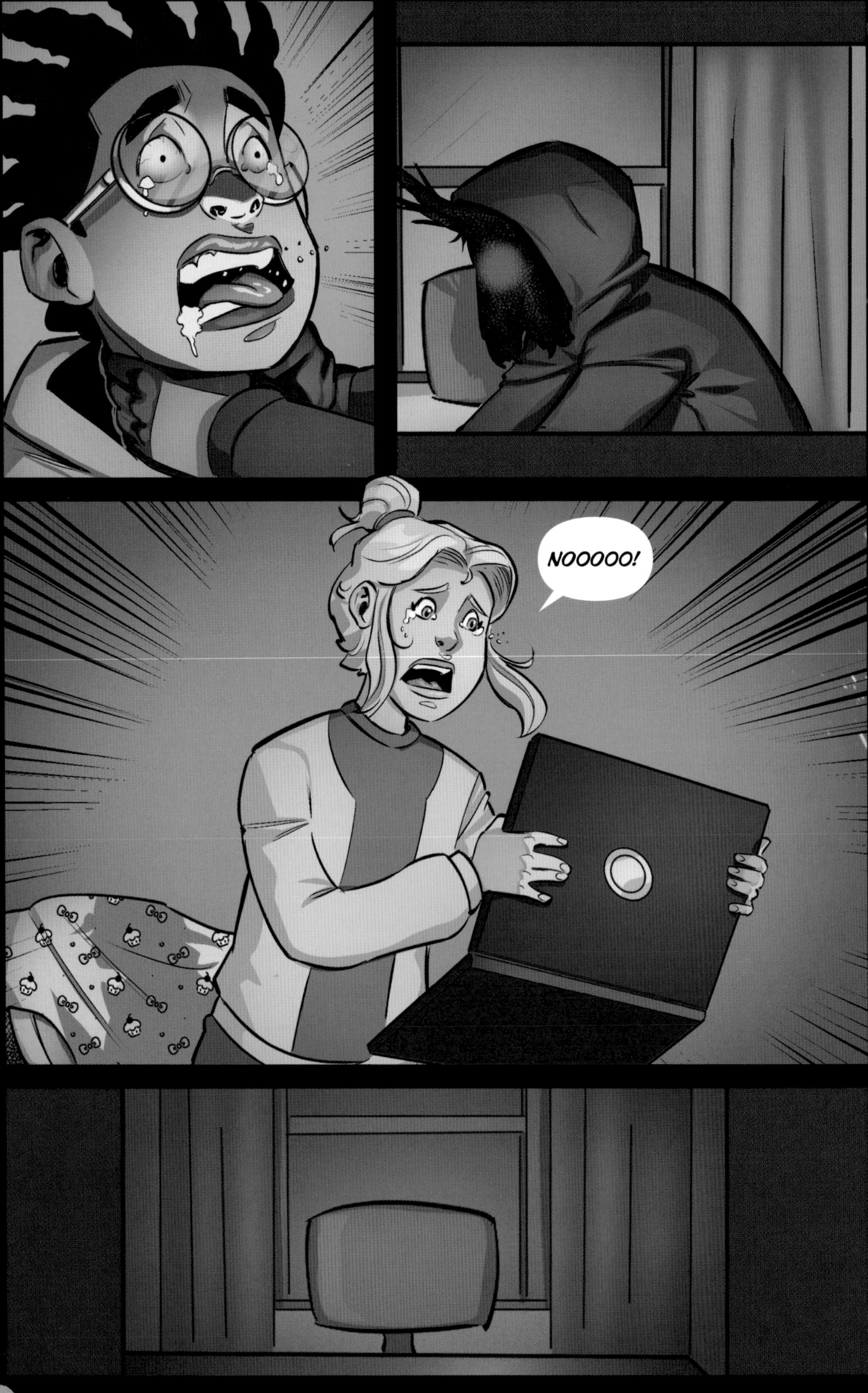
NOOOOO!

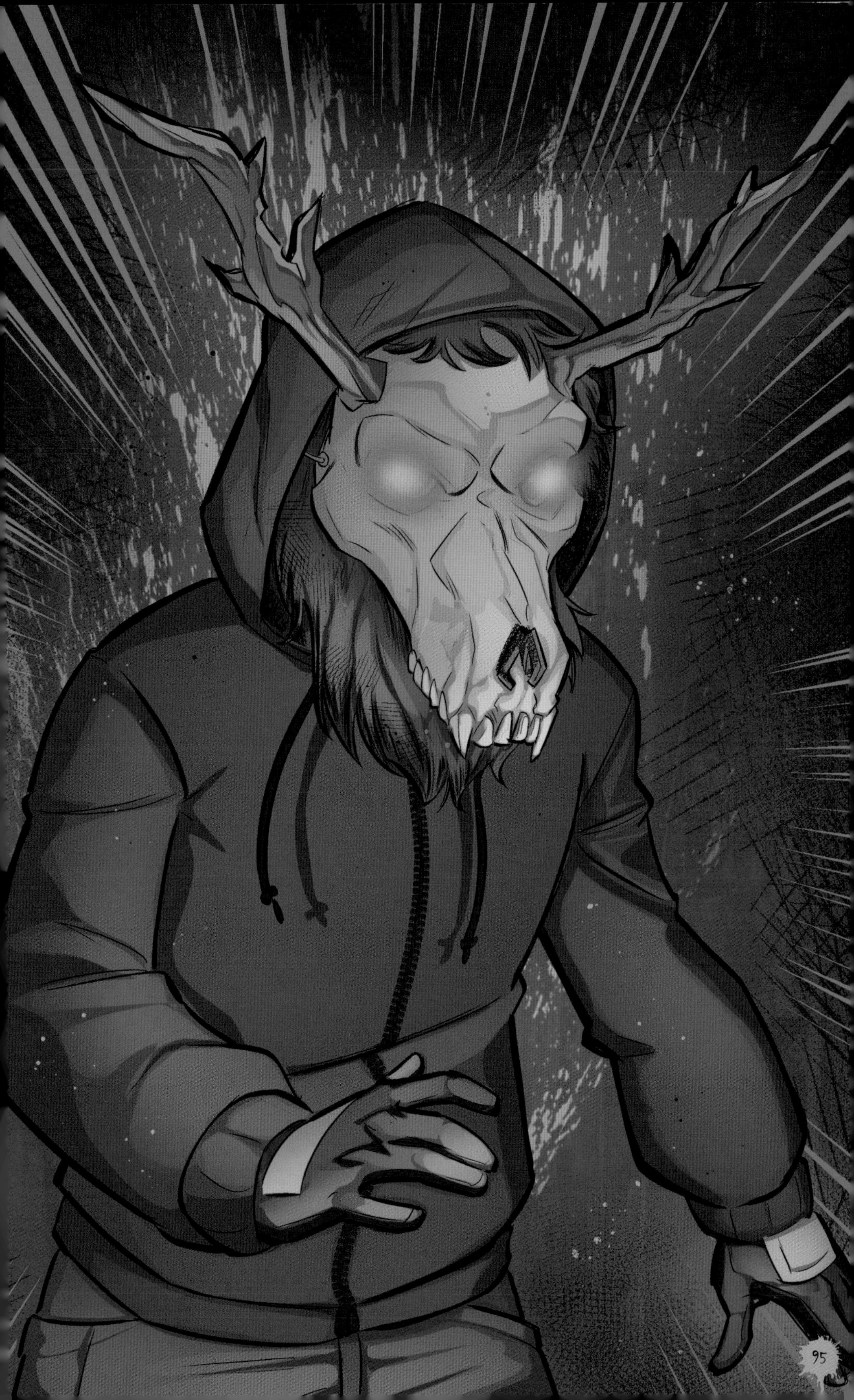

SPENCER...?

HEY, YOUR VIDEO'S FROZEN.

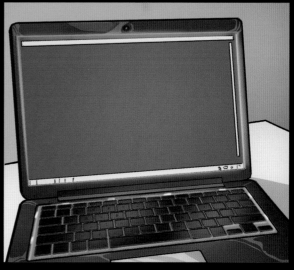

MAYBE THIS NIGHT REALLY IS *CURSED.*

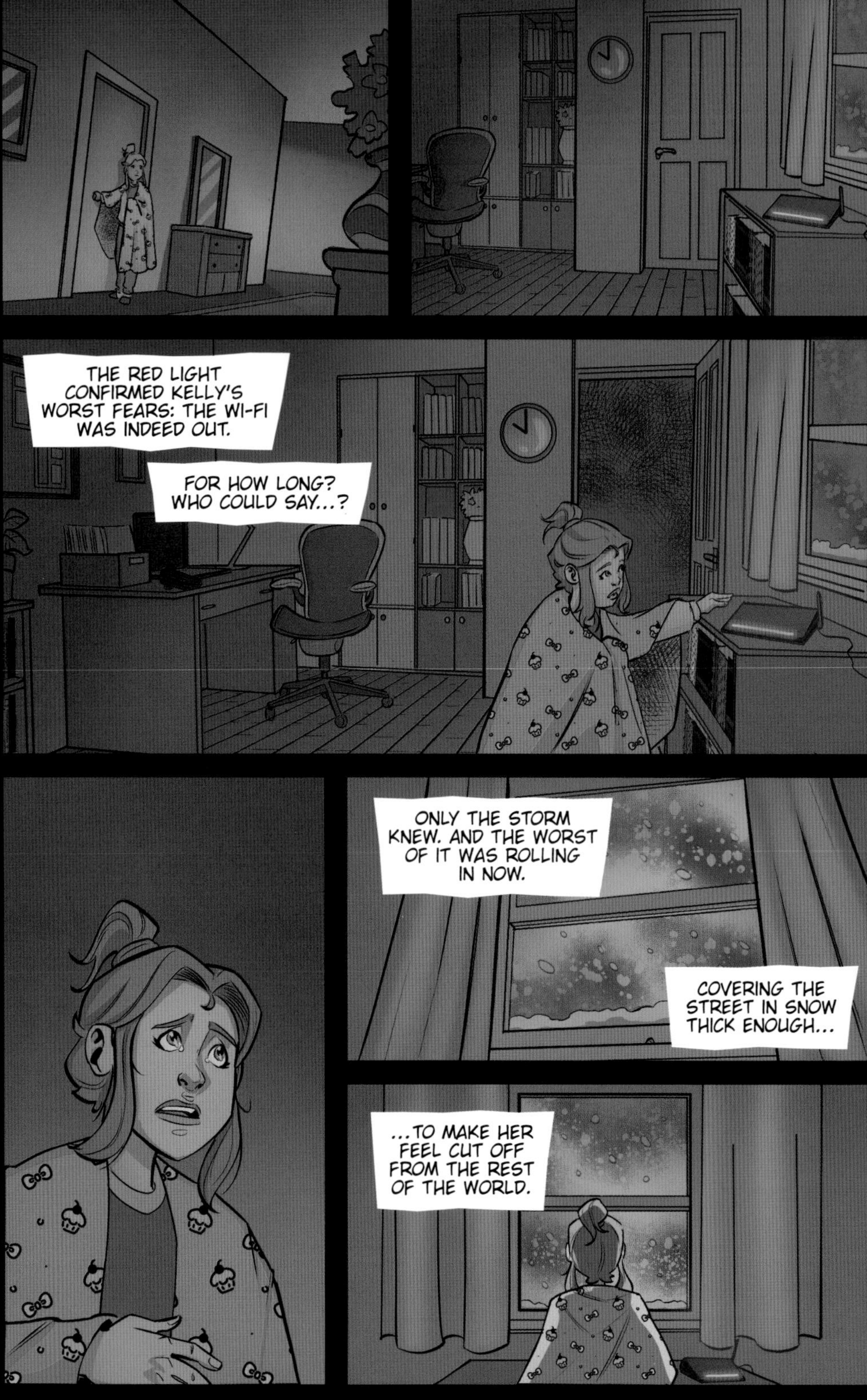
THE RED LIGHT CONFIRMED KELLY'S WORST FEARS: THE WI-FI WAS INDEED OUT.
FOR HOW LONG? WHO COULD SAY...?
ONLY THE STORM KNEW. AND THE WORST OF IT WAS ROLLING IN NOW.
COVERING THE STREET IN SNOW THICK ENOUGH...
...TO MAKE HER FEEL CUT OFF FROM THE REST OF THE WORLD.

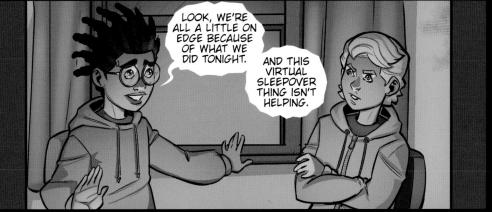

LOOK, WE'RE ALL A LITTLE ON EDGE BECAUSE OF WHAT WE DID TONIGHT.

AND THIS VIRTUAL SLEEPOVER THING ISN'T HELPING.

WHAT DO YOU MEAN?

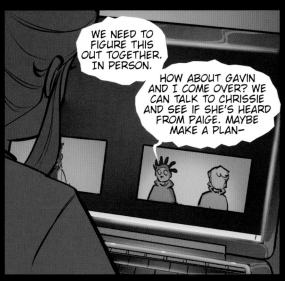

WE NEED TO FIGURE THIS OUT TOGETHER. IN PERSON.

HOW ABOUT GAVIN AND I COME OVER? WE CAN TALK TO CHRISSIE AND SEE IF SHE'S HEARD FROM PAIGE. MAYBE MAKE A PLAN—

OKAY, JUST... HURRY.

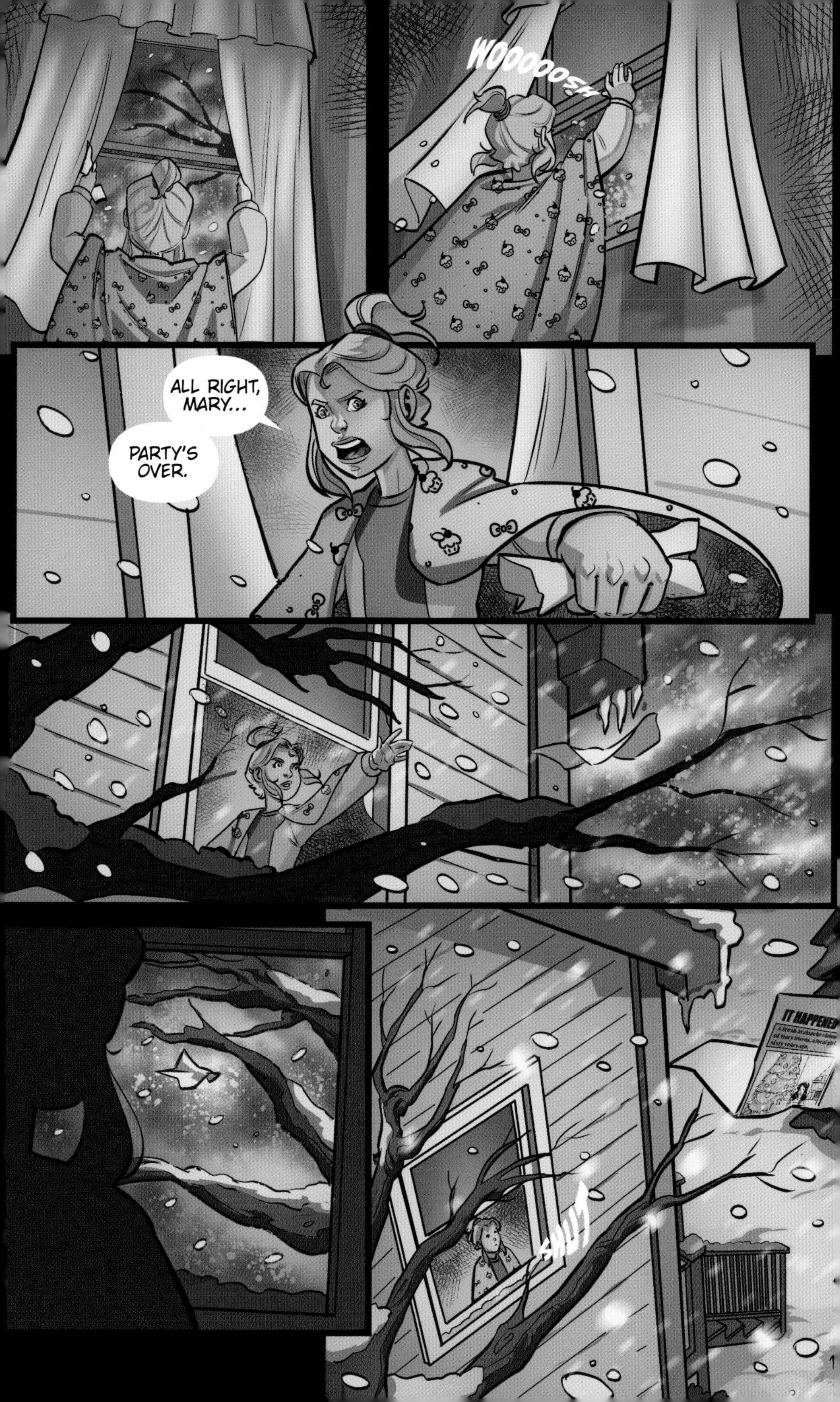
WOOOOOSH
ALL RIGHT, MARY...
PARTY'S OVER.
SHUT

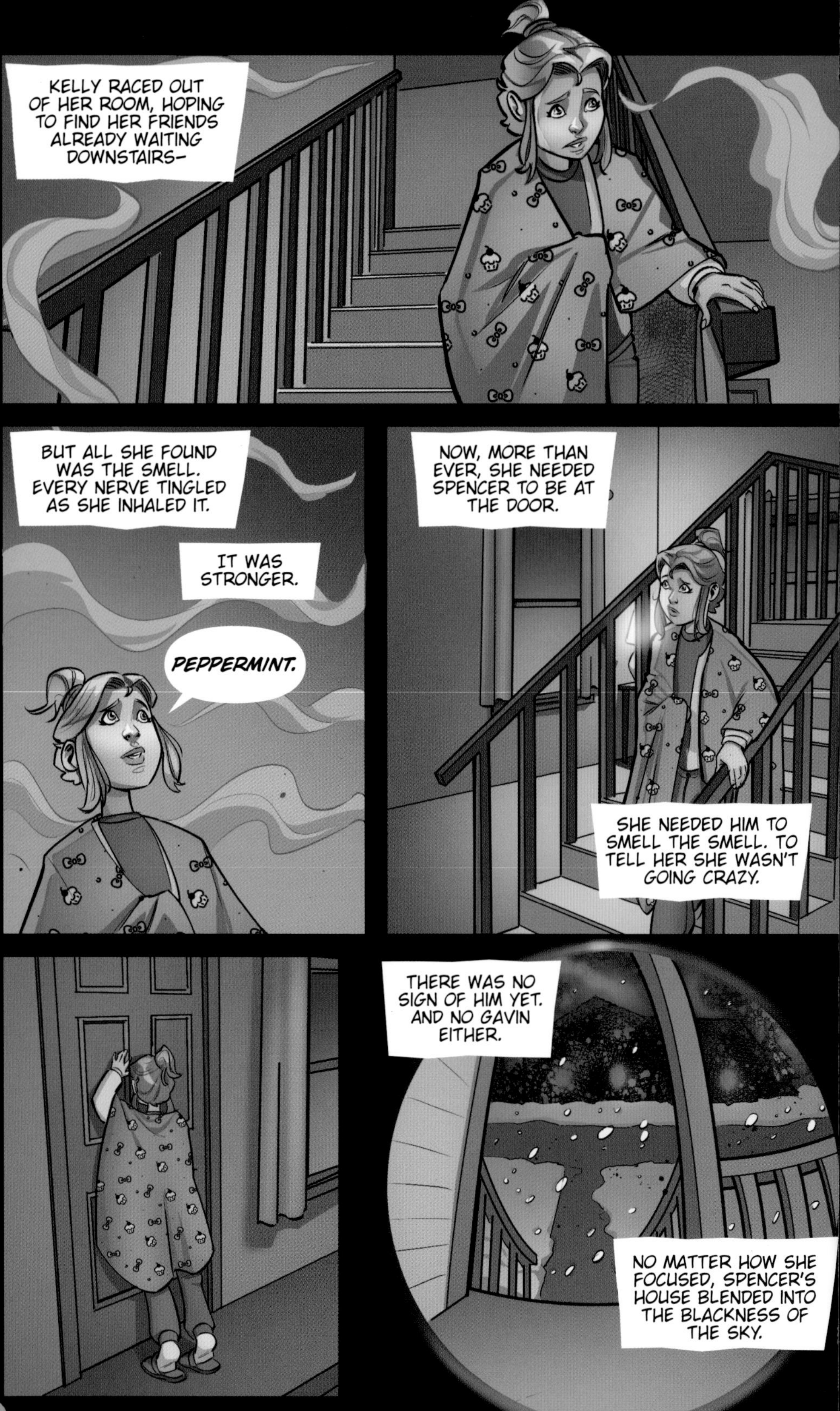
KELLY RACED OUT OF HER ROOM, HOPING TO FIND HER FRIENDS ALREADY WAITING DOWNSTAIRS–
BUT ALL SHE FOUND WAS THE SMELL. EVERY NERVE TINGLED AS SHE INHALED IT.
IT WAS STRONGER.
PEPPERMINT.
NOW, MORE THAN EVER, SHE NEEDED SPENCER TO BE AT THE DOOR.
SHE NEEDED HIM TO SMELL THE SMELL. TO TELL HER SHE WASN'T GOING CRAZY.
THERE WAS NO SIGN OF HIM YET. AND NO GAVIN EITHER.
NO MATTER HOW SHE FOCUSED, SPENCER'S HOUSE BLENDED INTO THE BLACKNESS OF THE SKY.

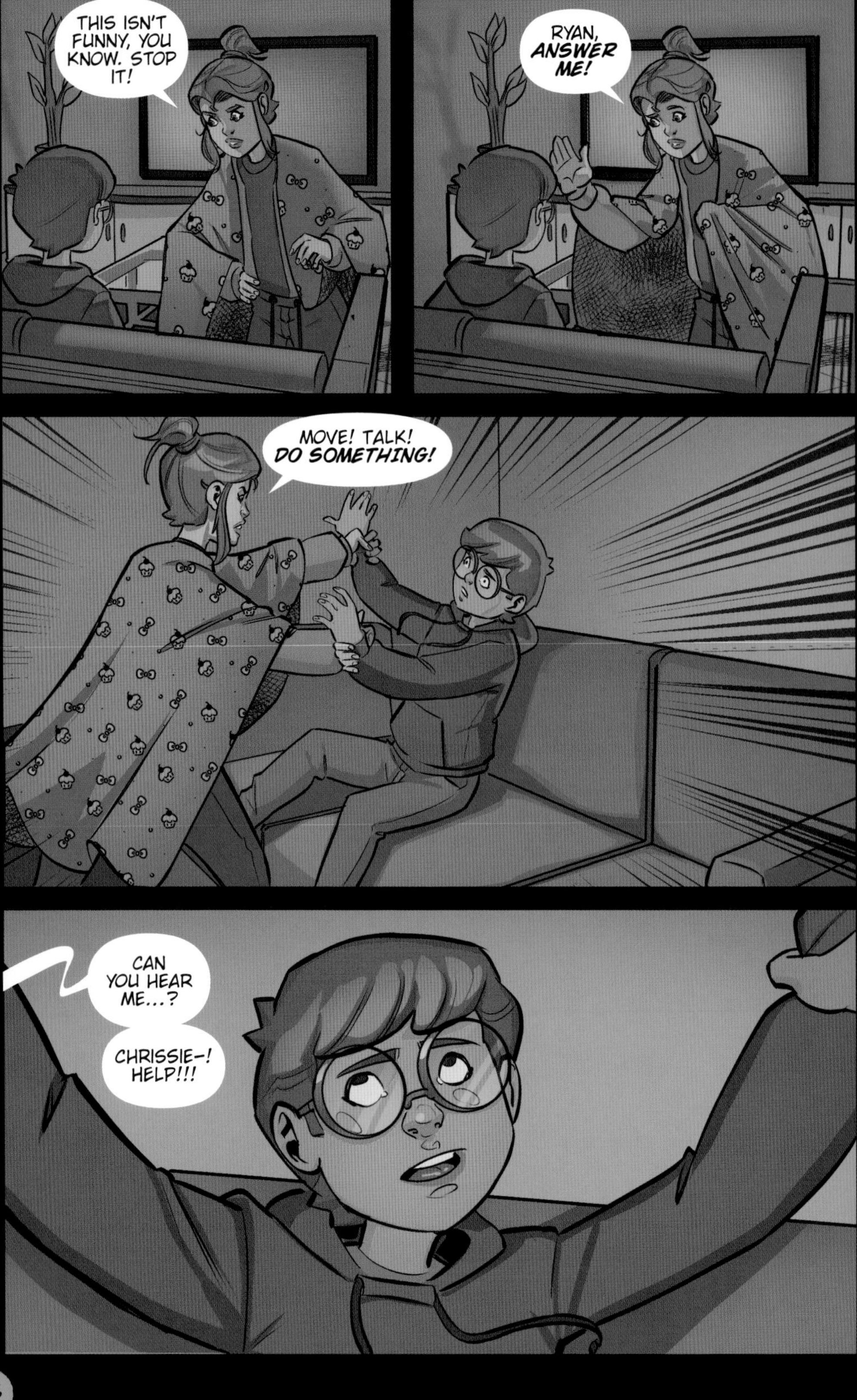
THIS ISN'T FUNNY, YOU KNOW. STOP IT!
RYAN, ANSWER ME!
MOVE! TALK! DO SOMETHING!
CAN YOU HEAR ME...?
CHRISSIE-! HELP!!!

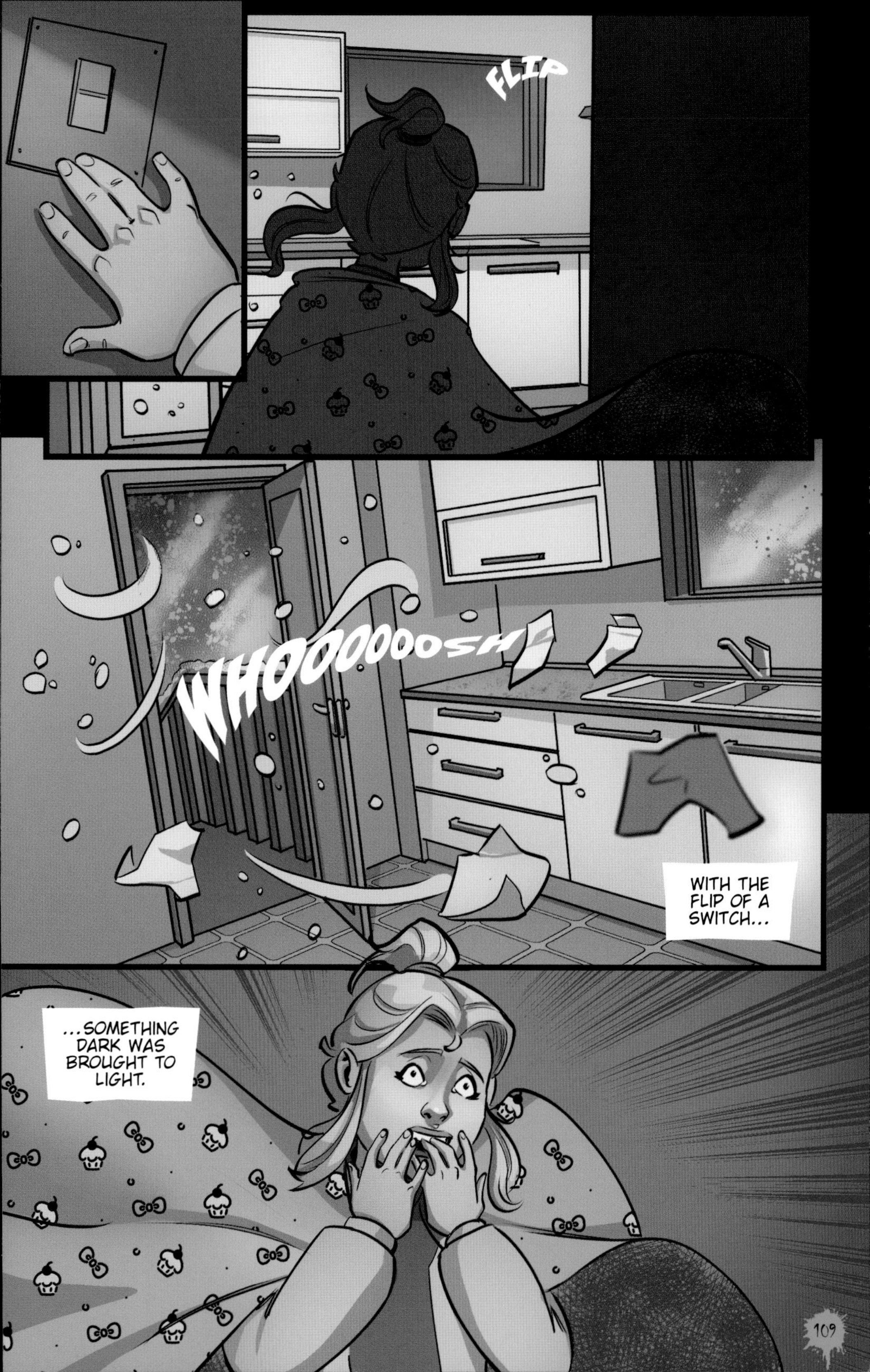
FLIP
WHOOOOOOOSH
WITH THE FLIP OF A SWITCH...
...SOMETHING DARK WAS BROUGHT TO LIGHT.

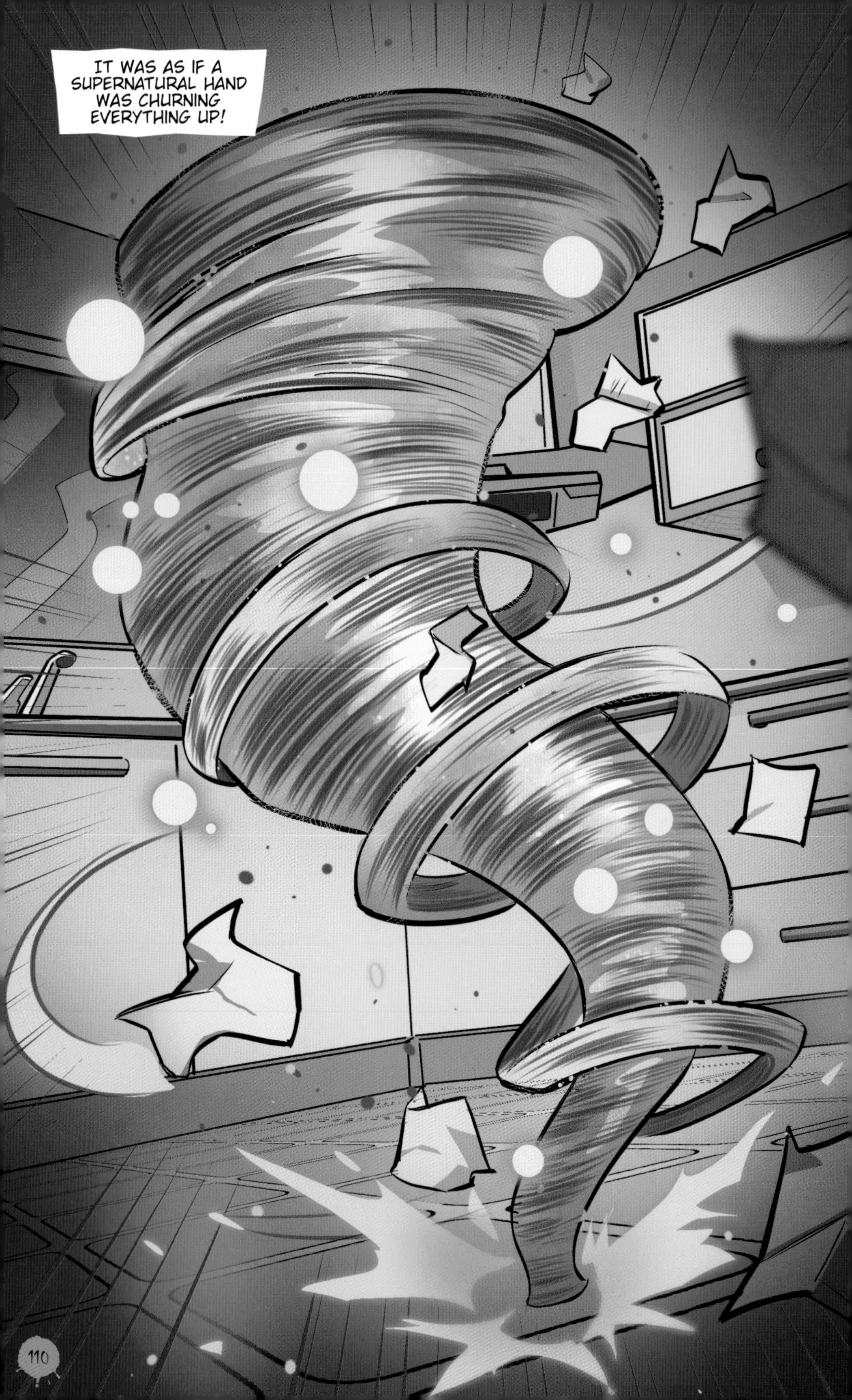
IT WAS AS IF A SUPERNATURAL HAND WAS CHURNING EVERYTHING UP!

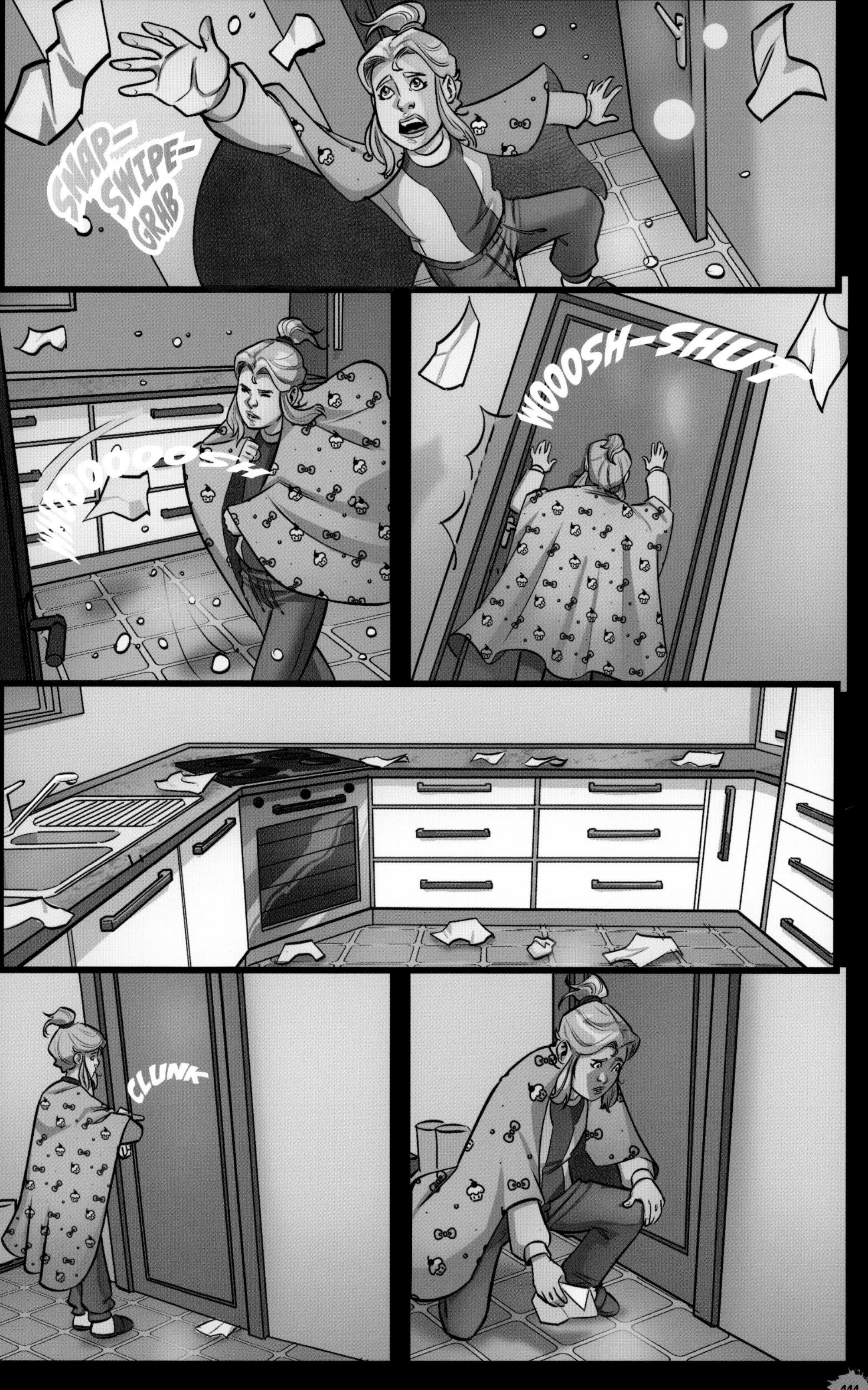
SNAP-
SWIPE-
GRAB
WOOOOOOOSH
WOOOSH-SHUT
CLUNK

CHAPTER 9

KELLY STARED AT THE FAMILIAR FACE ON THE PAGE ONCE MORE.

SHE AND THE GIRL WERE REUNITED. ONE. A BOND UNBREAKABLE.

HELLO AGAIN, MARY.

DESPITE TWIRLING IN THE SNOW, MARY'S PICTURE WAS SOMEHOW BONE DRY...

IT HAPPENED HERE!

...aimed the life al girl, almost

...SAVE FOR A WET PATTERN ON THE TOP CORNER. *ALMOST LIKE A BOOT PRINT*, KELLY THOUGHT.

SHE HAD SEEN *CHRISSIE* WEARING SNOW BOOTS INSIDE EARLIER.

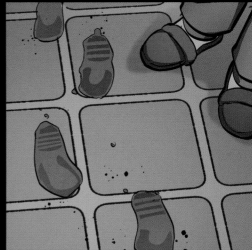

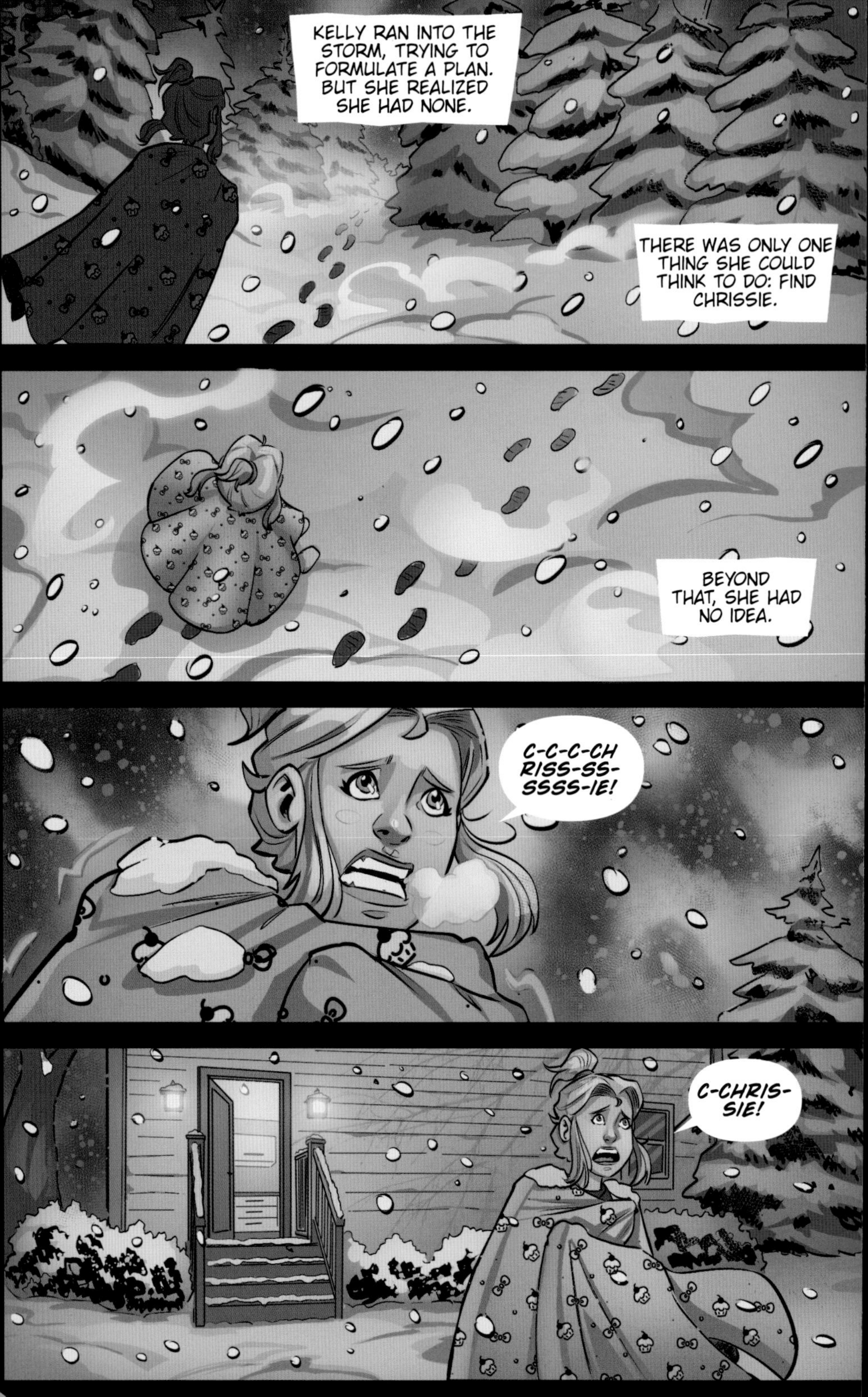
KELLY RAN INTO THE STORM, TRYING TO FORMULATE A PLAN. BUT SHE REALIZED SHE HAD NONE.
THERE WAS ONLY ONE THING SHE COULD THINK TO DO: FIND CHRISSIE.
BEYOND THAT, SHE HAD NO IDEA.
C-C-C-CH RISS-SS-SSSS-IE!
C-CHRIS-SIE!

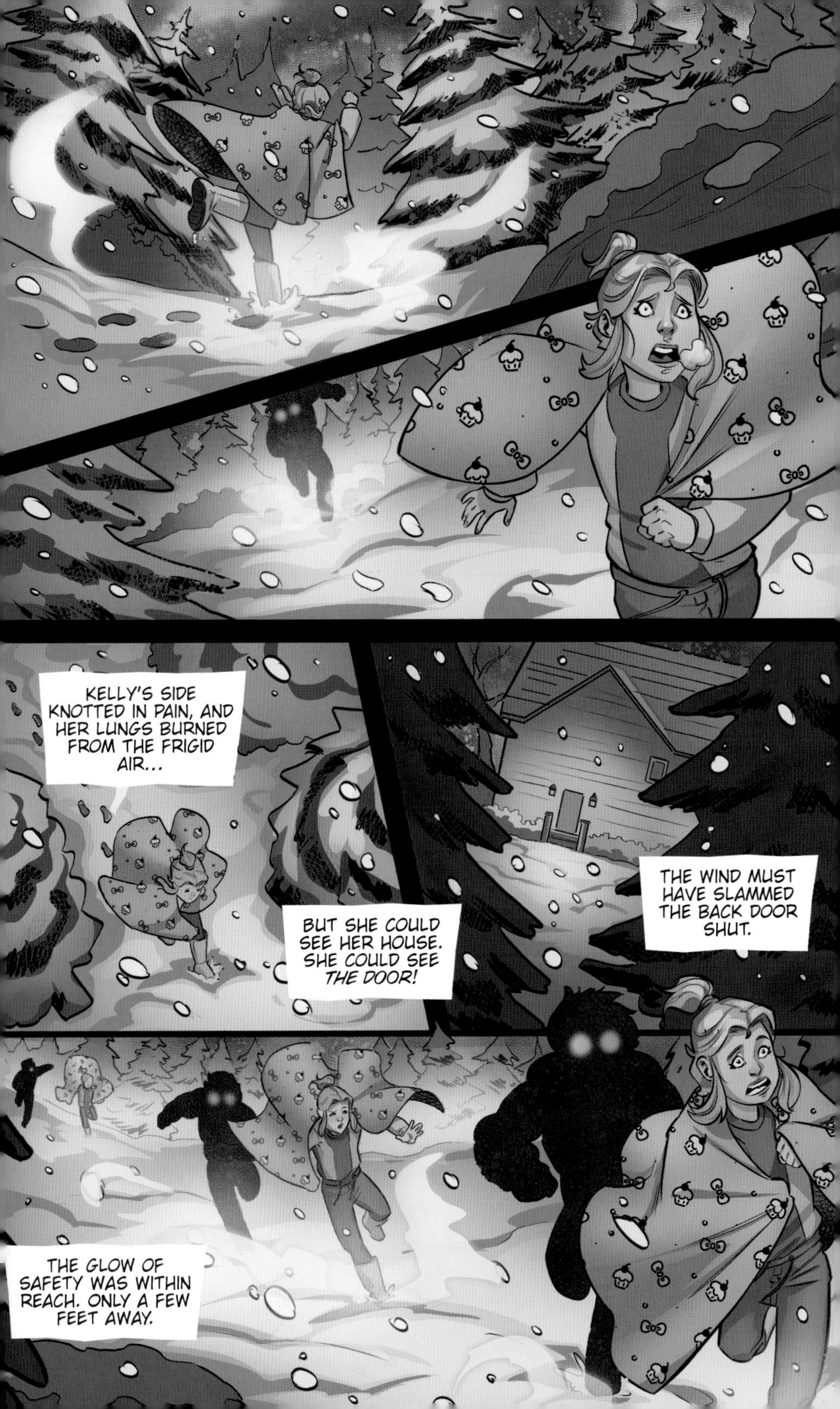
KELLY'S SIDE KNOTTED IN PAIN, AND HER LUNGS BURNED FROM THE FRIGID AIR...
BUT SHE COULD SEE HER HOUSE. SHE COULD SEE *THE DOOR!*
THE WIND MUST HAVE SLAMMED THE BACK DOOR SHUT.
THE GLOW OF SAFETY WAS WITHIN REACH. ONLY A FEW FEET AWAY.

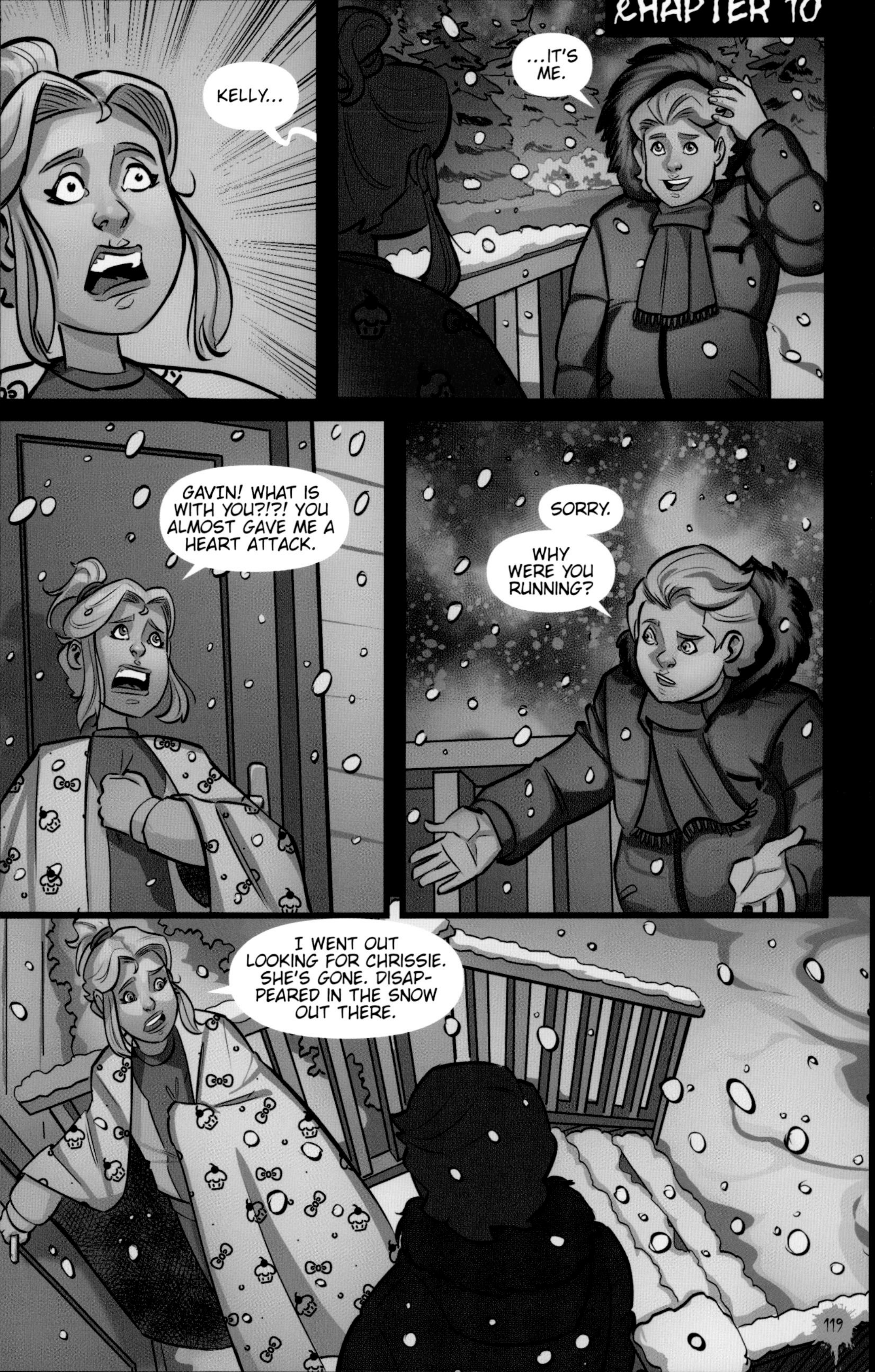
CHAPTER 10
KELLY...
...IT'S ME.
GAVIN! WHAT IS WITH YOU?!?! YOU ALMOST GAVE ME A HEART ATTACK.
SORRY.
WHY WERE YOU RUNNING?
I WENT OUT LOOKING FOR CHRISSIE. SHE'S GONE. DISAPPEARED IN THE SNOW OUT THERE.

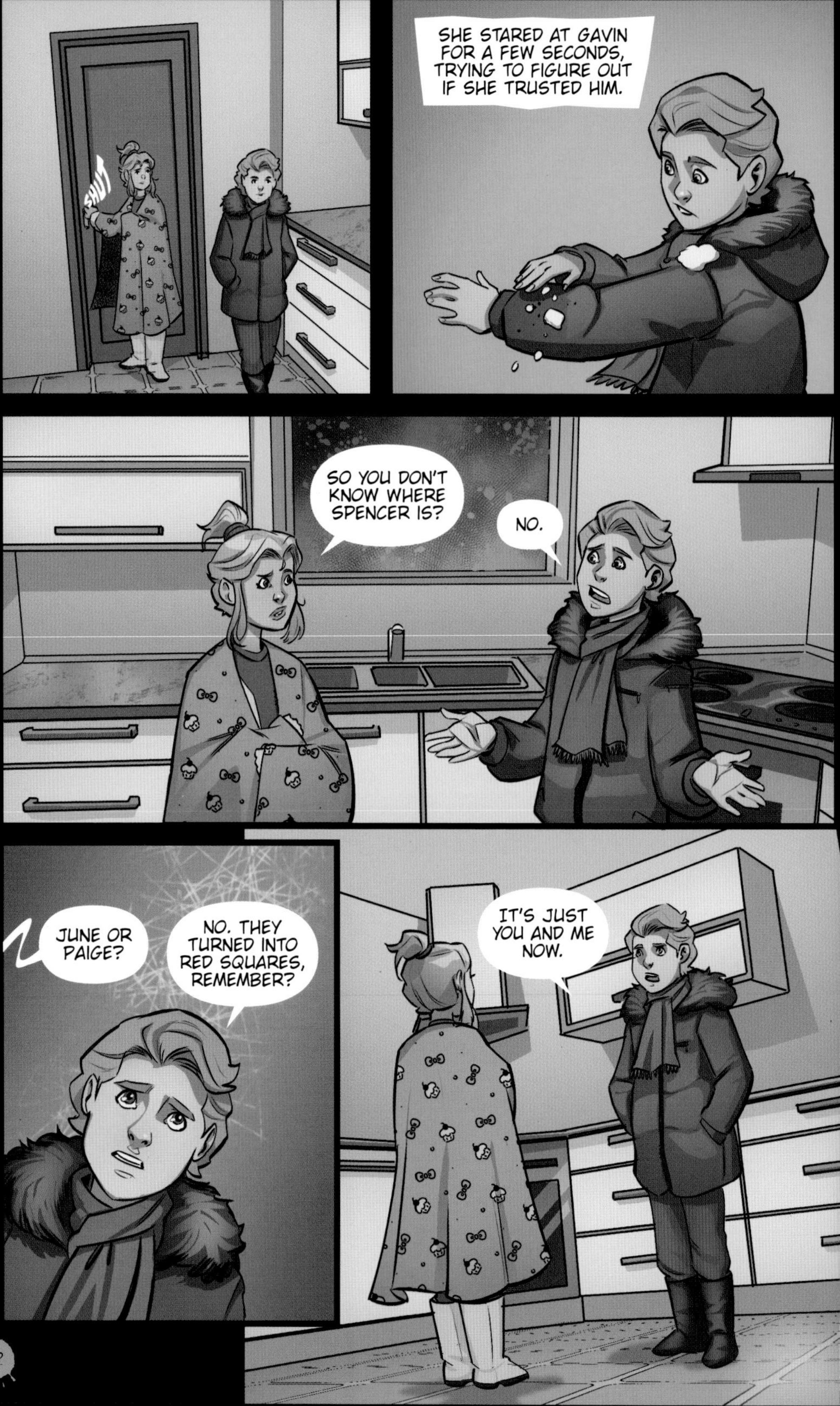
SHUT
SHE STARED AT GAVIN FOR A FEW SECONDS, TRYING TO FIGURE OUT IF SHE TRUSTED HIM.
SO YOU DON'T KNOW WHERE SPENCER IS?
NO.
JUNE OR PAIGE?
NO. THEY TURNED INTO RED SQUARES, REMEMBER?
IT'S JUST YOU AND ME NOW.

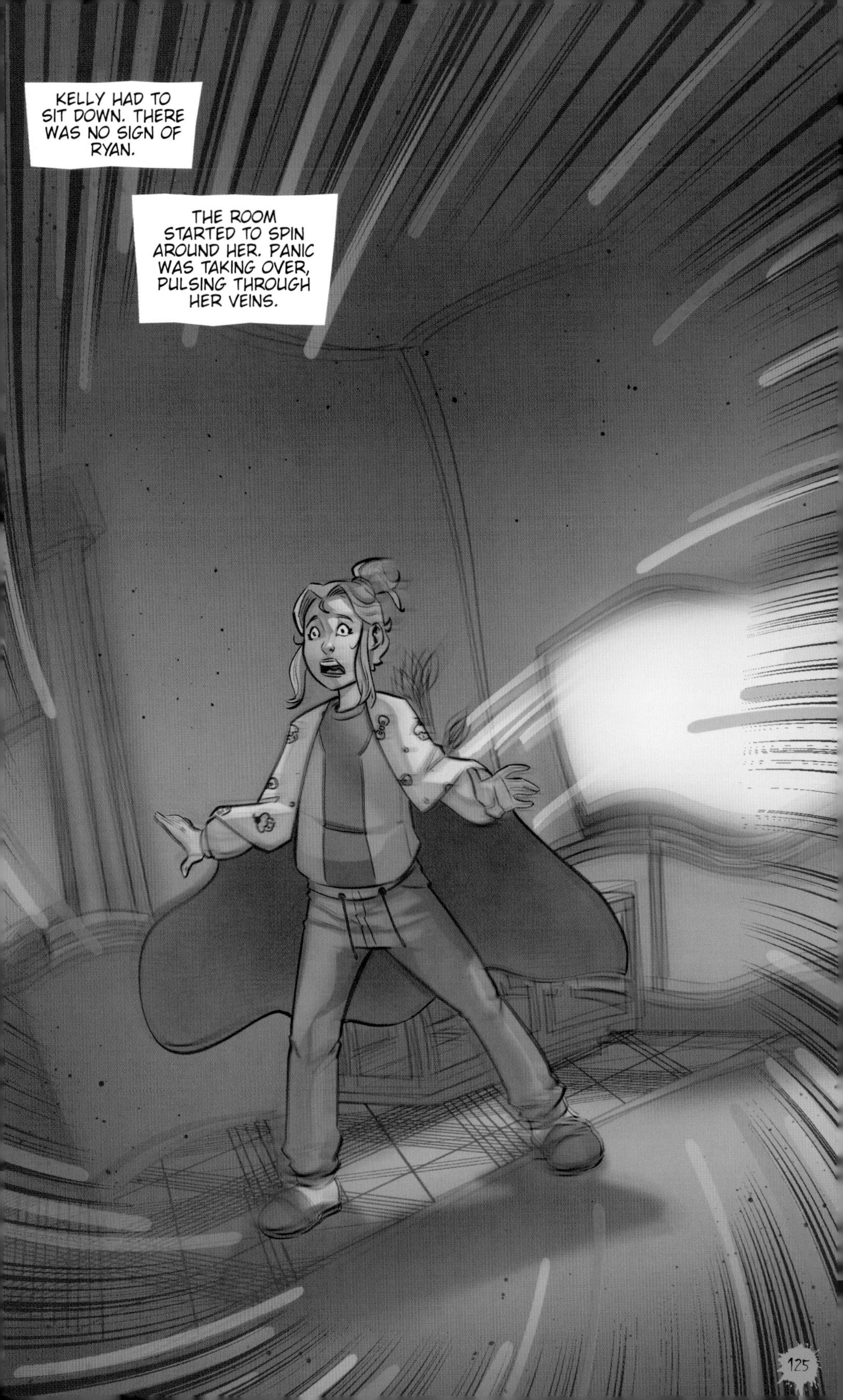
KELLY HAD TO SIT DOWN. THERE WAS NO SIGN OF RYAN.
THE ROOM STARTED TO SPIN AROUND HER. PANIC WAS TAKING OVER, PULSING THROUGH HER VEINS.

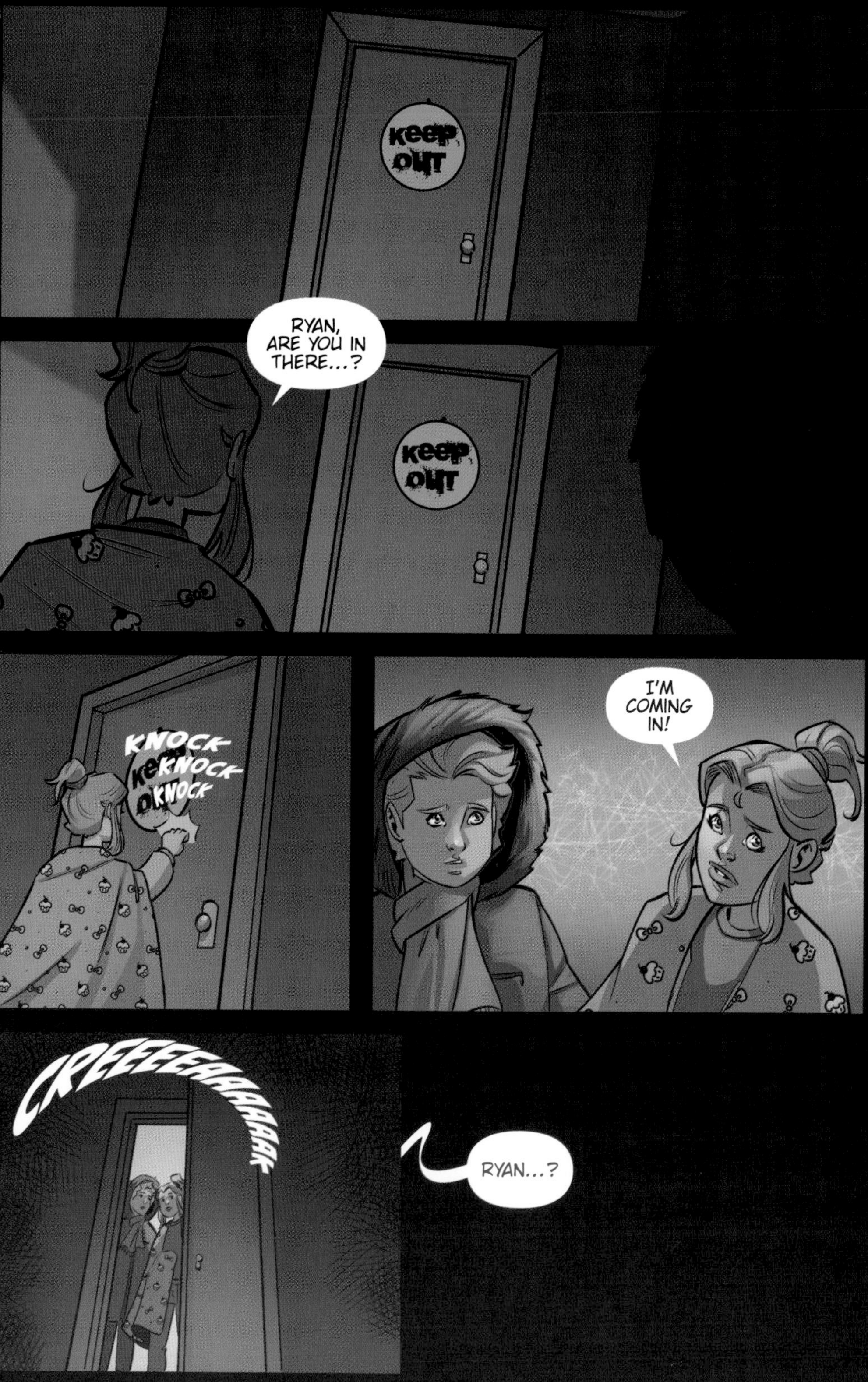

KEEP OUT
RYAN, ARE YOU IN THERE...?
KEEP OUT
KNOCK KNOCK KNOCK
I'M COMING IN!
CREEEEAAAAAK
RYAN...?

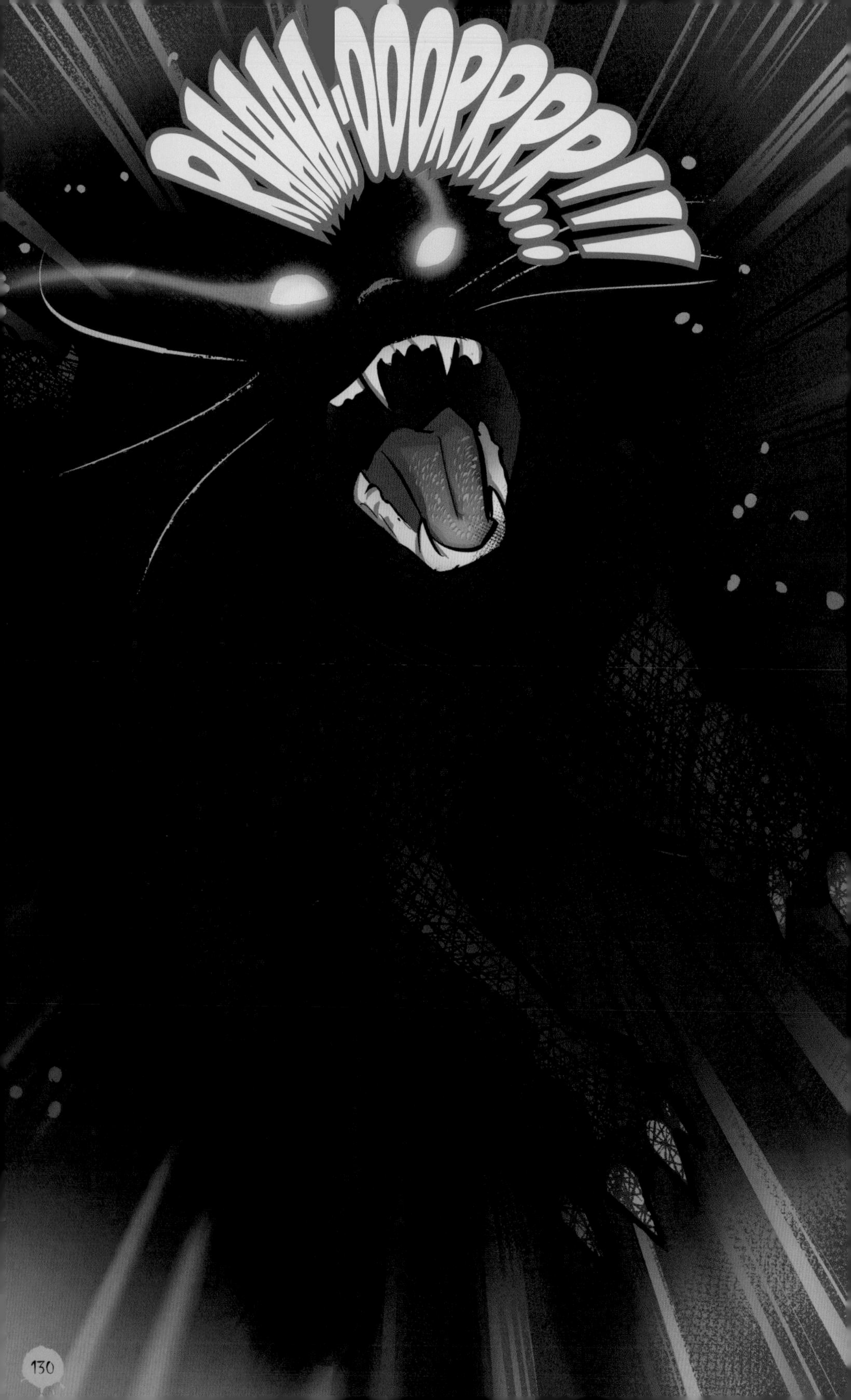
RAAAH-OOORRRR...!!!

135

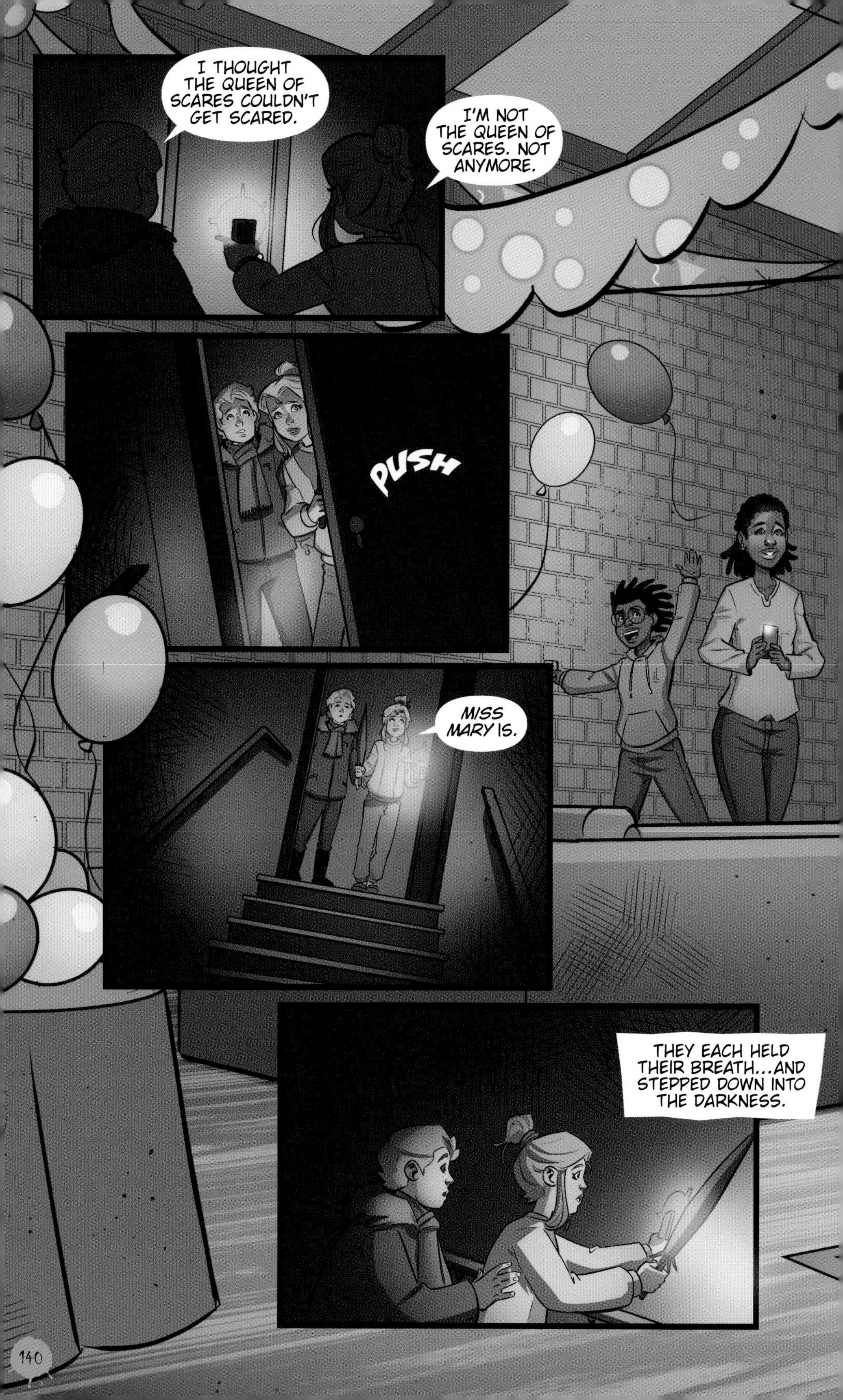
I THOUGHT THE QUEEN OF SCARES COULDN'T GET SCARED.
I'M NOT THE QUEEN OF SCARES. NOT ANYMORE.
PUSH
MISS MARY IS.
THEY EACH HELD THEIR BREATH...AND STEPPED DOWN INTO THE DARKNESS.

CHAPTER 12

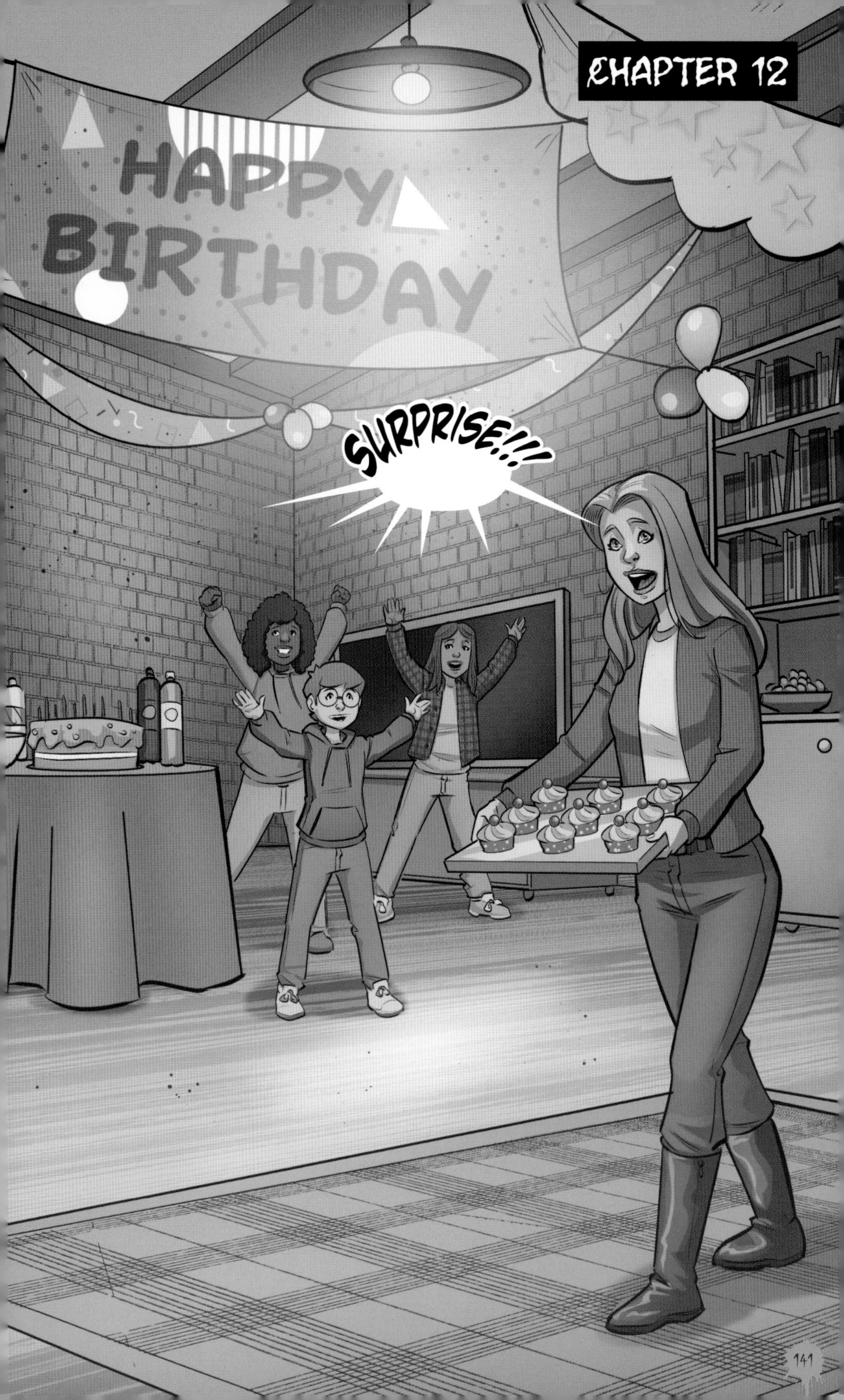
HAPPY BIRTHDAY
SURPRISE!!!

THAT'S WHY HE WAS PERFECT FOR THIS. HE WAS ALREADY SLEEPING OVER AT MY HOUSE, AND SINCE YOU DIDN'T KNOW HIM, HE COULD MESS WITH YOUR HEAD.

YOU CREEPED ME OUT BIG-TIME. ESPECIALLY WHEN YOU CAME OUT OF THE BUSHES, RUNNING.

CHRISSIE!

WE WERE WAITING TO SNEAK IN HERE FOR THE PARTY...

WE WERE WAITING TO SNEAK IN HERE FOR THE PARTY...

CHRISSIE UNLOCKED THE SIDE DOOR FOR US...AND SPENCER'S MOM WAS ON HAND TO SUPERVISE.

I PLAYED ALONG, BUT I WAS ALWAYS LOOKING OUT FOR YOUR SAFETY, HON.

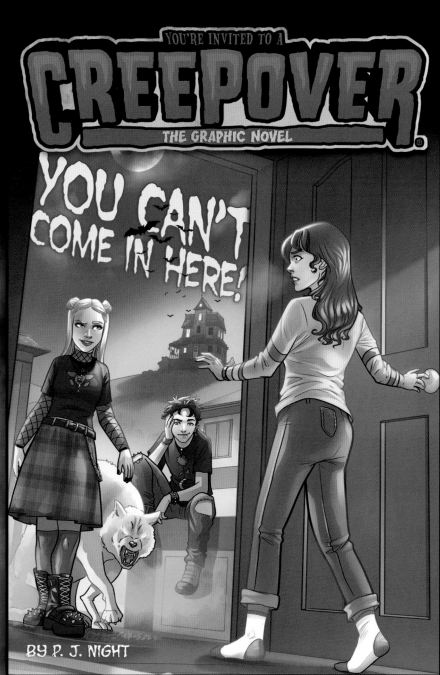

CHAPTER 1

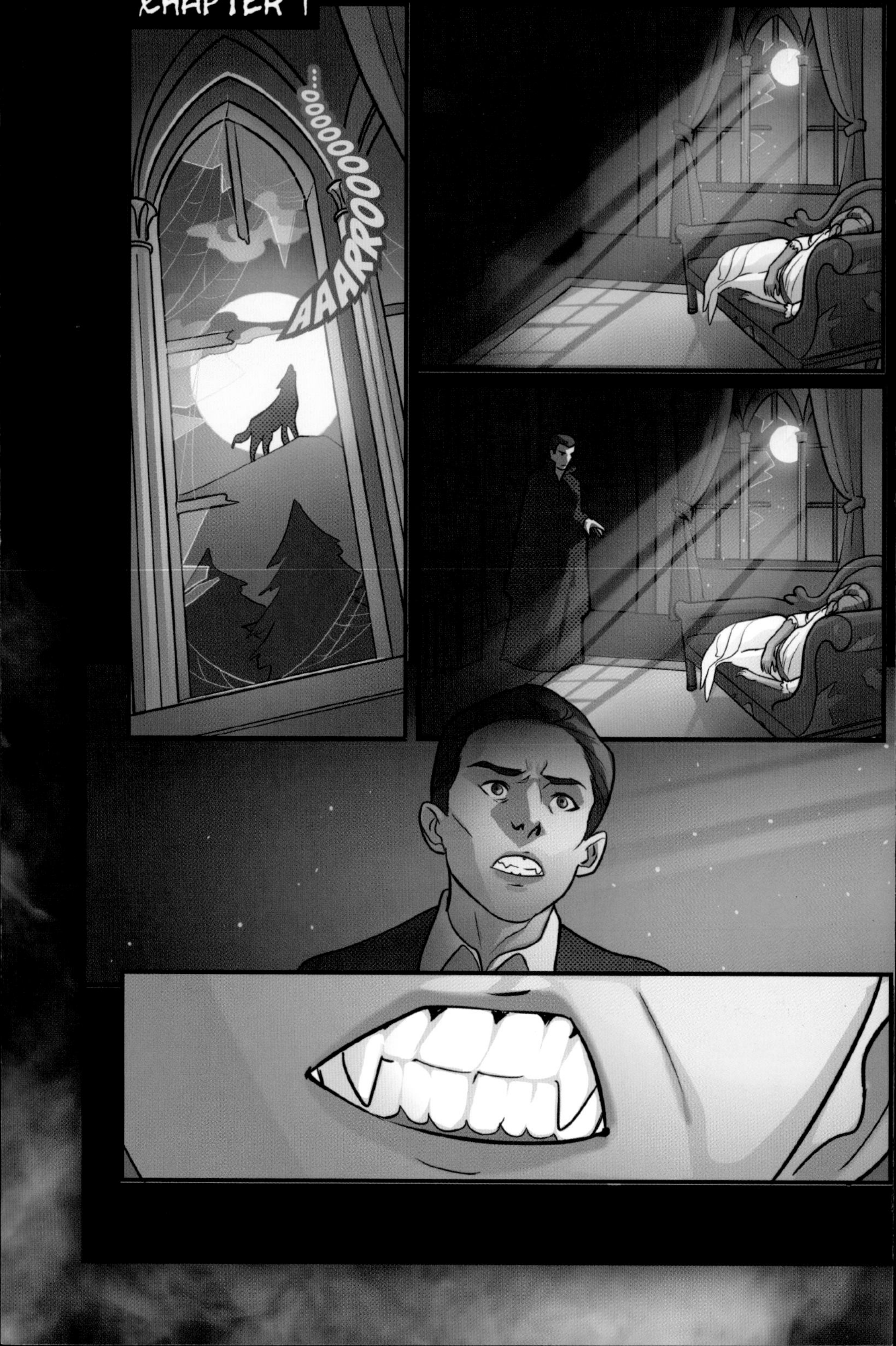
AAARROOOOOOOO...

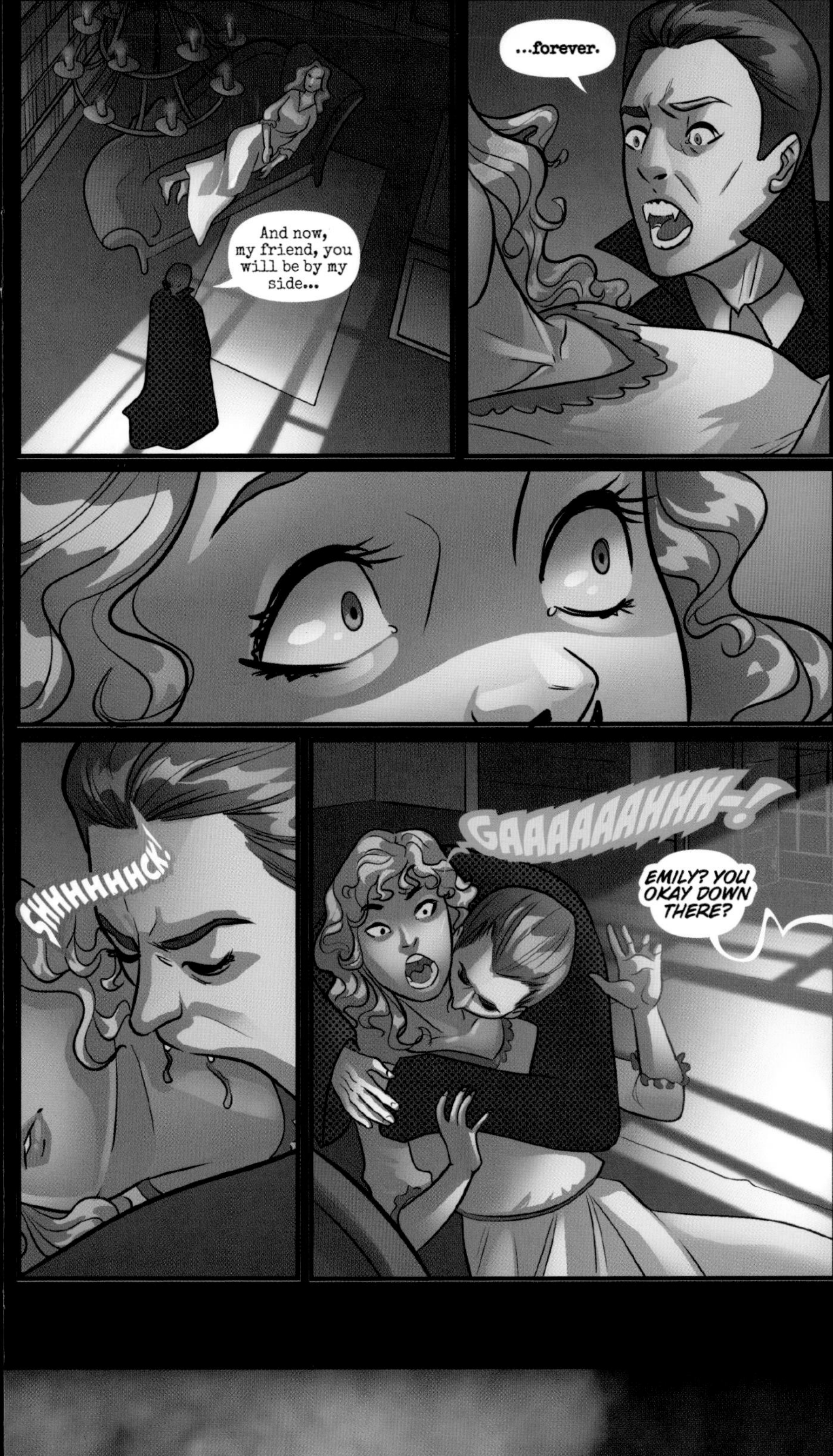

And now, my friend, you will be by my side...
...forever.
SHHHHHCK!
GAAAAAAHHH-!
EMILY? YOU OKAY DOWN THERE?

AND DON'T MISS

YOU'RE INVITED TO A

CREEPOVER®

THE GRAPHIC NOVEL

THE SHOW MUST GO ON!

COMING SOON!